SINCLAIR IN COMMAND

*Submariner Sinclair Series
Book Three*

John Wingate

Also in the Submariner Sinclair Series
Submariner Sinclair
Jimmy-The-One
Nuclear Captain
Sub-zero
Full Fathom Five

SINCLAIR IN COMMAND

Published by Sapere Books.

20 Windermere Drive, Leeds, England, LS17 7UZ,
United Kingdom

saperebooks.com

Copyright © The Estate of John Wingate

The Estate of John Wingate has asserted his right to be
identified as the author of this work.
All rights reserved.

No part of this publication may be reproduced, stored in any retrieval system, or transmitted, in any form, or by any means, electronic, mechanical, photocopying, recording, or otherwise, without the prior written permission of the publishers.
This book is a work of fiction. Names, characters, businesses, organisations, places and events, other than those clearly in the public domain, are either the product of the author's imagination, or are used fictitiously.
Any resemblances to actual persons, living or dead, events or locales are purely coincidental.

ISBN: 978-1-80055-229-6

To S.W. and C.J.W. and all those others who might be tempted to accept their heritage of freedom without recalling the cost.

Many incidents in this book are true. All characters are entirely fictitious, but if anyone who took part in these sterling days should recognise himself, the fact is coincidental and I offer my apologies.

The Author

THE SHIP'S COMPANY OF HIS MAJESTY'S SUBMARINE *RUGGED*

Lieutenant Peter Sinclair, R.N., Commanding Officer

Lieutenant Tom Benson, R.N.R., First Lieutenant

Sub-Lieutenant Ian Taggart, R.N.V.R., Navigating Officer

Sub-Lieutenant Geoffrey Brocklebank, R.N., Third Hand

C.P.O. George Withers, Coxswain

C.E.R.A. Reginald Potts, Chief E.R.A.

P.O. Jack Weston, Second Coxswain

P.O. James Haig, P.O. Telegraphist

P.O. Rodney Slater, Torpedo Instructor

E.R.A. Joseph Saunders, Outside E.R.A.

Acting P.O. David Elliott, Higher S/M Detector

Leading Seaman Michael Flint, Leading Torpedoman

Acting Leading Signalman Alec Goddard, Signalman

Able Seaman George Stack, Gunlayer and 'chef'

Able Seaman Henry Bowles, Gun Trainer

Able Seaman William Hawkins, Seaman

Ordinary Seaman Tom O'Riley, Ward Room Flunkey

Ordinary Seaman John Smith, T.I.'s Mate

S.P.O. George Hicks, Stoker Petty Officer

Stoker Patrick O'Connor, Stoker

Ordinary Seaman Henry Keating, Telegraphsman and Telephone Operator

COMMANDO

Lieutenant George 'Hank' Jefferson, U.S.N.

CHAPTER 1

The Yank

In Malta, 1943, two men were walking down the dusty road which runs across the head of Torpedo Creek. This turquoise stretch of water concealed the Tenth Submarine Flotilla's Torpedo Depot, where the torpedo stocks were stored. An old crane clanked at the end of a tumbledown stone jetty, alongside which a submarine was secured. Her bows pointed towards the road, and above them a steel-blue torpedo swung slowly from the jib of the ancient crane. An officer stood on the fore-casing, plumbing the 'fish' over the fore-hatch, while two ratings manned the steadying lines from the jetty. The officer's arm flapped, the harsh sound of the ratchet clanked across the water, and the torpedo began to disappear down the fore-hatch, its tail cocked into the air.

"Isn't that *Rugged*, Peter?"

The two men had halted to watch the evolution. The burlier of the two displayed the three pips of a Commando captain on the shoulder-tabs of his khaki shirt, and he turned to watch his companion as he asked his question.

Lieutenant Peter Sinclair, Royal Navy, did not seem to hear. His grey eyes were soaking in every detail of the little submarine even to her trim, for he could see by her draught-marks that she would be about right when the 'fish' were loaded. He had recently been her First Lieutenant and now he felt cut off from her. Even though he was the spare Commanding Officer in the Flotilla, he yearned to be with *Rugged* again, for what was the point of passing his

Commanding Officers' Qualifying Course and doing six months' 'ping-running' in P.612 if he was not going to get a boat? But then he grunted as Captain Jan Widdecombe's elbow struck him in the ribs.

"Is that *Rugged?*"

"Yes — and she's nearly kitted up for sea, Jan. She's sailing the day after tomorrow. Tim Cardew's got her, the lucky blighter."

Jan Widdecombe's burly frame moved forward down the road and Peter Sinclair followed reluctantly. Both officers were dressed in the unofficially accepted rig-of-the-day: khaki short-sleeved shirts, khaki shorts and stockings, and black or brown shoes. Peter's battered cap was tucked beneath his left arm, but Jan carried no headgear.

"Hang on, Jan!"

Peter Sinclair rejoined his old friend and together they slowly left the turquoise waters behind. To their left great mounds of stone sprawled untidily, monuments to the dead entombed beneath the shattered buildings. Although the attacks of the Luftwaffe had become less frequent recently, a day rarely passed without some visit from the black-crossed monsters.

Jan picked his way through a pile of rubble which sprawled across the pavement. Pools of shade were already beginning to flow across the dirty road, for the worst of the heat was over, and a gentle breeze had begun to flutter through the square holes that had once been windows in the walls of these now roofless houses.

Ahead of the two friends stretched a narrow causeway which joined the shore to Manoel Island. The leper colony of Lazaretto had once nestled beneath Fort Manoel, and now these ancient stone buildings functioned as a base for the Tenth Submarine Flotilla. The boats of The Fighting Tenth, the proud name of the flotilla, made their sorties from here, so the area was a natural target for enemy bombers. On the south side, the deep waters of Lazaretto Creek separated Manoel Island from the battlements of Valetta. Sliema lay on the north side of the creek from which it took its name. In peacetime many a destroyer captain's reputation had been made or broken here, for skill in ship-handling was needed when going astern up Sliema Creek.

"Where're you going, Jan? Aren't you coming back to Base?" Peter Sinclair asked his friend. There had been tensions between them the whole afternoon, and Peter could not put his finger on the cause. Jan had been strangely silent, and now he had strolled past the entrance to the causeway and was heading for Sliema.

"Come on, Peter. There's plenty of time before supper, and I want you to meet a friend of mine who's in digs in Sliema."

Peter shrugged his shoulders. He quickened his pace to catch up with the Commando, and together they approached the waterfront of Sliema. The indigo water washed against the yellow sandstone wall which ran in a gentle curve along the edge of the creek, and along this ran the road. Children were shouting and laughing in the sunlight as they scampered in the rubble, engrossed in their own make-believe. On a patch of bare earth ahead of them a few goats scrabbled, and it was towards this end of the waterfront that Jan was walking.

"What's his name, Jan?"

"*Lootenant George Jefferson*, *U.S. Navy*. Hank, for short."

"Good Lord!" Peter exploded. "What's a Yank doing in Malta? Bit hot for him, isn't it?"

Jan Widdecombe raised his eyebrows and turned slowly towards Peter.

"You'll have to judge. You see, I'm leaving in two days for the Burma front and he's relieving me."

For several paces there was no sound but the shuffle of their footsteps on the dusty road. Jan, his trusted friend of two previous cloak-and-dagger stunts, actually leaving Malta? It couldn't be possible.

"You're pulling my leg!"

"I'm not, Peter. I've already had Jefferson understudying me on two trips, one to Lampedusa, and a repeat performance to Pantelleria."

"Is he any good?"

"Yes, he's a good chap. He's living in that flat with the red door, just past those goats."

"But, Jan, be your age! How *can* he take your place here? The Yanks don't even know what war is yet."

The line of houses which forms the northern extremity of Sliema is built upon the rocks of the northern shore of Malta, and the Luftwaffe sometimes took advantage of the cover these dwellings afforded. So it was not surprising that on this sunlit evening, the two lone ME109s, which were flying low over the sea from Sicily, caught the defences of Malta unprepared. The fighters swooped up from behind the houses and hurtled over the crowded waterfront, their yellow-snouted engines snarling and spluttering.

Peter and Jan recognised the emergency a split second later than the Maltese on the waterfront who had already run for the shelter of the buildings or had hurled themselves to the ground.

Fascinated, Peter watched the Messerschmitts turn tight on their tails over Sliema Creek. They hovered motionless for a moment and then the leader fell out of the air to point its hideous yellow snout directly at the Sliema waterfront.

"Down, Jan!" Peter yelled. The two friends hurled themselves towards the stone parapet and rolled over and over upon the road. Peter heard the familiar stutter of machine-guns and he covered his head with his hands. The fighters were tearing in from behind them and from the corner of his left eye Peter watched the road ahead of him.

Above the spitting of the fighters' guns, he was dimly aware of a curious fluttering. The soles of Jan's shoes formed the major part of Peter's view, but from where he lay he saw lines of bullets kicking up the dust as they threshed past to the left. Tiny dust clouds whorled upwards as the bullets whocked by, and then the murderous fire got in amongst the goats.

Peter held his breath. His stomach sickened as the leading 109 shuddered overhead. The machine pulled up sharply to clear the houses and then, as Peter heard the second fighter swooping down upon them, he saw a white kid skip away from the stricken goats. It bleated pathetically for a moment as it searched in bewilderment for its dead mother. Then it started to wobble off jerkily down the road.

A little girl was running out from a doorway. With hands outstretched and with tears streaming down her face, she shouted to her kid as she ran down the centre of the road towards it. The animal turned towards the familiar sound, skipping towards its young mistress. As the two were reunited in the centre of the road, Peter heard the machine-guns opening fire behind him.

Peter could not shut his eyes to the murder about to be committed. The guns stuttered behind him as the roar of the engine grew louder. He heard the *whock! whock!* of lead as it splayed against the stone farther up the road.

The girl was clutching the kid desperately, when the red door of a house abreast of her suddenly opened. A huge figure streaked across the intervening gap. His right arm was stretched out and as he flashed across the road he swept the child up in the crook of his arm. Peter saw the line of bullets kicking up dust whorls down the road and he looked away as he saw them reach the tall man who was now rolling over on his side, the child clutched to him. Peter was glad that the dust smothered the actors in this ghastly scene.

Then Jan was on his feet, running up the road and yelling at the top of his voice:

"Hank! Hank!"

Peter tore after him. The noise of the 109s' engines was suddenly blanketed by the line of houses as the fighter dipped below their rooftops on its way out to sea, and then silence fell upon the shambles.

There drifted down upon the waiting onlookers, the feint bleating of a little kid. Still and clear in the silence it echoed against the buildings. And then, as the dust settled, Peter heard the whimper of a child in the stillness.

She lay in the dust on the far side of the American, protected from the bullets by the shield of his body. His gangling arms clutched her to him, so that she should not break away from him when he fell. She was crying softly, trying to reach the kid that tottered unsteadily towards her.

Peter reached Jan just as he was turning over the inert body of the American.

"He's alive. I can't see any bullet wound," the Commando said, and then the tall American suddenly regained consciousness. He shook himself and passed a hand over his reeling head.

"Sit up, Hank. You're okay," Jan said. "You're okay, Hank."

"Is this Jefferson?" Peter asked quietly.

Jan nodded. A mug of water was brought by a weeping Maltese woman, and he trickled the fluid between the American's lips.

"He's got guts," Peter said.

"What d'you think of my relief now?" Jan murmured.

Peter was silent for a moment as he watched the man's eyes flickering.

"A good Commando needs more than bravery, Jan. You know that."

Jan was silent a moment. Then he looked long at Peter as he supported the American across one arm.

"Please yourself, Peter. But one day you may be glad of Hank."

Peter Sinclair left Sliema after dark, having helped Jan put Jefferson to bed. The American Naval lieutenant was now sleeping, apparently none the worse from knocking himself out. Jan and Peter had bid each other God-speed, each knowing that he had to go his different way, so they did not waste time with emotion. The chances of their meeting again were less than ever.

Peter jumped as three enormous rats scampered from the dark mass of masonry that was heaped by the side of the road.

"Bigger than the cats, they say," he murmured to himself. "The island is on starvation diet now."

He swore softly as he started down the causeway to Lazaretto. *The folly of this war*, he thought, *the waste and cruelty of this wanton destruction*. He was in a black mood when at last he reached the base. He climbed up the sandstone steps to his cabin on the balcony floor, but paused for a moment outside his own cabin door, marked by the tally: 'Spare C.O.'. The Flotilla's new Staff Officer came towards him, a pink slip of paper fluttering in his left hand. He was Peter's ex-Captain, Lieutenant Joe Croxton, D.S.O., D.S.C., Royal Navy, one-time Captain of *Rugged*.

"Hullo, Peter, where've you been? Couldn't find you anywhere."

Peter smiled wearily.

"Watching other people preparing for sea made me chokka, sir, so I went ashore. I've said cheerio to Jan Widdecombe and met his relief."

"He's a Yank, isn't he?"

"Yes. He's a good hand."

"But he's got a job on, taking Jan's place."

"That's what *I* think, sir. It's a pity, but there it is."

Peter Sinclair was irritated by the grin that was creasing Croxton's leathery face.

"What's so funny, sir? The picture of a frustrated Spare C.O.?" he asked peevishly.

"Tim Cardew has gone sick with suspected rheumatic fever — these sandstone caves we live in, I suppose."

"What's amusing about that?"

"Nothing, except that you're *Rugged*'s new Captain."

For a moment Peter said nothing.

"You're not pulling my leg are you, Joe?" he asked quietly. "That wouldn't be fair."

"You know I'd never do that," Joe laughed, as he thumped Peter on the shoulder. "Look, here's your appointment," and he handed Peter the pink signal-sheet.

"'From Captain "S", Tenth Submarine Flotilla, to Flag Officer Submarines,'" he read. "'Lieutenant P. Sinclair, R.N., is appointed to H.M. Submarine *Rugged*, in command *vice* Cardew who will be flown home as soon as possible. My 161219 refers. Time of origin 161825.'"

Peter felt a tap on his back. When he looked up, he found that Joe was already disappearing down the steps which the first C.O.s had decorated with the carved crests of their boats. These stone blocks were already memorials to the famous names which had gone before but not returned.

Peter slowly walked to the edge of the balcony. He stared across at the battlements of Valetta looming in the darkness. Below him the water lip-lapped against the island and against the bobbing pontoons that ran out to the lean silhouettes straining at their moorings. He thought he could distinguish *Rugged* in the gloom.

"My first operational command of a submarine," he murmured. "May God bless her."

CHAPTER 2

First Patrol

Peter had never known it to be so hot. He had difficulty in looking through the periscope for any length of time because the sweat ran down from his eyebrows to blur the eyepieces.

"Down periscope."

The tube gleamed as it slid downwards into the well. It was glassy calm up top, so he waited before his next look.

Peter could not feel that he was actually experiencing reality, the whole tide of events seeming ethereal and dreamlike. But here he was in command of one of His Majesty's submarines — and *Rugged* at that! He could not believe his luck. It was generally accepted that a First Lieutenant did not become Captain of his old boat: experience proved that it did not work because the ship's company knew too much about their new Captain's idiosyncrasies.

Fate had stepped in however: Captain 'S' had no alternative but to give the appointment to Lieutenant P. Sinclair, Royal Navy, and judging by the welcome his troops gave Peter, it was no bad decision.

"Up periscope."

For over an hour now Peter had been slowly closing the North African coastline, but it had not yet come in sight. Perhaps his young Navigator, Sub-Lieutenant Ian Taggart, R.N.V.R., had gone badly wrong with his Dead Reckoning — the chap had had practically no experience as yet and Peter found himself continually checking Taggart's calculations. This was Peter's first landfall as Captain and he regarded the outcome somewhat superstitiously.

Peter swept round the horizon, first in low power to see if there were aircraft about, then, as he came on to the expected bearing of the land, he twisted the periscope handle with his right hand and the high-power lens clicked into focus.

He had never seen it so calm: the heat shimmered on the horizon line making it difficult to separate the sky from the horizon. The surface of the sea was silvered like a mirror and, when he swung the periscope aft, he could see the black swirl from the slick of the periscope as it sliced through the water.

When Peter looked again he was not surprised to see his first smudge of land.

"Bearing THAT — land," he said quietly.

"Red two, sir," reported Saunders, the calm Cornishman who had been the Outside E.R.A. since the boat was commissioned.

"Looks like the Kerkennahs all right, Pilot. Down periscope."

Peter slowly made his way to the chart, his face a study of unconcern, although it was difficult to affect nonchalance when surprise and delight hammered away inside him. About him he could feel the glances of approval that passed between the older men: not much doubt about it, their new skipper knew his onions as far as navigation was concerned — and that was important in this inhospitable Mediterranean with both sides laying minefields indiscriminately all over the seabed. Yes, they were pleased to have him as their new 'Old Man' even though he was five years younger than Croxton had been when he left — but then Croxton was getting on in age for a Commanding Officer of an R-boat.

Peter snapped his fingers and the periscope slid upwards. Even in the short interval since his last look, the blur on the horizon had hardened into a recognisable shape to stretch like a yellow ribbon above the horizon of the sea. He shut the handles and the steel tube slid silently downwards.

Yes, he had been lucky, for they were definitely the Kerkennah Isles: he'd seen them once before when he was Joe Croxton's First Lieutenant. Ah! but that had been a different kettle of fish — he had felt then that he had a large weight on his shoulders, but now there was no comparison. Half-a-million pounds' worth of submarine in his hands and thirty-five men's lives — their safety depended upon his split-second timing and skill. In the atmosphere around him, Peter felt the warmth of their trust and it was comforting.

But above all these feelings, a fiercer, more elemental fever ran hotly. To destroy the enemy, that was their task and their duty. To help obliterate the hideous evil of the Crooked Cross and its attendant ideologies, that was why they were sweating under the sea off the North African coast. To halt the cruelties and oppressions that the Nazis and Fascists were spreading over nine-tenths of Europe was the duty of Britain, and in this year of 1943 it was the stark realisation in these men's minds. If they failed there would be no homes to which to return, no parents, no wives or sweethearts to welcome them. The enemy had other destinies for the conquered.

No, there was no cynicism in 1943. Each man and woman knew what they were fighting for and what they should be fighting against.

"Who's on watch next?" asked Peter, his mind returning to the task in hand.

"I am, sir," the First Lieutenant replied.

"Come and have a look then, before I turn over to you," Peter said. "Up periscope."

Yes, thought Peter, *Captain 'S' has been kind to me, sending me on a quiet billet like this for my first patrol as a C.O. I'm glad it's a quiet one, because I don't feel at all confident yet and don't know how I'll make out if there's an attack.*

"Right, sir. I've identified the Kerkennahs," Benson's voice broke in upon Peter's thoughts.

"Take over, please, Number One; I'm going to get my head down. Continue on this course until you are two miles due north of the island, then shake me. We may run into something coming out of Sfax."

"Aye, aye, sir."

It was eight thirty-three a.m. when Peter left the Control Room.

"Captain in the Control Room!"

For a fraction of a second Peter was bewildered by his sudden awakening. He heard the summons from the Officer of the Watch, but in his semiconscious state he listened for Joe Croxton, his Captain of past months, to slither past the Ward Room table and into the Control Room.

Good lord, it's me! flashed through Peter's brain, and he started up from his settee where he had been sleeping. In the Control Room he saw Benson snapping the periscope handles shut and, as the shining steel tube slid downwards, Peter caught Benson's eye from behind the trembling hoist wires.

"Bearing?" snapped Peter.

"Red eight-o, sir. I can't make out what it is."

Peter snapped his fingers. The periscope hissed upwards. For a second in time Peter felt his knees go weak and his stomach turn to water. Was this the prelude to his first attack? What was he about to face in the next second when the periscope broke surface?

He grabbed the periscope handles as they slid upwards, and their familiar feeling of massiveness restored his confidence. *Here we go*, thought Peter, *any minute now ... there goes the water draining off the glass ... it's a streaky whiteness, now it's clearing, ah! now I can see! Flick over the right-hand periscope handle for high-power — click! that's better. Now for a quick all-round sweep for aircraft ... none about, that's good ... now I can concentrate on the object.*

"Put me on the bearing," Peter ordered.

The Outside E.R.A. firmly adjusted the periscope to red eight-o.

"On, sir."

For a moment Peter searched on either side of the bearing, but could see nothing. The sea shimmered a silvery-grey and to his left the coast of the northern island of the Kerkennahs stood up clearly, barely five thousand yards away. He could see the whiteness of the houses against a darker section of the land. Then sweeping slowly to the right of the island, his eye clapped suddenly on to what appeared to be a small matchbox standing on its end.

It can't be, thought Peter, *it can't be! I'll wait a second and have another look.* He slammed the handles shut and the periscope had hardly reached the well when he snapped his fingers. As the tube swirled upwards again, Peter grabbed the handles and set the periscope on the bearing.

The glass broke surface, whiteness streamed into Peter's right eye, the circle blurred, then rapidly cleared to reveal the sharp image of ... the conning tower of an advancing U-boat, the most difficult target of them all.

"Diving stations!"

Peter's controlled voice was tinged with excitement as he gave the vital command for the first time. Then suddenly he felt nervousness and fear dropping from him like a mantle. It was up to him now, and the stakes were high. A U-boat, the undersea pirate whose ruthlessness was notorious, and who, if Peter missed, might well survive to sink more Allied ships and drown thousands of men.

Already he could identify her jumping wires, and the bulge of her bows was just showing above the horizon. Peter had little time, for she was doing about eighteen knots. *Rugged*'s Captain jumped into action, the training and drill of the previous months giving him automatic confidence.

"Target U-boat, bearing THAT. I'm twenty degrees on her starboard bow. Speed eighteen knots. Range eight, down periscope."

While the Third Hand, Sub-Lieutenant Geoffrey Brocklebank, fed the information into his Fruit Machine by twiddling the knobs, the hands rushed aft to man their diving stations. Jostling, bustling, and bent double as they stooped to avoid jabbing their skulls into protruding valve spindles, they silently changed places with those who had been on watch.

"Stand by all tubes, depth setting fourteen feet. What's my course for a hundred-and-twenty track and what shall I be off track? Up periscope."

As Peter watched Number One wrestling with the trim — the depth was twenty-one feet at this moment — he could feel the unspoken support of his ship's company around him. This was how they liked an attack to be carried out, with torpedoes and not with the gun — more like the Croxton technique.

When the lens cleared Peter was delighted to see how well placed he was.

"Twenty feet, sir!" reported Benson anxiously.

"For Pete's sake keep her down, Number One. She mustn't sight my stick," and Saunders, the Outside E.R.A., gently lowered the periscope as he saw his Captain's thumbs turn downwards on the periscope handle.

"Flood Q!" Number One jerked towards Saunders.

"Flood Q, sir! Q flooding, sir."

Peter banged the handles shut and the periscope swished downwards. He moved to the attack periscope at the after-end of the Control Room and Saunders started to raise the smaller tube. Peter's eyes anxiously watched the Coxswain wrestling with the after-planes — twenty-one feet and still not going down — only another three feet upwards and the standards would break surface. Peter stopped breathing momentarily while he watched Benson savagely fighting for control.

"All tubes ready, sir!" the Sub shouted from his Fruit Machine. "Course for a hundred-and-twenty track, three-one-o. Distance off track, six hundred yards…"

"Starboard ten, steer three-one-o," Peter snapped. "What's my D.A.?"

"… Range eighteen hundred yards, sir. D.A., red ten," the Sub continued.

"Stop flooding! Blow Q!" Number One's voice sounded above the orders which rang about the Control Room. "Vent Q inboard."

"Up periscope!"

Peter was now kneeling on the deck so that he should show as little periscope as possible, and as he grabbed the handles he could see from the corner of his eye that the trim was under control again. But had he waited too long, had the target already slipped past his firing angle, his D.A.?

"Asdic gives eighteen knots, sir," Elliott reported.

"Very good…" and Peter suddenly found his eyes focusing, first on a blurred, black object, then, aeons later, on the sharp image of an advancing U-boat.

"Course three-one-o, sir."

"Very good…"

He would never forget the sighting of his first target. There she was, barely six hundred yards away as she swept grandly by, blissfully unaware of the terror that lurked in wait for her.

"Put me on my D.A.," Peter ordered.

The Outside E.R.A. swung the periscope off the target by five degrees and now Peter could not see her.

"Down periscope!"

The attack periscope descended to the lip of the well.

"Loud H.E. passing up the port side, sir," Elliott reported.

"Up periscope — put me on my D.A."

Number One's voice cut into Peter's consciousness.

"Twenty-eight feet, sir."

Peter groaned out loud.

"Don't dip me — I must see now."

"You're on now, sir," Saunders's quiet voice murmured in his Captain's ear, as Peter wrenched at the periscope handles. He kept his thumb up to get the full height of the periscope. It would be fatal to be blind at this vital moment.

"Twenty-nine feet, sir," Benson reported desperately. "May I speed up, sir?"

The maddening request cut through to Peter's racing brain, just as the glass broke surface.

"No, certainly not, they'll see us."

But even as Peter was blinded by the blue-green water which drenched the glass, he had seen all that he needed. She stood up as large as a house, and, as the whiteness of her wake frothed at her stern, he could see the bare-chested figures of several sunburnt Italians on the bridge. They were singing their hearts out, and, as her bows scythed across the graticule of the periscope, Peter saw one of them suddenly stretch out his hand and point excitedly towards him.

"Fire one!" Peter snapped.

There was a sudden jolt as the first torpedo shot from its tube.

"Fire by time interval," Peter continued.

A slight pause, then three more jolts in quick succession.

"All torpedoes running, sir!" the Sub reported from the tube-space telephones.

CHAPTER 3

The Fortunes of War

Alberto Francini, Capitano di Corvetta, Commanding Officer of the Italian submarine *Lystra*, was not the first to see it. His thoughts had been hundreds of miles away, with his black-eyed Maria to be precise. He had recently taken his fuel-carrying submarine to Benghazi where the cargo was discharged direct into the Afrika Korps tankers which were waiting on the jetty. In his mind's eye he could see them now: no sooner were the pulsing hoses disconnected from one full truck than the next in line drew up to take his departing predecessor's place. Yes! Rommel certainly was short of gasoline because of the Royal Air Force and the British submarines. Ha! But he'd fooled the enemy and now he was on his way home for more fuel — and Maria! Ah! Maria, she would be having their fourth child at any time now and how they longed for a little girl... Alberto Francini smiled happily to himself.

No, it was Lorenzo Pollino who first sighted it, and it was his hysterical scream that first jolted the Capitano from his reveries.

"*Guarda!*" Pollino screeched, and his hand pointed just for'd of the starboard beam.

Pollino is a loud-mouthed braggart, thought the Capitano, *but, although there should be no British submarines inside the Kerkennahs, I suppose I'd better look through my glasses — Pollino does seem unusually excited, though.*

"Periscope, on starboard beam!" Pollino, the bullying Petty Officer, shouted frantically.

But by the time that Alberto Francini had lined himself up on the bearing of Pollino's outstretched arm, the periscope had dipped. The Capitano could see nothing.

"You're dreaming, Pollino," he shouted jocularly. "You should think more of your job, eh, Lorenzo Pollino?"

But at that moment even the Capitano di Corvetta could not fail to sight the first two torpedo tracks. They were streaking towards him, two bubbling fingers of frothing water, the first barely fifty yards away.

"*Santa Maria!*" he cried, his eyes bulging in their sockets. His heart stopped beating as he watched, fascinated, mesmerised in terror. There was nothing he could do.

Morelli Tupini, on the other hand, did all he could — more than he believed possible, in fact, for he was only a little man. But he had a burning love of life and he was determined not to die — not he!

He was the Helmsman of the Watch in the Control Room, some fifteen feet below the surface of the sea, and he was looking forward to going off watch. This had been a deadly dull passage and he wanted sleep. The trouble was that the more he slept the more he wanted to sleep, and at the moment he could hardly keep his eyes open. Bumbling along on the surface always gave him the willies — the Capitano said that their speed was quite safe for them and that's why they went on the surface if they could. But Morelli Tupini glanced over his shoulder at the lower hatch of the conning tower — he never felt safe with these British submarines about.

A peculiar grunt — a hollow shout of excitement came from the bell-mouthed voicepipe and Morelli leaned forward to hear better.

There was a sudden roar, a flash of yellow light and he found himself up to the neck in cascading water. With only one thought in mind he fought his way to the conning tower ladder, and having only six feet to cross, he was there in a split second, only one other floundering body having preceded him.

He screamed as the water cascaded in a torrent about his head, and then he felt the first rung of the ladder slide under his foot.

"I'm going to live…" He was astonished at his calmness now that Death was breathing down his neck, and he felt his lungs near bursting as they clamoured for air. He would have to climb faster if he was to gain on the water — and then suddenly he felt his fingers groping for the lip of the upper hatch.

As he grappled in the darkness, his hands brushed against a human leg. He clutched it and desperately tried to pull himself up. Suddenly his mouth was above the surface and he gulped air; and simultaneously the threshing leg above him kicked out savagely at his clawing hands. He let go and found himself gulping down fresh air. He trod water while the spasmodic twitchings of his body subsided as he gradually collected himself.

"I mustn't lose my head — panic kills…" he kept repeating to himself through chattering teeth, and then he saw an arm flailing in the maelstrom of floating debris.

"The Capitano!"

Morelli Tupini shouted and struck out for his drowning Captain, but as he reached him he heard a high-pitched voice yelling hysterically from somewhere behind them.

"Let the silly blighter drown!" it raved. "He could have saved us if he'd bothered."

Morelli recognised the voice as Pollino's. He ignored the crazed Petty Officer and continued trying to take the dead weight of the unconscious captain between his hands. He kicked out with his legs to try and reach a wooden board that bobbed nearby, but he was forced to lie on his back. As he did so he caught sight of a blue, steel tube poking vertically through the oily wreckage. Like the eye of a cobra about to strike, the glass of a periscope brooded down upon them, vindictively witnessing their death throes. It was very close and Morelli pictured the faces gloating at the lower end of the instrument.

"Americani!" he whispered hoarsely, and with his free hand he hurriedly crossed himself. He had often heard of the atrocities carried out by the Americani — had he not often listened to the stories told by the announcer on the Rome Radio? He shuddered involuntarily and shook his fist at the ugly lens. *Rather the Inglesi than the Americani*, he thought, *but either would be better than drowning.* He yelled at the top of his voice as he felt the weight of his captain dragging him down. But what was the use? They could not hear him, the devils! Tears were streaming down his oily face when he decided he could endure no more.

The three hits jounced *Rugged*'s pressure hull like the vibrations of a giant steam-hammer. For a second there was silence as the men reeled to the shock, then a spontaneous cheer rang through the little submarine. Men clapped each other on the back and in the tube-space and fore-ends there was jubilation.

"What did I tell you, Smithy?" Able Seaman Bill Hawkins shouted, a grin splitting his rugged face.

"O.K., Bill, you win! Our old subbie is making out all right — a U-boat on his first patrol."

"It's just a matter of luck," Petty Officer Slater interrupted. "You've got to be in the right place at the right time."

"And then use torpedoes," Hawkins added.

Slater was grinning foolishly.

"Come on, you loafers, get cracking! Drain down all tubes — the Old Man will want to reload in a moment," and he drove them back to their duties.

But in the Control Room a new problem had arisen.

"There's not much left up top, Number One," said the Captain quietly. "Poor devils."

"Breaking-up noises, sir," Elliott reported, his eyes fixed to the Asdic dial. "No H.E."

The cheering was as suddenly replaced by a shocked hush as each man could hear for himself the sickening reverberations of the disintegrating U-boat as she plunged into the depths. It was too real, too vivid, and surely it was merely a matter of fortune that they were born Britons rather than Italians — and then, might not the tables have been reversed? Of keener sensitivity were some men than others, but to one, Able Seaman Hawkins, the exploding bulkheads hundreds of feet below them meant less of the enemy to fight another day, and remembering his personal tragedy he rejoiced. Even the success of this catastrophic sinking would not replace his wife and two children — no, there was iron in Hawkins' soul.

Peter broke the silence.

"There are three survivors, Number One. They are hollering like mad and can see our stick. It looks as if one poor devil is trying to support one of his wounded," Peter announced briefly. Then he turned to Ian Taggart, the Navigator. "How far are we from the Kerkennahs?"

Peter's instincts were confused. His immediate reaction was to allow the survivors to drown; for surely they had deserved their fate? The Italians would have passed them by had the positions been reversed, and anyway, land wasn't so far off — any aircraft that was around would catch *Rugged* like a sitting duck if she surfaced to pick up survivors. All this flashed through Peter's mind as he turned to his Number One.

"What about it, Number One?" asked Peter. "Shall we let them drown?"

Before Benson could reply there was a muffled growl from Able Seaman Bowles who was on the wheel, and it did not go unnoticed.

"Let the murderers drown, sir. We don't want to risk our necks for the likes of 'em," and the singsong voice of the Glasgow ex-policeman grated in Peter's ear.

"I was asking the First Lieutenant for his opinion and not yours, Able Seaman Bowles," he said brusquely.

There was silence for a moment, and then the Coxswain spoke up respectfully from the after-planes.

"If you'll excuse me, sir, but I think a lot of us would like to pick 'em up if we could, if you understand me."

"Thank you, Coxswain."

"Northern end of the Kerkennahs, three and a half miles, sir," Taggart interrupted.

"Very good, Pilot. All round H.E. sweep, please, Elliott."

"I think we should pick them up if we can, sir," Benson said. "Apart from humanitarian reasons, they might be of use to us."

"But we'll have to be slippy about it: they are bound to send out aircraft after seeing and hearing the explosions," Peter continued. "I'm going to surface now, but I'm not risking the boat if anything appears. Stand by to surface!"

"Stand by to surface, sir," Number One repeated. "Check main vents."

"Second Coxswain and Able Seaman Bowles in the tower," the Captain ordered. "Provide heaving lines."

"Ready to surface, sir."

"Surface!" Peter rapped as he left the periscope. "Follow me up, Second Coxswain."

"Surface. Blow one, blow six," Benson ordered, and, in the darkness of the tower, Peter could hear the air singing along the high-pressure lines.

"Eighteen feet, sir," from down below.

"Open up!" Peter shouted to the signalman standing above him in the darkness.

The rattle of the clips as they were released, the sudden rush of air past him, the dripping and splashing of water, and then the blinding daylight of the world above. While Acting Leading Signalman Goddard dashed to open the voicepipe cock, Peter swept his eyes around the horizon.

"Rescue party on the fore-casing! Over you go, Second Coxswain," and then Petty Officer Jack Weston, his gleaming teeth grinning through his black whiskers, vaulted over the bridge side, followed by Bowles's huge bulk, each with a heaving line coiled around his shoulders.

"Buck up!" Peter said, and he swept his arm fore-and-aft, outside the bridge, so that the survivors would come alongside.

The single man was the first to reach the slippery pressure hull. He tore his hands on the rust-splotched roundness of the black hull, and then the coils of a heaving line snaked on top of him. He rapidly wriggled into the bowline and was hauled slithering and floundering on to the wet fore-casing where he was grabbed by Bowles. To his amazement Peter saw the man arrogantly give the Fascist salute, then, to Peter's joy, he watched Bowles punch him on the nose. The Fascist toppled backwards into the water where he remained, dangling in the heaving line while the rescue party recovered the other two survivors.

In all, the whole rescue took four and a half minutes, but to Peter's mind as he searched the horizon to the south-westward, where he could see the blur of Tunisia, the operation seemed more like four and a half hours. He was glad when Bowles's enormous fist plucked the damp Fascist from the water to carry him over the bridge and hurl him down the conning tower hatch. Peter followed, diving the boat as he shut the hatch over him.

The passage of the three Italians was marked by an oily slime and this led, snail-like, to the warmth of the Engine Room. There Pollino cowered in front of Stoker O'Connor, grovelling on his knees before the disgusted Irishman.

"Merc-ee, Americani, merc-ee!" the Fascist Petty Officer blubbered, tears streaming down his oil-blackened face as he clutched the stoker's sandals.

The Irishman was bewildered and embarrassed.

"Get up, ye Wop, ye. What d'ya take me forr, the Lord God Almighty?" and he flung the wretched man a handful of cotton waste to wipe his face.

Meanwhile, Second Class Seaman Morelli Tupini, although still believing that he was in for a bad time, showed dignity in his pathetic loyalty and devotion to his half-drowned Captain. Morelli insisted on their caring first for the unconscious man, and not until the Coxswain had forced a tot of rum between the Italian Captain's grey lips did the little man start to clean himself with the waste.

"We not Americani, we Inglesi," O'Connor said and, when he saw the slow smile of relief spreading over Morelli's face, he added with a sardonic grin, "Why, what's the matter, mate?"

Morelli drew his fingers across his throat.

"Americani, si, si!" he muttered as he nodded violently.

"Don't be so flippin' wet, Wop," O'Connor said kindly. "You no listen to propaganda, you believe no lies," and he pushed a bucket of warm water towards the naked man.

As the warmth of human kindness that lies deep in every sailor welled to the surface so, gradually, the stories of the three men were pieced together. Cigarettes, to be smoked later, were proffered to all except Pollino, and the men in the fore-ends took an instant liking to Morelli.

Alberto Francini, ex-Capitano of the Italian submarine *Lystra*, was accepted as a prisoner-of-war into the Ward Room, where he slept in the First Lieutenant's shirt and in the First Lieutenant's bunk.

"I've got to sleep hot bunks with you, Pilot," Benson groaned.

"I feel sorry for the Wop in your shirt," Taggart grinned. "But what's Alberto trying to say?"

The Italian Captain was gabbling excitedly at Peter, who sat alongside him, a slight smile on his face as he watched the swarthy, blue-shirted Sicilian.

It appeared that the man was a professional sailor, had been Master of his own ship before the war and now had been conscripted into the Marine. He was particularly upset because, as far as Peter could make out, his wife was expecting their fourth child and the news of the loss of her husband would be a grievous blow to her. Would Signor Capitano Inglesi *plees* radio Alberto Francini's safety so that his wife could be reassured?

At last Peter understood, and when he nodded his comprehension the Sicilian opposite him burst into uncontrollable sobs of relief. Peter steadied the man's heaving shoulders and left the Ward Room.

"When's our next routine, P.O. Tel.?" he asked James Haig in his tiny office.

"Half an hour's time, sir."

"Right; I'll come up for a transmission. I'll send in the Navigator with the enciphered groups."

"Aye, aye, sir."

On his way back to the Ward Room, Peter had a quiet word with Benson.

"I'm going to send this signal, Number One, for the enemy must know where we are anyway. There's not much risk, for we're a long way from the Trapani First Eleven. Do you agree?"

"Yes, sir. But are you mentioning Alberto's survival?"

"Here, see for yourself. Cipher it up quickly and give it to the P.O. Tel."

With a secret feeling of pride at his first sinking, Peter handed his First Lieutenant the pink signal sheet.

"'To Captain "S" Ten from *Rugged*,'" Benson read. "'Italian U-boat *Lystra* sunk 350 Kerkennah Isles 3.5 miles. Three survivors, including Commanding Officer. Request inform enemy authorities as Madame Lystra is expecting a bambino shortly.'"

"Aye, aye, sir," and Benson smiled as he went for'd with the signal.

"I'm going to shift billet, Number One," Peter added. "We've stirred it up around here and I think we'll do better farther up the coast. Pilot!"

"Sir?"

"Let me know the course for the Kuriate Lighthouse."

It was an uneventful night, and by nine o'clock the next morning *Rugged* had rounded Cape Africa and was abeam of the graceful lighthouse that rose from the ocean like a slender wand, gleaming white for both friend and foe. Peter took *Rugged* within five miles of the lighthouse, then set course for Sousse. He guessed that shipping might be concentrating in the little port, because the German Afrika Korps was now on the run, driven out of Cyrenaica by General Alexander. Their transport was forced to use the coastal roads and bottlenecks were known to exist in Sfax, Teboulba, Sousse and Hammamet. The Malta Wellingtons had bombed Sfax two nights previously, so the chance of there being chaos in Sousse was good.

As the bearing of Monastir drew slowly across, the township of Sousse came into view, a higgledy-piggledy conglomeration of white buildings, strung across a low cliff. Peter whistled as he looked through the periscope, across the mirror-like surface of the blistering sea and towards the arm of the breakwater which stretched towards him, grey stoned and uninviting.

"Down periscope, stop starboard. Diving Stations and Silent Routine," Peter ordered and then he turned to his First Lieutenant.

"There's not a breath of wind up top, Number One. It's a glassy calm so I must be careful with the stick. I'm going right up to the harbour entrance because they can't have mined it. There's too much shipping activity."

"Hope not, sir," and Benson grinned.

"We might get a crack at some of the coastal stuff inside the breakwater," Peter added, "but watch your trim, for heaven's sake, Number One. I shall only be able to use the stick for seconds at a time — it's like a mirror up top."

"Aye, aye, sir."

"Not a sound from anyone, as they may have hydrophones out — pass the word. Up periscope."

Peter was running with perspiration and he had to use his sweat-rag continuously as he swung up and down with the constant periscope work. The arm of the breakwater gradually became larger, a strip of water opened up as the entrance came into view, and then appeared the short arm of the farther breakwater.

"Down periscope. Phew! it's hot — I've never seen it so calm. The slick from the stick looks like a black finger oiling its way towards the harbour. They must be blind if they don't see us, Number One."

"They might not expect a visitor quite so close, sir."

"Maybe. Up periscope."

Peter's throat was dry as he had another quick look. He felt that he could almost put his hand out and touch the stonework of the breakwater and then, through the gap of the entrance, he sighted the inner harbour.

"What a shambles!" he murmured. "And there's a coaster inside, a sitting duck. Stand by Number One, and blow up all tubes!"

Major Johann Hoffmann was uneasy. He felt that all was not well with the Afrika Korps; that Rommel was being let down by the politicians in Berlin. Even his own 88mm Field Gun Battery had been forced to halt because it was starved of petrol. The supply lines were so vulnerable to sea attack from the Royal Navy based on Malta that Rommel was always looking over his shoulder to see how far he could travel on his dwindling petrol supplies.

Major Hoffmann groaned. How jubilant they had all been six months ago! Now they were driving westwards, westwards all the time. Yes, he had been lucky to reach here with his battery, and he looked with pride across the harbour at the town where he picked out the gun emplacements, dispersed so efficiently along the waterfront. Even though the twisted steel girders of the bombed warehouses blocked the working of the port after the Royal Air Force attack last night, the bombers had failed to knock out any of his guns, and, from his control position at the end of the breakwater, he felt a surge of affection for the battery he had led continuously throughout the African campaign. With his second-in-command, the ostentatious Leutnant Rinnor, he had forged an efficient unit for the Afrika Korps: the different functions of the superb 88mm were well known to the enemy. Anti-aircraft, anti-tank, light field artillery and even mounted in F-lighters to protect the coastal convoys, these 88s were proving themselves the most versatile of guns — and Major Hoffmann looked across the harbour nostalgically.

"*Achtung!*" Leutnant Rinnor barked. "U-boat's periscope!"

Hoffmann spun round, and his desert-trained eyes picked up the sliver of steel just sliding beneath the placid surface of the sea — barely five hundred yards away.

"It's gone," Rinnor yelled.

"Alert all guns, Leutnant! Load with high explosive, impact fuse."

Rinnor spun the handle of the field telephone and passed his orders to the guns dispersed round the harbour. He was proud of the effectiveness of his training, and this he showed when he reported back to the Major.

"All guns ready, *Herr Major*!"

Hoffmann did not bother to use his field glasses, for the periscope had now reappeared plainly on the mirror-like surface. Already in the back of his mind he was wondering whether he would be the first officer in the Afrika Korps to sink a cursed British submarine.

"*Achtung!* There!" and Hoffmann's body froze stiffly as his arm stretched out towards the periscope which was moving slowly towards the harbour entrance. "Range four hundred yards. Fire when all guns are bearing."

Rinnor, however, was screaming down the telephone:

"Where the devil are you, Number Five? For the Führer's sake, buck up and report when you're on!"

The phone crackled.

"Open…"

But the slender tube had disappeared.

"Cease firing!" the frustrated second-in-command bellowed. "Wait for the next sighting."

But it was not so easy for the Fifty-Ninth 88mm Battery. Each time that the periscope appeared, one of the guns would fail to sight it; when they were all 'on target' the tube would vanish with only an eddy breaking the surface to mark its previous position.

Hoffmann's Teutonic self-control was slipping fast, the nearer the submarine approached the harbour entrance.

"Alert all ships in the harbour," he bawled. "If you can't get all the guns on, Leutnant, open fire by local control," and he swung round angrily towards his second-in-command. "We've got to stop the *schweinhund!*"

"All guns, Local Control!" Rinnor shouted, and his eyes swept towards the emplacements. He smiled secretly to himself as he counted the five lean barrels silently traversing the harbour.

"Some squarehead is pretty worked up on the end of the breakwater, Number One," Peter Sinclair remarked as he stood by the attack periscope. "He's dancing up and down with excitement."

"Probably sighted our periscope, sir. Maybe he'll whistle up the Luftwaffe."

"Numbers one and two tubes ready, sir," Brocklebank reported from the Fruit Machine.

"Very good. I'll fire when my bows are pointing at her engine room. Put me on zero D.A."

Peter was crouching on his knees and as the tube slid past him, he hauled himself up from the corticene-covered deck. The Outside E.R.A. swung the periscope on to the fore-and-aft line, and then the glass broke surface. A split second of this heat and the lens cleared. "Ah, there she is!" Peter whispered to himself. The coaster lay beam on to him, a sitting duck, low in the water and bulging with supplies for the Afrika Korps. But, with the cranes lying drunkenly on the quayside after last night's air attack, she could not unload.

What a target! Peter could even see the cooling water of her generators discharging in a spout over the side, and across the ship's counter he glimpsed the blurred letters of her name.

"It's almost immoral, it's so easy," he remarked as the periscope slid downwards. "Stand by!"

The graticule was just crossing the midship superstructure when their whole world broke into ear-splitting pandemonium.

Brocklebank saw his Captain's lips move:

"Fire one! ... Fire two!" and the Sub pulled the firing switches.

The boat jumped twice. Peter saw Elliott's astonished face as he quickly wrenched off his earphones, his mouth opening and shutting soundlessly as he tried to make himself heard above the din. The young Captain was bewildered and, as he glanced at Benson, his first thought was of exploding tank-traps, laid on the seabed.

"Christopher Columbus, I've got it! Shelling!" and Peter strode between the periscopes. "Starboard twenty! Forty feet, quickly, Number One."

"Speed up, sir?"

"Yes."

"Group up, half-ahead together. Take her to forty feet, Coxswain," the First Lieutenant ordered.

As the boat quickly sank another ten feet, the shelling seemed to draw aft, even though the swirl from her propellers must have shown clearly on the surface.

With barely a split second between them, the blast of two explosions crashed against the pressure hull, to be followed by a succession of tinklings and whistling water noises.

The racket of the gunfire disappeared dramatically and in the sudden silence a cheer rang from the tensed-up men in the submarine.

Peter took her out a mile before coming to periscope depth. A quick look showed a black cloud, streaked by red and orange flame, billowing upwards rapidly. Of the Germans at the end of the jetty there was no sign.

"I reckon that's one ship less for Rommel!" Peter exulted. "Down periscope, eighty feet. What's my course for the Gulf of Hammamet, Pilot? We might catch them bending there."

But they were to be disappointed. After eight blank and frustrating days in the Gulf, *Rugged* was recalled to Malta.

Captain 'S' was waiting for them on the jetty and by him stood his 'Staffie', Joe Croxton, *Rugged*'s first Captain.

I suppose this is one of the moments in life which I shall never forget, Peter reflected as he glanced at his periscope standards. From the top of the attack periscope, *Rugged*'s Jolly Roger fluttered, black, and sinister with its red and white symbols stitched upon it: white bars for supply ships sunk, a blood-red for warships. The black rectangle of hessian streamed proudly, and upon it a new symbol had recently been sewn by the privileged signalman — a large red 'U'. Beneath the Jolly Roger, from its bracket at the after-end of the bridge there fluttered the White Ensign, flapping in the breeze. Peter felt a surge of pride as he looked down at the figure of Captain 'S'.

"Well done, Sinclair," he said, and the eyes twinkled up at the young man leaning over the bridge side. "Not bad for a beginner! But you'll have to watch your step on your next patrol."

"Why's that, sir?" Peter laughed.

"Harry Arkwright's gone sick and I've no one to replace him except Joe Croxton who insists on relieving him. I want an Iron Ring round Tunis: they're rushing in supplies fast and doing all they know in a last bid to save Rommel."

"How long have I got to kit up with torpedoes, sir?"

"Twenty-four hours. Joe's preceding you in *Restless* tonight."

Peter looked long at 'S' who seemed to be bubbling over with suppressed merriment.

"What's the catch, sir?" Peter asked, sticking out his neck.

"You are at the eastern end of the Ring and Joe Croxton is your next-door neighbour!" chuckled Captain 'S'.

CHAPTER 4

Attack and ...

It was not the fault of the minelayer *Sea-unicorn* that she missed her wireless routine. She was being hunted at the time, having laid mines off Hammamet and now she was returning home by the Pantelleria route. She had picked up a submarine contact on her Asdics, and as no boats of the Tenth Flotilla were scheduled for today, *Restless* having passed through yesterday, the Captain of *Sea-unicorn* decided that he would stalk and destroy the lurking U-boat.

The Control Room in *Rugged* was very quiet. Peter was gliding his submarine through the blazed trail at sixty feet, and he knew from his last look that the wedge of Pantelleria was but three miles distant on his starboard beam.

"Silent Routine," he ordered.

Intelligence had reported, and the boats of the Tenth Submarine Flotilla knew from experience, that the enemy had laid hydrophones on the shallow shelf of the seabed which ran out south-easterly from the island fortress of Pantelleria. It was simple for the listening enemy to hear the careless submarine, and then the covey of E-boats waiting in the harbour would tear out to hunt the intruder.

Peter never liked this business of creeping through enemy minefields and the sooner it was over the better.

Although he was bound for a patrol of intensive activity — a certainty this, in the Bay of Tunis — his spirits were low. He felt a curious premonition of disaster as he leant over the chart table, double-checking his position. The south-eastern extremity of the long island, yellow in the morning sun, reared boldly above the horizon, the cliff falling steeply into the sea. The land then fell away gently to the north-westward until the sloping plateau joined the blue Mediterranean. Sighting it had stirred Peter, for the last time he had seen it had been when, as Joe Croxton's First Lieutenant, he had helped to put Jan Widdecombe's Commandos ashore under the steep cliff.

"Asdic transmission, red six-o, sir."

Elliott's report shattered the silence and snatched Peter from his moodiness.

"Asdics?" he asked incredulously. He hadn't seen any destroyer when he went deep, and Elliott usually picked up their propeller noises before the enemy gained contact.

"Yes, sir, I'm positive. They're in contact."

"Well, I'm jiggered! Port ten, steer two-nine-o."

"Transmission interval fifteen hundred yards, sir."

Peter went over to the chart. He looked again at his position and was certain he was on course.

"Take her up slowly, Number One. Periscope depth."

"Periscope depth, sir."

If there's nothing in sight, thought Peter as he watched the depth pointers creep back, *the transmissions can mean one of two things. Either the 'loops' have remote-controlled Asdic sets out on the spit here, or else a U-boat is stalking us. But I never knew they had transmitting Asdic…*

"Transmission interval decreased to one thousand yards, sir. Still in contact," the H.S.D. reported quietly.

"Course two-nine-o, sir," Able Seaman Bowles growled from the wheel.

"Still in contact?"

"Twenty-eight feet, sir; twenty-seven…" from the First Lieutenant.

"In contact, sir. Green one-seven-o."

"Up periscope."

What a weird business, Peter thought, as he swung the lens around the horizon, first in low-power for aircraft, then slowly in high-power. But apart from the yellow island now sliding across his stern and the silver of the surface shimmering with heat, there was nothing to be seen.

It's uncanny, Peter thought to himself. *We're being stalked by a submarine and I can't throw him off. He's almost within firing range now and I can't do anything about it. But surely Pantelleria should pick him up? And, as they haven't sent out patrols, this must be a U-boat they know about.*

"She's using British procedure, sir," spoke Elliott calmly from the set. "Range eight hundred yards."

Peter moved swiftly. She'd be firing at any moment now, but he dare not speed up or the listening stations ashore would pick him up.

"Sixty feet. Port five, steer two-seven-o. Pilot, give me the sailing orders. Not a sound in the boat, Number One. We're being stalked by an expert, and if we can't throw him off, we're sunk."

"Lost contact, sir, right astern."

"Very good, all-round sweep."

"Aye, aye, sir."

Peter flicked over the pages of the sailing orders until he read the last page but one. 'Own movements,' he read. 'Wednesday, 21st May. *Sea-unicorn* homewards from Hammamet via Pantelleria channel…'

He threw the orders to Taggart and turned to face his First Lieutenant.

"It's Bill Harris, in *Sea-unicorn*, homeward bound from a mine-laying patrol. You know Petty Officer Jenks is his H.S.D.?" Peter said gravely.

"The chap that stalked and sank the U-boat in an underwater attack in the Skagerrak?"

"Yes."

Elliott's back stiffened on the stool by the Asdic set, and Peter felt the hair on the back of his neck begin to bristle. At any second, the torpedoes from the minelayer would spill out into the depths to seek out *Rugged*.

"Regained contact, sir. Range five hundred yards, green one-four-o, gaining bearing."

Peter acted.

"Transmit on Asdics the Identification Reply for the day," he snapped.

Elliott had been waiting for this and, as he looked towards the Navigator, his fingers felt for the transmitting key.

"Q for Queenie," Taggart blurted.

While all eyes in the Control Room were fascinated by the long fingers jerking out morse identification — dash-dash-dot-dash, dash-dash-dot-dash … the silence in the Control Room was complete. Benson had to bite his tongue, while Saunders, fighting for self-control, turned his back on the Control Room and faced his panel. To be blown asunder in the depths, particularly by one's own friends, was a horrible end, too ghastly to imagine. And on those lean fingers, tapping the ebony key so confidently, depended their salvation. No, Saunders could watch no longer — he wanted to scream his lungs out.

"Sixty feet, sir," Benson's voice reported, and the matter-of-fact tones brought sanity back to the situation.

Elliott's fingers were motionless, the slight fuzz of black hair gleaming in the sweat between the knuckles. Then Peter saw him clutch the earphone over his left ear.

Ah! Here it comes! thought Peter. *So this is the end. She's fired her torpedoes!* And he turned his head to hear the approaching prelude to annihilation.

"Letter R for Roger transmitted twice, sir," Elliott reported, but for the first time Peter detected a tremor in the H.S.D.'s voice.

"Very good. Carry on with your all-round sweep. Starboard ten. Steady on three hundred."

Peter sighed. Then the whole Control Room relaxed, subdued conversations being continued quietly from where they had been left off.

"All part of the daily round, I suppose, but I do wish Bill Harris would stick to mine-laying," Peter murmured as he made ready to leave the Control Room. "What's the course for Cape Bon, Pilot, once we clear Pantelleria?"

"Two-nine-six, sir."

"Alter course to two-nine-six when the northern tip of Pantelleria bears o-nine-o. I'm going to get my head down. Who's on watch?"

"I am, sir," Taggart replied.

"Shake me when you sight Cape Bon."

"Aye, aye, sir."

The island of Zembra lies some ten miles west of Cape Bon, and it was towards this black outline that the Captain of H.M. Submarine *Rugged* steered his ship. He had picked up Cape Bon in the late afternoon, but it was not until dusk that he rounded the white lighthouse which stood up so high and so clearly on this massive headland, the nearest point to Europe still available to the Afrika Korps, and soon to be the scene of such savage fighting. Europe was only ninety miles away, but Rommel might as well sigh for the moon if the Italians could not control the seaway between Marittimo Island and the Bay of Tunis — the 'Tunis Run' as it was known to the Fighting Tenth.

Between Sicily and Tunis the enemy had laid vast minefields and through these they maintained swept channels for their own convoys. Down the Tunis Corridor they poured all the shipping they could muster: supply ships with war stores, ammunition ships, troop ships and oilers, and, even in the air overhead, the great lumbering air transports known as Heinkel Boxcars.

The convoys passed up and down this corridor in an unending stream, and on either side of them steamed the overworked Italian destroyers, sleek and dangerous watchdogs, ready to pounce on the lurking submarines of the Fighting Tenth, soon to be augmented by the larger boats from the Eighth Flotilla at Algiers.

But the Italian Admiralty suffered one disadvantage: the Tunis Corridor, though impregnably defended through the minefields, had to pass through a bottleneck off the island of Zembra. This focal point was barely twenty miles wide, for, with the island forming a physical barrier to the eastward, dangerous rocks bounded the western extremity. It was here that the Iron Ring was marshalling, with *Rugged*'s extreme easterly position five miles due west of Zembra. Five miles west of her, Joe Croxton, who had arrived yesterday in *Restless*, then *Renegade*, and, at the western end, John Easton, Peter's old First Lieutenant, in *Rapid*.

Quite a 'Rugged' party, Peter thought as he searched the darkness ahead. *Lucky there's no moon, because zigzagging on the surface within five miles of each other, they would be standing up like houses. Ah, there's the lighthouse on Zembra! Lighthouses look so white and clean, even in the darkness — but there's one consolation: trimmed down like this, I'm not likely to be sighted with Zembra for a background*; and on his port beam he felt he could almost touch the black mass jutting from the sea, its outline silhouetted sharply against the starlit sky.

"Bridge?"

The summons took Peter to the voicepipe and he heard Taggart reporting on their last bearings.

"This fix puts us right on the line, sir, and one mile to the east of our westerly limit. Mean course for the zigzag, two-seven-o."

"Very good. Using five degrees of wheel, weave forty degrees either side of the mean line. Slow ahead together."

Peter felt happier now that he was on his billet at last: it was good to feel that the man for whom he had the greatest respect and admiration, the man who had taught Peter all he'd ever known about wartime patrols, was within five miles or so. And if Peter remembered the experiences he had shared with Joe Croxton, he ought not to go very far wrong.

"Keep your eyes skinned, lookouts," Peter reminded them. "This is one of the hottest corners in the Med."

Murmured "aye, ayes" from the bridge-sides reassured him, and it was good to see the outlines of the lookouts crouching over their binoculars. It was upon the sharpness of their eyes against those of the enemy that their very existence depended, so in submarines the best men for the task were selected as lookouts, irrespective of rating, be it seaman or stoker, wireless operator or signalman. Only hourly tricks were set because of the strain of concentration, although the Officer of the Watch stood two hours, as against the four-hour watch in surface ships.

"Permission to ditch gash, sir?" came the nightly request up the voicepipe.

"Be quick about it," Peter said to Brocklebank who was the Officer of the Watch. "We can't afford to get caught here."

"Permission granted," the Third Hand shouted above the drumming of the diesels. "Buck up."

Then up from the darkness of the conning tower came the clatter of buckets and bins, the sour smell of rubbish and the whisper of oaths. Ordinary Seaman Smith stood astride the upper lid, then he reached down for each bucket and passed it to the waiting Hawkins on the leeward side of the bridge. There was a heave in the darkness, the clatter of tins as they bounced off the pressure hull and the flutter of rubbish as it hit the water. So the process was repeated until all the gash was ditched, all the tins punctured carefully at each end so that they would sink quickly to leave no tell-tale floating evidence on the surface.

Tonight there seemed to be an unending stream of rubbish and Peter was becoming restless as he peered into the darkness. He knew that the convoys would be timed to pass through this focal point at night and he did not want to miss an opportunity by being cluttered up with the gash party.

Then there was a hoarse report from Able Seaman Hawkins in the starboard wing.

"There's plenty of gash 'ere already, sir, by the looks o' things," and he stood poised, bucket in mid-air and ready for the next fling.

Peter looked over the side and, sure enough, there was the usual motley collection of British rubbish — bobbing 'Carnation' condensed milk tins, broken-up dried fruit boxes, cotton waste. He exploded with laughter and broke the spell of foreboding that was clouding the bridge.

"It's Joe's gash, of all his confounded cheek!" Peter chuckled. "*Restless* has come up to the edge of our area to ditch his gash and has beaten us to it!"

"We'll get him tomorrow night, sir," Brocklebank smiled in the darkness without taking his eyes from his binoculars. Then suddenly his body jerked.

"Red one-six-o, sir, darkened ship!" he shouted.

Peter swung round and lined himself up behind the Officer of the Watch the better to pick up the bearing.

"Gash party clear the bridge! Stop the generators, group up, slow ahead together."

The eyepieces of his binoculars bored into his eye sockets and the circle of vision slowly delineated, the night sky quickly separating itself from the deeper darkness of the sea. Then, as he slowly swept across the horizon line from right to left, the blur of Brocklebank's head intervened. He knew then he was nearly on the bearing, and he felt his heart pounding with the excitement of his first night alarm as a Commanding Officer.

"Have you still got him?" Peter asked irritably, his glasses searching hungrily.

"Yes, sir. I'm on now. She's crossing our stern jumping wire now, range about a thousand yards. Zembra is behind her, sir. She's only a blur and I can't make out what she is."

Feverishly Peter slid his glasses across the horizon line until the island of Zembra showed blacker than the sea. Ah! there was the island, dark and gaunt, its outline jagged against the luminous sky; sweep back again, steady — there she was — now he'd got her in his circle of vision.

"Hard-a-starboard, full ahead port, sound the night alarm!"

While the little submarine trembled to the added power and swept towards the escaping ship in a sharp curve, Peter strained his eyes for signs of other vessels — destroyers in particular or perhaps an elusive E-boat.

"Eyes skinned, everybody," he heard himself saying. "Keep a sharp lookout for her escorts! Full ahead together."

He was surprised to hear his voice so steady on this, his first night encounter. It was a most unnerving attack, for the submarine relied entirely upon her cloak of invisibility to close the target, and on the surface she was hideously vulnerable. But now that Peter was in action he felt different. When he heard the distant summons of the alarm rattlers down below, he felt his blood racing, and a fierce joy swept over him as he gripped his binoculars.

"Stand by all tubes!" he shouted above *Rugged*'s own wind as it started to ruffle his hair. "Sub, set the torpedo sight."

"Aye, aye, sir."

Peter was glued to his glasses but Brocklebank and the lookouts continued searching their own sectors. As *Rugged* swung her bows on to a closing course, Peter began to distinguish the target.

Ah, that's better! he thought, *she's clearing Zembra now.* And there she stood, silhouetted starkly along the horizon, a bone in her teeth and black Zembra sliding away astern of her.

"Hell's bells!" Peter blurted. "That's why she hasn't got an escort: she's in ballast, Sub!"

And, true enough, the nearer *Rugged* closed the more apparent it became that she was unladen, empty, with her antifouling showing boldly above the water, and her ship's side standing like a house against the horizon.

Rugged was now at full speed and within five hundred yards of the tramp's port quarter.

"What a temptation!" Peter whispered. "It's a pity 'S' ordered us not to waste torpedoes on empty ships."

He smiled to himself as he distinguished every detail: her rusty side with the boats already swung out on their davits, ready to abandon ship; the Italian ensign fluttering in the darkness; the smoke curling from the tall funnel standing so squarely amidships; and the boiling wake which frothed and danced with its phosphorescence in the blackness.

"Break off the attack! Stop both!"

Peter dropped the glasses from his eyes and sighed. He watched the ship slip into the night which quickly enveloped her.

"Starboard ten, start the generators. Group down, slow ahead together," the Captain ordered wearily. "Steer two-six-five, resume normal weaving on either side of the mean line."

He moved to the after-end of the bridge where he crouched down in the dampness.

"Keep your eyes skinned, Sub, I'm going to get some sleep. Tomorrow may be a busy day."

And so it proved to be.

But apart from star shell and depth-charging away to the westward — *probably John Easton*, Peter thought — *Rugged* had an uneventful night and she dived at first light.

It was a dawn that Peter would never forget, for this was to be a day that would leave its memory indelibly scarred upon his soul. And as he looked around him for the first time on the birth of this new day, he felt unusually keyed up. As he stood by the upper conning tower hatch, one foot already feeling for the brass lip, a section of his mind told him to relax; but the other part prodded him to an acute awareness of his surroundings and in that instant before diving Peter came close to the Things Unseen. The eastern sky was suffused with a duck egg green, and against this pastel dawn the outline of the island of Zembra gently receded to merge into the mainland of Cape Bon which advanced from out of the night. The mountain ranges pushed themselves forward to announce their domination; dark azure and purple they were in the promise of sweltering heat, while, far away to the southward, the haze of La Goulette and Tunis shimmered in the freshness of the morning. To the westward, the gloom of the night was quickly dispersing, but upon the surface the young Captain could see nothing, try as he might to sight *Restless*. He took a long draught of the fresh air and his nostrils thrilled to the fresh tang of the early offshore breeze, laden with the elusive scents of a strange shore.

"Dive, dive, dive!" he shouted down the hatch, and as he swung off into space, shutting the open lid down upon him, he glanced at his watch on his left wrist. It showed half past five.

"Twenty-two feet, sir."

"Good morning, Number One."

"Good morning, sir," and Benson flicked his order instrument to 'pump'.

"Eighty feet."

"Eighty feet, sir."

And so the next day began, the regular routine of another day's wartime patrol. Peter watched the pointers glide round the gauges.

"Did you get the 'box' right up, Number One?"

"Stop pumping. Yes, sir, we just finished the charge," the First Lieutenant replied. "Eighty feet, sir."

"Good — we may need every amp we can find today. I have a hunch it's going to be a busy one," said the Captain as he climbed out of his Ursula suit, the signalman taking the clothes and binoculars. "Steer two-seven-o, stop starboard, and send the hands to breakfast."

To Peter, this was always one of the most pleasant moments of the day. After the tension of the night, it was good to feel the orderly routine continuing quietly around him. He brushed his hair by the heads door while men moved by him, busily substituting white bulbs for the red. "Excuse me, sir," Flint, the L.T.O., murmured as he crouched on his knees by his Captain's feet to take another battery reading. There was a certain friendliness and respect in his tone which was reassuring to the raw young Captain. Peter stretched himself to shake off the tiredness from his aching joints, and he knew that by the time he slumped on to the Ward Room settee, O'Riley's face would be smiling down at him from around the curtain.

"Good morning, sir. It's a fair lovely breakfast this morning, sir."

"Good morning, O'Riley. You cooked it, I suppose?"

A pause, while the Ward Room flunkey scratched his black hair.

"In a manner of speakin', yes sir, I did."

"Baked beans on fried bread?"

"Yes, sir, that it is. How did you guess?" asked the irrepressible youth from the Gorbals, disappearing through the bulkhead door.

Peter was feeling drowsy and as his head nodded with lassitude, the Sub's head poked round the corner.

"The H.S.D. reports H.E. approaching on a wide arc from three-five-o, sir."

Peter rose and stumbled into the Control Room, but the fluttering in his stomach belied his calm exterior.

"What do you make of it, Elliott?"

The H.S.D. paused before looking up.

"I think it's a fast convoy, sir. The H.E.'s on a broad front and is increasing rapidly."

Peter looked at his watch — five minutes to six. There should be enough light to see through the periscope but he would have to chance a collision from deep.

"Periscope depth," he said quietly. "Diving stations!"

Half-finished cups of tea were hurriedly pushed aside to stand steamily on mess-tables and in oily corticene corners, while men tumbled to their diving stations, silently cursing to themselves as *Rugged* swooped upwards at a steep angle.

"Twenty-eight feet, sir."

"Up periscope."

The initial feeling of stage fright was fast slipping away, but whenever the periscope slid upwards for the first sighting in an attack Peter was always to feel this watery feeling flowing through his innards and there was nothing he could do about it — *rather like going in to bat, first wicket down*, he thought grimly as he clutched the periscope handles. A flick of his thumb and the steel tube stopped abruptly; then he settled the upper half of his face more comfortably into the rubber shock guard and light excluder. A piercing shaft of light, blurred vision as the water drained off the sloping lens, and then suddenly clear focus. Yes, it was light enough to see all right, and he spun round in a low-power sweep. To the westward nothing; to the south, the grey-green haze of the Bay of Tunis, then, quickly, into the eastern sector where the island of Zembra monopolised his circle of vision. Not so sinister was it by daylight, mottled green and brown, with lighthouse perched up high and gleaming pink in the rays of the rising sun, while just clear of the northern tip, and forming a distant haze of mauve, the headland of Cape Bon disappeared into the distance. He swept across the north-eastern sector, the blue Mediterranean sparkling in the freshness — and there, yes, a dot, flying from left to right.

Peter flicked the handle and the lens changed to high-power.

"Bearing THAT — aircraft, Cant 52."

"Green one-six-five," the Outside E.R.A. reported quietly.

Back in low-power, Peter continued his sweep across the northern sector but this time he did not stop.

"Phew!" he whistled. "Down periscope. Start the attack. Stand by all tubes."

There were not many men whose hearts did not sink into their boots when they heard this order, so oft repeated. "Start the attack!" — the crash of cymbals before the crescendo, the prelude to such vital alternatives — success and survival, or failure and annihilation: it depended upon how long your nerve could stand it.

"Start the attack!"

As Peter heard himself calling his men to action, all the training he had been given up in Rothesay and Inchmarnock, the real-life attacks he had carried out on the battle fleet off Scapa Flow, all the many weeks of intensive training he had been given flooded back upon him as the periscope flashed upwards for the second time. He felt his team standing around him, waiting for him to transmit to them his own oral interpretation of what he was about to see.

"Bearing THAT, leading ship of convoy."

The picture that flashed into his mind seemed unreal and as dreamlike as the miniature target in the attack-teacher that advanced relentlessly along the tramlines at Blockhouse. There they were, the little ships upon the blue sea which frolicked with a whisk of white horses in the offshore breeze of the morning. *A perfect sea*, he thought; *they shouldn't sight my periscope in this*. Then the wide front of the convoy, flanked by three weaving destroyers with their white cross-trees gleaming above the horizon, the nearest apparently about a mile off.

"Target bearing THAT, large trooper, eight thousand tons — I'm ten degrees on her port bow."

He clapped the periscope handles shut and the tube slid downwards. He looked at Brocklebank who was feeding the Fruit Machine with the information.

"I'll try and get a range on my next look, Sub. She's doing about twenty-four knots, judging by her bow wave. There are so many aircraft there's no point in worrying about them," and Peter grinned as he slipped his hands into the pockets of his shorts. "The whole convoy is running us down fast, so I need all the time I can get. Port fifteen. What's my course for a hundred and twenty track?"

He flicked his fingers.

By now his movements had become instinctive and he felt a controlled elation sweeping over him as he grabbed the stick.

Ah, that's better! I can see now. There ... a 'weaver', right ahead of me, her camouflage extraordinarily efficient with her white and green dazzle-bars criss-crossed; but the break in her bridge superstructure gives her away, he thought. *Yes, she's crossing my bow and going like a bat out of hell; ah! another weaving destroyer steaming in the opposite direction, then two buzzing anti-submarine aircraft, growing larger every minute. They'll soon be up on me.* "Down periscope!"

"Course for a hundred and twenty track, two-three-o, sir. D.A., red twelve," the young Sub said, his voice rising with excitement and then, as the mauve indicator lights flickered on one by one above his head, "All tubes ready, sir!" he reported.

Peter was enjoying this now, all nervousness gone. Perspiration ran in runnels between his eyes; he dashed the drops away as the upper glass drained off and then the picture on the surface sharpened into focus.

The destroyers were much closer, their fo'c'sles and bridges now clearly in sight. *Rugged* was broad on the bow of the nearest, but, even as he watched, the dazzling whiteness of her side changed imperceptibly as she altered course towards him. He could plainly see her listing over to starboard as she heeled on her continuous weave. *I can ignore the other two,* Peter calculated, *they're farther off — but this first one is the menace.* Then out loud he gave his fresh estimations of the course and speed of the target before slamming shut the periscope handles.

"Range eight hundred yards, sir."

"Thank you, Sub. How many degrees to go?"

"Thirty-five, sir."

Peter jerked round towards Elliott.

"What speed on Asdics?"

Elliott looked up, but shook his head.

"There's too much H.E., sir, but I should say that by the noise it's a fast convoy."

Peter felt his heart beating faster, for already he could hear the rhythmic pounding of propeller noise as the enemy thrashed towards him.

"Stand by all tubes! Up periscope."

Now what? thought Peter. *Will the situation be the same or will that destroyer baulk me?* His eye was glued to the eyepiece even before the periscope cleft the water. Then suddenly the dark blueness flashed to white, and slowly, much too slowly, the scene drifted into focus as the heat of the day dried the drenched lens.

Peter slithered round on his heel as he swept in low-power — even in this magnification the destroyer was looking too close. He just caught sight of a receding Cant 52, its ponderous bulk winging downward in a lumbering turn. He flicked to high-power and suddenly the picture jumped at him.

The whole set piece had now rolled down upon him, the position changing with every moment. The nearest destroyer stood up hugely, her side exposed broadly to *Rugged*'s itching torpedoes as the lean greyhound swung away across the bows of her troopship in the last leg of her weave.

I've only the trooper to base my estimations upon, Peter thought, *so thank heavens she's steering a steady course...*

Then suddenly his stomach sank as the target's silhouette began changing rapidly. Peter swore beneath his breath while he watched her swing rapidly towards him.

He banged shut the handles of the periscope, but, before the lens dipped, he caught a quick glimpse of the trooper as she altered course. Gradually the angle of the break on the bridge superstructure closed as she swung: *is she altering*, Peter wondered, *or am I imagining things?* Then the grey flatness of her bridge slowly crossed the vertical line of the modern foremast, ugly in its stumpiness and with its derricks rearing skywards. Her bows swiftly curved towards him, and as *Rugged* crossed her fore-and-aft line, Peter could see the white mountain of water creaming at her stern. From this angle, looking up at her as she bore down upon him in her juggernaut splendour, Peter was amazed to see her lifeboats already swung out on the davits.

She's taking no chances, he thought, and he flicked his fingers from the periscope. *Ah! that's better, she's settled now. Perhaps she'll give me enough time to get in a shot.*

"That's fine," he said out loud, "bearing THAT; I'm ten degrees on her starboard bow. Starboard ten. That's the range. What's my course for a sixty track?"

I must get a crack at her before she alters again, Peter thought, and he swivelled round on his heel to sweep the horizon in low-power.

"Bearing THAT, number two destroyer — bearing THAT number three," and he banged shut the periscope handles.

The second destroyer was now bearing straight down upon him, barely four hundred yards away.

"I'll have to go deep and get inside her, Number One. She'll run us down on our present course. Emergency change of depth — eighty feet!" Peter snapped. "Group up, full ahead together."

"Flood Q!" barked the First Lieutenant.

The emergency order crackled through the boat, and as the klaxon blared for the emergency change of depth, the bulkhead doors swung shut. The depth-gauge pointers started to swing, and the submarine took on a steep bow-down angle. Peter grabbed the rung of the ladder for support.

"Course for a hundred and twenty track, sir," Brocklebank shouted above the roar of Q tank venting inboard. "O-one-two. Distance off track, four hundred yards: your D.A., red eight."

"Loud H.E. port quarter, sir," Elliott said, his face a study of grim concentration as he crouched over the dials, his earphones pressed to his head. "H.E. starting to move up the port side."

"Eighty feet, sir!"

Peter could hear the destroyer rumbling overhead now, and even as the clatter died down over his starboard bow, to leave faint whistlings and hollow water noises, he gave the order to come up from deep.

"Periscope depth! Group down, steer o-one-two. Slow ahead together," and he looked anxiously at his ship's head: she was only on north at the moment and still had twelve degrees to swing.

"Oh, God," Peter whispered to himself, "am I too close and is she gaining bearing on my D.A.?" Slowly the compass card ticked round, o-o-five … o-o-seven… He glanced at the gauges — fifty feet and swinging upwards: he could feel the deck rising beneath his feet.

"H.E. passing up the port side, sir!"

"Hell's bells!" Peter swore, "she's gaining on me," and he snapped his fingers for the periscope. "Put me on my D.A."

As the tube flashed upwards he felt he'd missed his chance — the target was already sliding up his port side, too fast, too quickly for him. He'd got too close, he'd bungled his first real attack.

Then suddenly all was light and the water was streaming from the glass as the periscope broke surface. And in the next second his mind registered an unforgettable sight, one that would stir his imagination to his dying day.

The blue water stretched away to the brightness of the sky and horizon. Little fleecy clouds sailed across the cobalt sky, and as all this flashed through his mind, a huge, terrifying image swept into view from left to right.

"Struth!" Peter whispered, "she's close!"

Then suddenly his circle of vision started to fill up, the hairline of the graticule cutting vertically across the stern of the troopship. She had a jackstaff, he noted, a modern capstan evidently, and then, just abaft the break of the fo'c'sle, banks of lorries were roped down securely, the lines criss-crossing like a spider's web.

"Fire one! Fire by time interval, flood Q, eighty feet!" Peter rapped. "I daren't speed up, Number One, or I might hit her, I'm so close!"

While the venting inboard of Q roared into his consciousness, the sea engulfed his vision, but not before a last glimpse was indelibly registered upon his mind — he was much too close, he had known that.

"Two fired, sir!" the Sub shouted in the din.

Yes, too close, and Peter's face was grim as he felt the shock wave of the second torpedo. She was one wall of ship, a mass of light grey plating as she swept by, the auxiliary discharges cascading from the outlets to send spouts of foam spurting from the sea. Lines of troops were thick upon the upper decks — he could plainly see them in their cork life jackets — Germans they were, he reckoned, not Wops, and for some unexplained reason he was glad.

"Three fired, sir."

The bow-down angle was steep now that she hurtled downwards.

Yes, it's terrifying how impersonal this killing business becomes, he thought. *Yet I'm glad that it's the real enemy we're after this time: they looked so cocky in their Afrika Korps uniform.*

"Number four..."

But Brocklebank was inaudible, for at that moment a deafening *crash!* shook the boat from stem to stern. As Peter rebounded from the shock, he braced himself; it was as well that he did so, for there followed two more explosions in rapid succession, their blows knocking off the cork from the deckhead and putting out the main lighting.

In the dim paleness of the emergency lights, Peter looked around him. In the Asdic corner Elliott had removed his phones and was rubbing his ears, while at the telegraphs, Ordinary Seaman Keating was hauling himself up from the deck, an amused grin upon his youthful face. The rasping and battering continued for a few seconds, and then for a brief space all was quiet.

"Where is she now, H.S.D.?" Peter asked calmly.

Elliott quickly replaced his earphones and paused before replying.

"Stopped, right ahead, sir. I can hear only breaking-up noises." Then he stiffened and when Peter watched him, his heart sank.

"Destroyer in contact, sir. Green nine-o."

Peter cocked his head, and sure enough the sinister whisper of the Asdic 'pings' pervaded the hearing of everyone on board.

"Dammit, Number One," Peter swore, "I thought they'd give us more time than that! Shut off from depth charging."

Benson's strained face smiled. "Probably our Trapani First Eleven, sir. They'll be only too pleased to have another go at us," and he turned towards his gauges where the pointers were sliding slowly round the dials. He was worried because he had not had enough time to catch a trim.

"I'll either have to speed up, sir, or pump — I'm afraid I can't hold her."

Peter swore beneath his breath. He felt instinctively that they were in for some intense heat and he did not want to let the hunter have it all his own way.

"Speed up, if you must, Number One," he replied, "but as little as possible for they're bound to pick up the noise. Port ten."

"Port ten, sir." The voice of the helmsman, Able Seaman Bowles, was like music in Peter's ears, and the young Captain smiled as he glanced towards the man. The broad back was towards him, and lines of sweat ran in rivulets down the oily flesh to disappear into the soggy band of his khaki shorts. With his sandy hair jutting upwards, the cast of this Briton's head was stubborn with its faint air of truculence. *Give the British sailor a good leader*, thought Peter as he looked at the massive shoulders, *and he could conquer the world* — yes, there was comfort for Peter in the man's ruggedness.

I've had no time to escape from my firing position, Peter thought bitterly, *because I was too close and could not speed up — and now we shall all pay for my error of judgement.*

"Still in contact, green one-seven-o, sir," Elliott reported. "H.E. increasing, range about eight hundred yards."

Peter had to think quickly — he could hardly be farther than a few hundred yards from his firing position.

"Steady as you go," he rapped. "Silent Routine."

"Course, sir, one-nine-o."

The last clips were being swung home on the bulkhead doors, but gently and without noise. Each man knew that within a few minutes patterns of depth charges would rain down towards them. Each man was careful, silent and thoughtful.

Peter looked at his watch. He was amazed to see that it was only nine o'clock — "and I haven't had breakfast yet," he muttered.

Elliott looked up from his set.

"H.E. increasing, sir," he said. "Destroyer running in to attack."

CHAPTER 5

Counter-Attack

"Transmission interval decreased, sir — range five hundred yards, destroyer running in to attack."

Elliott's taciturn report sent Peter's heart racing. Most of those on board *Rugged* had now survived twelve patrols in her, twelve wartime patrols in one of the hottest areas in the world. For nearly a year, week in, week out, they had been living upon the knife edge of their nerves, and Peter could register the difference in attitude with that of twelve months previously.

Their thirteenth patrol, this, and for some unexplained reason Peter had been experiencing a secret dread — a foolish superstition, he told himself, that this was to be their last; and now, "Destroyer running in to attack…"

Peter knew in his heart that this was to be an accurate and savage attack, and his stomach heaved with apprehension as his eyes quickly checked the instruments.

"Port ten, open main vents," he ordered, surprised to hear his voice unwavering. *I suppose I'm deadened to fear by now*, he thought, *and if my number turns up, I've had it, that's all* — and he forced his mind away from dangerous thoughts to concentrate upon the job in hand.

Then from aft he heard a faint tinkling, a distant clatter and whistling that quickly swelled into the crescendo that they now all dreaded.

From the corner of his eyes, Peter watched Elliott — that calm and dependable Englishman from Surrey. *He never shows any emotion*, Peter noted to himself, *and yet he must be loathing this as much as any of us by now.* Unruffled, the black-haired man slowly and deliberately removed the headset from his ears: the noise was too great for him to supply any useful information, and when the charges detonated he did not relish split eardrums. Elliott had once seen the result of this, in a friend of his, and he did not welcome the same experience. He carefully placed the earphones in his lap — they would remain undamaged there when the charges came — and slowly folded his arms. He waited, and, as he half turned towards his Captain, his lean face lit up with a quiet smile. *Heavens*, Peter thought, *what trust that man has in me;* he *trusts me to get him out of this, and if Elliott does, then I reckon I can have confidence in myself* — and Peter squared his shoulders.

But there was little that he could do now — just wait; wait for the catastrophic explosion that might split them asunder within the next few seconds. He gripped the burnished steel rung of the ladder to brace himself, straddling his legs apart the better to withstand the shock. He glanced quickly around him. Yes, they were all waiting; tense, expectant, intelligent men with imaginations — Saunders, the Outside E.R.A., stood, wheel spanner in hand, waiting by his panel and ready for immediate action: the blighters weren't going to catch him bending.

The noise was now overwhelming. The deep rumble changed to a rhythmic beat as the propellers pounded overhead, the background of queer whistlings and clatterings forming a crazy devil's opera. But even through the sound of thrashing screws, they all heard the distant 'slap' of the depth charges when they hit the surface of the sea.

"Probably from the throwers," Peter murmured, his imagination picturing the hectic scene that must be, at this second, being enacted on the surface. The sinking troopship, stern rearing from the water, would already have dipped her bows below the sea that sparkled in the morning sun. She must be under way, and she would be dragging the boats that dangled from their falls with her. The Lilliputian figures manning the lifeboats would be tumbling helter-skelter into a sea which frothed and boiled from the bursting tanks in the stricken ship. A fire would be raging from below, the flames already orange-bright and licking up the bridge, the paintwork blackened by the torpedoes' explosions — great gouts of steam would be streaming from abaft the funnel, and at her stern the propellers would be revolving, churning their unnatural medium of air and sky while, from the water immediately below, the swimmers would be staring upwards in terror at the scythe-like blades about to crush them...

Click! click! ... click! click!

Peter saw the young telegraphsman, Ordinary Seaman Keating, shut his eyes quickly and his lips were moving as he waited. *I wonder what he's saying*, Peter thought; *praying to his Maker, I hope, or perhaps it's because he wants his Able Seaman's rate next Tuesday — it's his birthday then, when he will have reached the ripe old age of nineteen. Poor kid, he certainly tumbled straight into it by joining us straight from the U.K. — but he looks years older already, the innocent roundness of a youthful face already replaced by the pallor and gauntness that seemed to go with this life of tension and semi-starvation. There were lines on the drawn face, scars of unique experiences that he would take to the grave with him — but he, too, has heard the detonators clicking home,* the Captain thought, and for a second Peter shut his eyes and prayed for deliverance.

Number One had both his hands in his pockets; he stood firmly astride, and, if he felt fear breathing down his neck, he showed nothing of it as he watched the two planesmen.

Neither did Chief Petty Officer Withers, the revered Coxswain of the boat, who sat at his shining handwheel, his grizzled head upright, a faint look of amusement playing at the corners of his controlled mouth — *I've been through this sort of thing so often before*, he seemed to say, *it's child's play*; and his amused contempt for the enemy inspired confidence in the less experienced.

"Stand by!" Peter warned.

Sub-Lieutenant Brocklebank's face was a study of controlled excitement. With one hand stretched out to his Fruit Machine for support, his brown eyes flickered excitedly; his eyes were unusual for they often danced with secret amusement. A typical Devonian he, from just below Three Bridges — and the very name conjured up for Peter happy days in his youth, when, a fly rod in his hand, he had stalked trout in the winking brown water.

God, how I dread being hunted now! thought Peter as the holocaust enveloped them. *It used to be part of the game*, he mused, *but now, after all this time, I loathe the heat. Depth charges are all right in their proper place, on a destroyer's upper deck, but at the receiving end down here, their fascination tends to pall.*

Above, below and around them, so that their sensibilities reeled from the pandemonium, the uproar rose to a terrifying crescendo as the hunter swept overhead; but, infiltrating through this hideous cacophony the insidious beat of the propellers pounded rhythmically, remorselessly, an unforgettable accompaniment.

Then suddenly she was past them, the roar quickly changing to a medley of whistlings and chucklings, as her stern, low in the water from her speed, frothed away from the tumbling depth charges. Peter instinctively glanced upwards, as did all around him. Now … yes, now … and he could have screamed with the tension and the agony of waiting for the moment of annihilation. At least, if they were hit, they would know little about it at this depth — the engulfing deeps would crush them out of existence, but…

A devastating shock squeezed the boat, so that no one was conscious of any explosion. The curved sides of the boat leapt towards Peter. He instinctively cringed from the impact and found his hands going forward to ward off the advancing calamity. Their whole world suddenly constricted, making them gasp as the air was knocked from their lungs by the violent compression. Then the steel curvature whipped, the bowed frames of the pressure hull trembled and the boat's sides sprung outwards again with a concertina effect.

As suddenly the lights flickered, then went out, and in the moment of darkness Peter distinctly heard the patter of cork as it dropped to the corticene, dislodged by the appalling shock of the first pattern. Simultaneously, he felt the whole boat lifted from under him — she seemed to be poised for a split second in time; then she was hurled through the water, lifted from below by a giant's hand, so that it felt as if she was tumbled on to her stern, bows down and with her after-ends sailing upwards through the depths, as if she wanted to topple over herself, stern-over-bows.

"My God!" Peter whispered to himself. "This is the end. There's nothing I can do," and he felt his knees go from under him as he staggered to slither along the deck, still half upright as he clung to the steel ladder. But as this support was now almost horizontal, he found his feet in the air, his back flattened by gravity against the ladder.

The luminous pointers on the depth gauges were a pinpoint of light as they glowed green, a focal point for all the unseen eyes in the darkness. Two hundred and ten feet on the for'd gauge, one hundred and sixty aft! She'd been hurled to this depth in less than a few seconds.

An emergency light flicked on by the telegraphs, fed by its independent dry cell, and a paleness shone upon the chaotic shambles that was the Control Room. The Captain was hauling himself upright, so that he faced aft, his feet wedged at the foot of the ladder, his head vertical, but not far from touching the bearing-ring of the attack periscope.

"She must be almost standing on her ends," he gasped as his eyes swept to the inclinometers, but the bubbles had disappeared, hard up against the stops. "At least a forty-degree bow-down angle. The electrolyte is bound to spill from the batteries" and with horror he realised the implication — death by choking from the chlorine gas that would writhe and curl towards them from the bilges, to snuff them out like candle flames.

The Captain waited no longer.

"Shut main vents!" he cried, "blow Number One Main Ballast!"

The signal lantern in the starboard wings of the Italian destroyer clattered feverishly, and across Tunis Bay there flashed an urgent message from Capitano di Fregata Cesare Ricasoli. A short man of about thirty-five, he felt proud of his appointment as Captain of his ship, the *Luca Tarigo*, a 'Navigatori'-class destroyer, one of the hardest-hitting destroyers in the Royal Italian Navy. Displacing 2,000 tons, with a waterline length of 351 feet and a speed of 38 knots, she was a powerful ship — and Cesare Ricasoli glanced affectionately at his armament: six 4.7 guns; three 40mm high-angle guns; six 21-inch torpedo tubes, and whole batteries of depth charges which, if need be, could be replaced by mines and mine-laying rails. Yes, she was a fine ship, but what gratified him even more was his appointment as Divisional Commander of the Second Division: four 'Navigatori' were under his command, the second half of the Trapani Flotilla.

Although the *Luca Tarigo* lay stopped, wallowing on the placid sea in the midst of the wreckage which floated accusingly around her, there was a smile on the face of the efficient little man who leant quietly against his bridge side. In his crumpled khaki shirt and in the battered thing he called his cap, he knew that he was the picture of self-assurance; he knew, too, that his troops loved him, not for his character, but because he was competent and successful. Hadn't this destroyer division, under his command, accounted for five of the accursed British Submarine Flotilla from Malta? Yes, he and his ships had practised this game so often that they worked like a gleaming machine, silently and smoothly, with seldom a hitch.

He was waiting for the *Ugolino Vivaldi* and *Nicolo Zeno* to join him from the other side of the late convoy; he had told the *Lanzerotto Malocello* to break off the attack and to proceed with utmost dispatch up to Tunis and to start forming up the return convoy that awaited them off La Goulette. Meanwhile he would finish off this submarine; he was in firm contact now, and it was only a matter of time — but that was the snag, he hadn't much of that commodity to spare for he had to take his division to help *Malocello* with the return convoy off Tunis.

He was a strange man, for, regarding him dispassionately on his workman-like bridge on that crystal-clear morning, you would not have guessed that he had feelings as sensitive as many of us. His eye took in the pathetic flotsam that floated upon the sea, deep ultramarine from its depth in The Bay, while from all sides the screams of stricken and drowning soldiers quickly diminished. A soldier, fully kitted up for immediate action, could not remain afloat for long, and Capitano di Fregata Cesare Ricasoli knew his orders: sink the submarines at all costs, whatever the sacrifice in survivors. He slowly lifted his melancholy eyes to the dark patches of swimmers who clustered, like the beginnings of a May swarm of bees, directly ahead of his ship and immediately above the lurking submarine.

The mountains to the eastward, blue and purple with the haze of distance, looked down with compassion upon the unfortunate Capitano di Fregata, while across the other side of The Bay, the cliffs brown in barren patches, waited for him to make his impossible decision. Even his friend, the sea, spared him not, for now the mirror-like surface was blistering hot, the heat dancing in mirages upon the glassy calm.

"Full ahead both!"

Cesare Ricasoli hurled off his cap and dashed the sweat from his forehead as he clambered to the binnacle. He would have to make certain of this submarine and sacrifice the remains of the Afrika Korps detachment that pathetically clung to life, and which were swimming ahead of him. He had a definite contact, and he would ensure that she would sink no more troop transports, or any other ships for that matter — yes, her destruction came first because she had not been given time to move off track from her firing position.

He felt the wind begin to ruffle his hair as his *Luca Tarigo* quickly gathered way, the throbbing from her enormous horsepower vibrating the bridge in anticipation. He glanced across at his consorts who were racing up to join him, then he settled down to the run in. Crouched low over the bearing-ring, and conning her with sensitive competence, he pointed his ship along the Asdic bearing. The background accompaniment of the impulses echoing from the Asdic cabinet and back from the submarine howled around him with the strange note that was the signature of this deadly technique, and Cesare thrilled again as he ran in once more to another attack. In his bones he felt sure that he'd got her and he was going to make no mistakes.

"Stand by throwers!"

His teeth gleamed whitely as he snapped the order, but even at that instant the Officer of the Watch screamed from the bridge and pointed towards the water. The destroyer was entering the dark cluster of swimmers and was scything her way through them mercilessly, so that they disappeared in the white smother of foam that was her wash.

"Five hundred yards, sir, lost contact!"

"Stand by racks!"

I shall pretend not to hear the screams nor the Officer of the Watch, thought Cesare Ricasoli; *with this speed, the noise of the wind slatting against the rigging should drown what I have no wish to hear,* and he crouched even lower over the bearing-ring, entirely engrossed with the course adjustments that he passed down the voicepipe.

"Two hundred yards, sir."

From the corner of his eye he saw Luigi, his young Officer of the Watch, cross himself and then tear his eyes from the water which was now so horribly stained, but, *my God! how dreadful it's going to be for the wretches when the patterns explode.* The same thought had crossed the mind of the young seaman who was now vomiting uncontrollably over the port wing.

"Fire!"

The telephone operator's mouth seemed to open and shut spasmodically, but the Capitano di Fregata remembered no sound. He dimly remembered the bark of the throwers and the gouts of spray as the charges hit the water amongst the densest patch of swimmers — and then he looked over the starboard bow for he could bear it no longer.

"Starboard twenty."

He took her out and away in a sweeping curve, the easier to regain contact after the explosions, but now, when he glanced at his hands he found them trembling.

Murderer! Murderer! ... Murderer! He could hear the cries now, as the horrifying truth slowly dawned upon the swimmers in the water, men who waited for an agonising death to strike when the depth charges exploded below them. Then Cesare Ricasoli wept.

The first explosion tremored a second later, and a huge hump bulged on the surface astern; boiled for a moment, then jumped skywards from the sea in a tapering spout to fall back in a fine spray. As the succeeding charges detonated, the Capitano di Fregata hid his face from the dreadful carnage in the water. But then he was suddenly aware of a gigantic explosion, greater by far than all the rest, so that the ship under him shivered from stem to stern. Cesare Ricasoli peered towards his boiling wake, and there before his eyes erupted a slowly rising mountain of water. It was terrifying.

"The charges have counter-mined each other somehow!" he gasped. "*Santa Maria!*" and he whispered as he crossed himself, "those poor devils in the water — and, as for the submarine, that's the end of her," and he looked away as nausea swept over him. He regained his composure and then forced himself to take his ship around the area in a wide circle: there might be the usual grisly evidence from the shattered submarine, and proof was always better than one's word with the Italian Admiralty.

His Officer of the Watch was the first to see it. The young man gabbled and stretched his hand out towards the edge of the discoloured circle. Cesare Ricasoli spun round and then his heart leapt: right on the southern perimeter of the circle two huge mushrooms of air suddenly frothed and bubbled from the depths. The surface continued seething for some minutes, but as the *Luca Tarigo* lost way the convulsion subsided to leave only a gentle hissing from the aerated water.

"Her tanks have exploded," the Capitano said quietly. "Record it in the log, Officer of the Watch. There's no point in lowering a boat to pick up evidence — the bits and pieces could just as well be from the poor devils in the troopship," and Cesare Ricasoli quickly looked away. He was now thoroughly sickened by the revolting carnage and he wanted to escape — even to his seasoned ship's company the spectacle was morale-disturbing.

"Wake up, Signalman! Answer the *Zeno*."

The man had been mesmerised by the sights which drifted by so pathetically on the water, but now he leapt for the lamp and the shutter clattered. He read the message out loud.

"'Congratulations on one more submarine destroyed,'" he read. "'Please leave the next one to *Vivaldi* and myself. We're getting bored.'"

The Capitano di Fregata turned on his heel and smiled.

"Let's get cracking," he said. "I want to have a wash and shave before we turn round for the next north-bound convoy. Officer of the Watch, tell the others to follow."

The lamp flickered once again, then three sleek greyhounds formed up in line ahead to disappear into the heat haze of La Goulette.

"Stop blowing!"

Above the whine of the high-pressure air, Peter's voice was only just audible. He had been noticing the length of time that the Outside E.R.A. had kept Number One blow open, and Peter did not want to waste air. If the high-pressure line was intact, Number One main ballast must be free of water by now — and being at the for'd extremity of the boat, she must surely start lifting her bows.

"Unless she starts to right herself now," Peter muttered to himself, "we're done." He closed his eyes to shut out the hideous picture which flashed across his mind: the buckling plating of the pressure hull, squeezed by these enormous depths; the engulfing deluge of disaster and the sudden pain of it all as the pressures squeezed the life out of them all.

"Oh God," he prayed, and for an instant his mind flew to his Maker. "Save us in Thy mercy, save us," and his eyes closed tight.

Benson, the First Lieutenant, seemed to be mesmerised by the stationary pointers on the depth gauges, hard up against the stops. *I'm sure the airlines are fractured by the shock*, he thought. *This is the end*, and then he, too, suddenly found himself praying. *It's queer to feel so calm about it all*, he deliberated within himself. *I always wondered how I'd behave and what it would be like*, and then he found himself on his knees as the angle made the deck shoot away from under his feet. His hands shot out and he felt the strong grasp of the Coxswain's arm groping for him.

"'Ere, sir, 'old on! I got a grip, 'old on," and in the confusion Benson dimly remembered the serene quality of Chief Petty Officer Withers's voice. No wonder the troops loved him.

It was dark, mercifully, in the fore-ends. The T.I., Petty Officer Slater, had cursed when the emergency lamp failed to operate as the lights were shattered by the first explosion. In his haste he had forgotten to bring the tiny flash lamp that he usually carried on him, so now he and his crew were being pummelled and battered in the darkness by the sudden angles which the boat was taking on.

"'Old tight, men," he had shouted as she plunged downwards from the last pattern. "There ain't no charge for this scenic railway!" and, as he crashed against the for'd bulkhead between the two tube-space doors, his knees buckled under him and he sat down, his legs stretched uphill and aft. Then he heard a gasp in the darkness and suddenly a tangle of arms and legs smothered him.

"Sorry, T.I.," Ordinary Seaman Smith apologised with a chuckle. "I didn't know it was you," and he disentangled himself from his Petty Officer to sit next to him.

"Are you all right, Bill?"

Slater suddenly remembered Able Seaman Bill Hawkins. If his bulk crashed down on them they would be winded for life. Then from somewhere above them there was a disgruntled growl.

"I'm coming down," Hawkins spoke from the darkness, "it's bloomin' stupid to be 'anging on up 'ere, T.I., like a perishin' parrot swingin' on its perch." There was a clatter as Hawkins dislodged the gash bucket which came bounding down on top of them, smothering them all with tealeaves and empty tins.

"You…"

But Slater's imprecations were knocked from him as the man fell down upon them.

"Sorry, T.I.…"

But there was one glimmer of light in the fore-ends: just above them on the deckhead and over the starboard rack was the fore-end deep depth gauge, and now the luminous numbers on the dial glowed comfortingly. The three men's eyes were instinctively mesmerised by their only glimmer of light and they each knew that the others were watching it.

"The pointer's hard up agin the stops," Smith said.

In the long silence that followed, each man allowed his own thoughts to run uncontrolled, for the darkness would conceal their expressions. The angle was steeper now, and Slater's heart beat faster: this was a crisis, worse by far than most counter-attacks. At this angle and at this depth he didn't see how they could regain control, even if the Old Man did blow main ballast. Slater prayed in the darkness. He was an intelligent man and he realised that he only just had control of his feelings; he wanted to give vent to his jangling nerves, taut-strung like a violin string. With the terror that swept over him in the darkness, from the realisation that the fore-ends would be engulfed first, there came an insane longing to scream and weep like a child, and he found himself trembling from the struggle of will over body.

"They're blowing main ballast ... listen…" Bill Hawkins's calm voice growled in the darkness.

"'Bout flippin' time too!" Smith added, a note of hysteria in his voice.

Slater turned his head to listen, and then he realised dimly that there was indeed a far off singing, an unbearably high note screaming above them. Suddenly there was a drumming above his head, and with joy beating fiercely in his heart he realised that the H.P. air was reaching Number One ballast tank.

"The line's intact — it's intact!" he shouted above the throbbing resonance. "Hawkins, Smithy, don't you realise it, the line's okay?"

In the Control Room, the young Captain felt that he could not bear the agony of waiting one second longer. If the H.P. airline was fractured...

But then he was nearly hurled off his feet by the sudden movement of the bows. Up they came, up, up and away from the yawning jaws of death.

Saunders's soft voice spoke from the panel. "The H.P. fines are all right, sir," he said, and Peter could see that the hand which held the wheel spanner was trembling.

Then, almost imperceptibly, the pointer of the deep gauge started to move back — two hundred and forty-five feet.

"Bubble's amidships ... now, sir," the First Lieutenant muttered.

"Blow Number Two main ballast," Peter ordered quietly.

At the close of a summer's day, the evening breeze sometimes stirs the leaves of the poplar trees; they shiver for a moment, rustling and whispering, and then to your finer sensibilities comes the delicious scent that only poplar leaves yield. The sigh of relief which momentarily rustled round the Control Room whispered for a moment, then was gone, like the movement in the graceful trees.

"Thank God," Peter muttered.

"Fore-planes are jammed, sir," the black-bearded giant reported unconcernedly from his stool. Petty Officer Weston sat gazing at his bubble, his arms resting motionless on the brass handwheel, the black hair matted close on his forearms like coils of wire.

"Fore-planes in hand."

Sub-Lieutenant Geoffrey Brocklebank spun the handle of the fore-ends phone, but for a moment there was no reply. He gave another twist to the instrument.

"Fore-ends? Are you all right? Yes? Right, fore-planes in hand," and Peter could see the tensed face, white and strained as it stooped over the mouthpiece. Suddenly Brocklebank looked up.

"Fore-planes in hand, sir."

"Tell them, 'Twenty degrees of rise on the fore-planes'," the First Lieutenant ordered.

Peter was talking quietly while he watched the gauges.

"One hundred and eighty feet... I shall have to vent, Number One, or we shall break surface."

"We can't afford that luxury," Benson laughed. "Better to let the bubbles give us away than the standards!"

"There'll be the devil of a lot of air, though," Peter continued. "But it can't be helped. I'll speed up while we vent — you never know, what with the mountains of escaping air and the noise of my propellers when I speed up, they might think we're done for."

"Let's hope so, sir."

Peter glanced at the gauge — one hundred and ten feet, and coming up fast.

"Open main vents!" he ordered. "Starboard twenty, steer three-five-o; group up, full ahead together."

Peter noticed with surprise that his hands were trembling and he quickly thrust them into his pockets. *It's the reaction, I suppose*, he thought. *I couldn't stand another battering like that.*

But the reservoir of human courage runs deep. It is as well that this is so for much was still to be demanded of *Rugged*, her Captain and her company.

CHAPTER 6

Pipped at the Post

Rugged's escaping air had indeed been taken by the Italians as marking her grave, and she gave them no chance to discover their mistake.

The Tunis Run, however, allowed the submariners little respite. Peter craved for a few hours of undisturbed sleep, but, what with the frequent reports of the approaching enemy and the reloading, he had little rest that night.

"Permission to ditch gash, sir?"

There was a long pause and then, from his corner at the after-end of the bridge, where he crouched in a cramped effort at fitful sleep, Peter heard Benson, the Officer of the Watch, grant permission. The buckets clattered as they were passed hand-over-hand up the tower, and then, just as Peter's eyelids drooped with the weight of sleep he jerked to his feet.

"Captain, sir!"

In three seconds Peter managed to clamber from his sodden corner to regain his position by the compass.

"What is it?"

Benson was looking over the side, but as he looked round towards his Captain he was chuckling.

"Sorry to bother you, sir, but I could not imagine what it was on this smooth sea."

Peter glanced along the waterline, and there, in the white slick that ran like a ribbon down the side of the pressure hull, bobbed and bounced the familiar tins from the stores of any British submarine while, slightly out on the port quarter, gliding up and down on the blackness of the sea, a small patch of gash announced its presence.

"Well, I'll be blowed!" and Peter chuckled in spite of his weariness. "Joe Croxton's pipped us again, right slap on the edge of our billet! Might as well add ours to his — get it over quickly, Number One."

The tell-tale evidence was soon ditched, and then there followed a night of frustrations. It was very dark and the silence was overpowering when the generators were stopped after the charge was finished. The island of Zembra loomed over them, stark against the splendour of the star-studded sky, and the only sound was the swish of the water as it swept down *Rugged*'s side. Peter was anxious at first lest she should be visible from above, but he was reassured when the continuous stream of aircraft lumbered overhead, low and oblivious.

"The Hun is certainly trying to get the stuff through," Peter muttered. "He's pouring troops across in these Heinkels," and once more he waited anxiously while another air transport rumbled overhead.

At three-fifteen in the morning there was a vivid flash away to the westward, followed by a dull glow — then depth charging. *Probably John Easton*, Peter thought — *it's quite a family party tonight!*

Rugged dived at dawn and once again the sun rushed out of the east. Then, apart from one north-bound convoy well to the westward, nothing tried to run the gauntlet and Peter snatched two hours' sleep before lunch. He could hardly keep his heavy lids open after O'Riley's breakfast of 'corned dog' and pickles, eased down by the First Lieutenant's vile bread. Benson had not used enough salt in this, his newest bake, and the stuff was tasteless. Peter strolled into the Control Room to recover, while throughout the boat came the snores and snafflings of exhausted men. He found the Sub nervously gripping the periscope and searching to the westward.

"What's up, Sub?"

"I think there's something on this bearing, sir." Brocklebank murmured.

Peter took over and, as he gazed, a smudge of smoke crept into the circle of vision.

"Bearing THAT, smoke."

"Green four-o, sir."

Three minutes later two aircraft had come into sight and, shortly after, the first cross-trees of escorting destroyers.

"They're too far to the west for us, Sub," Peter added from the periscope. "They're in *Restless*'s billet, I'll bet. Down periscope."

But eight minutes later there were two muffled explosions, and when Peter looked again he was amazed to see that the whole convoy had zigged towards him, and that it now seemed much closer — almost in range, in fact.

"They're coming our way, and must be cutting straight across *Restless*'s billet by now," he said. "Go to Diving Stations, Sub."

"Diving Stations!" Brocklebank cried, and Peter noted the excitement in the young officer's voice. *He's as whacked as I am*, Peter thought, *but I suppose he's not used to it yet — anyway, my own stomach has turned to water again with this lot coming towards me*. And once more he saw the familiar shapes of advancing destroyers.

The periscope streaked upwards, and Peter waited impatiently for the lens to dry — ah! there they were, close now and heading straight for *Rugged*. The bows of the leading merchant ship were shoving a wall of water in front of them and the whiteness of the flat face of the bridge was already gleaming above the horizon; astern of her he could just see her consort — she looked like an old A.M.C.

"Bearing THAT!"

He swivelled round on his heel, crouched over the handles of the periscope, for there was a glassy calm on the surface and Number One was adjusting his depth. The surface was shimmering with heat, its glaring whiteness undulating gently, like quicksilver.

"Watch your trim, Number One, for Pete's sake! There's a flat calm up top and they must be able to see our stick miles away. Down periscope. Starboard ten."

The Captain had already made his decision: he would run off track and place himself in a good attacking position, firing with a full outfit of four torpedoes from abaft the beam. He glanced at the compass, and then rapped out the information that Brocklebank eagerly awaited to feed into his Fruit Machine.

"There are several aircraft on the far side of the convoy at the moment," Peter snapped. "I'm right ahead of my target, an eight-thousand-ton ship doing about eighteen knots and she's steaming straight towards us from across *Restless*'s area."

Dimly Peter's mind registered that the hands had now settled down at their Diving Stations, an important factor because while they were still moving about the boat from one extremity to the other, the First Lieutenant could not catch his trim — and Peter smiled to himself when he remembered that O'Connor, the happy and well-covered Irish stoker, if he happened to be on watch in the Engine Room when Diving Stations were ordered, needed the transference of about twenty-five gallons from for'd to 'O' tank in order to compensate for his movement to the pump space in the fore-ends.

"Range about two thousand yards," Peter continued. "I may be wrong about her speed because it's difficult to see her bow wave from this angle. Blow up and stand by all tubes. Depth setting fourteen feet."

He flicked his fingers and the steel tube slid upwards. As he grasped the handles he saw the orange glow of the compass card ticking round the degrees.

"Bearing THAT!"

"Red one-four-o, sir."

"Range THAT! I'm fifteen degrees on her starboard bow. What's my course for a hundred and twenty track?" Peter spun round on his heel, the muscles taut in his drawn face. "There's one destroyer coming straight towards, about eight hundred yards; there's another broad on the target's bow about fifteen hundred yards." Peter glanced at his First Lieutenant. "I may have to ask for an emergency change of depth, Number One: this blighter's too close for my liking."

"All tubes ready, sir. Depth setting fourteen feet. Your D.A. green one-five," Brocklebank reported as the mauve tell-tales from the tube-space flickered on.

"I may have to fire from deep, so have your time interval ready. Stand by all tubes!"

Peter nodded at the Outside E.R.A. whose eyes were fixed upon every movement of his Captain's. The Cornishman's arm barely moved, yet the periscope once more slid upwards accurately, swiftly.

"Put me on my D.A.," Peter murmured.

The young Captain knew no apprehension now, so intense was his concentration — a split second out in timing and not only would he miss his target, but he was in danger of being run down by the destroyer. His heart banged against his ribs when he felt George Hicks, the Stoker P.O., firmly settling the periscope on the D.A. Peter could have screamed with impatience as he blindly waited for the glass to clear while the water drained off the sloping surface of the lens. Then the blurring of the image suddenly drifted into focus and the picture flashed into definition. He spun round for a quick sweep, then settled on his D.A.

"Thank God," Peter murmured aloud to himself, "the destroyer has weaved away and has already crossed our bows, but there's a reconnaissance aircraft flying towards on our starboard quarter. I'll have to risk him. Hullo, what's this? My target ship hasn't altered course yet, but a flying boxcar, one of those enormous Heinkels, is lumbering over her."

"Steady on two-one-o, sir," the helmsman reported.

"Very good ... stand by..." Peter snapped.

These last few seconds were always excruciatingly tense. So much could go wrong: the target could alter course or speed, the periscope could be dipped by bad trimming, or worse, the submarine might break surface to show her standards, but even more likely, a prowling destroyer or aircraft would intervene.

Peter would never forget this attack all his life. He was in a perfect position. He could see the destroyer from the corner of his eye — safely past him she was, her stern low in the water, and half hidden by her bubbling wake, the mass of her superstructure heeling outwards as she altered course in a close turn. Her light grey sides were dazzling in the sunlight and Peter could see the heat shimmering above her two funnels.

The target was now displayed in all her naked splendour, racing by like an express train, her side dazzle-painted in black, green and brown. *I've estimated her course right*, Peter thought; *the break in her bridge gives her away. She's moving all right, just look at her auxiliary discharges spouting into the sea! What a grand sight she is, with the gulls wheeling, white and gleaming in a screaming motley about her cruiser stern! But I must watch out for the other destroyer coming up on her port quarter. That flying boxcar does look absurd though, bumbling over the ship — look, I can see some seamen waving at it. Good God! What's happened now?*

As Peter watched, a column of water spouted at the target's bows, some hundreds of feet into the air, smothering the for'd end of the ship in a blanket of mist and steam. At the same time, Peter was dimly conscious of a steam-hammer *clang!* against the pressure hull, and then, a few seconds later, another jolt, and a smaller column of water leaping at her stern.

"My God!" Peter whispered to himself.

An astonishing sight met his eyes when the mist cleared away, streaming plume-like from the bows of the target because of the way she was carrying. While he watched, a hollow rumble reverberated through the submarine, and then the bows of the eight-thousand-ton ship seemed to jump, jerked by a superhuman force. A sheet of orange flame flashed suddenly, just as the flying boxcar was approaching her foredeck. Then, to Peter's horror, the aircraft exploded in a ball of fire to topple, a flaming wreck, into the gantries just for'd of the bridge.

"The poor wretches," Peter muttered, "they must be fried alive. Down periscope."

Peter's face was ashen when he left the eyepieces; his men had never seen him visibly shaken before, but then, mercifully, such appalling horrors were not often actually witnessed.

"Two torpedo hits," Peter said, "and the bows of the target have disintegrated from one of them, bringing down the boxcar. I must confess that this is the first time I've heard of a submarine torpedoing an aircraft!"

There was a chuckle around the Control Room.

"Must be *Restless*, sir. Perhaps she knew we were just going to fire!" the First Lieutenant said.

"Well, she's certainly pipped us, Number One. Up periscope, let's see what's going on now."

Peter's mind rejected the terrifying sight, paralysed for a split second by the horrible consequences of the torpedoing. Half the great ship had disappeared, her bows already gone. The explosion had cleft her fore-part in two, opening her up like a sardine tin. The deluge had done the rest and, with the way that she was carrying and with her propellers still thrashing the sea, she was relentlessly driving herself under water, like a vast, wounded whale. The bridge had already disappeared, and over the funnel, like some nursery toy, there flapped gently one wing of the unlucky Heinkel. Then suddenly she was gone.

"I just can't believe it," Peter whispered as he gripped the handles of the periscope the better to control himself. All he could see now were the pathetic remains of another wartime casualty, the common denominator of both sides in this war at sea: floating debris, tragic in its helplessness — the bobbing heads of those who had miraculously survived, the Carley floats that danced in the boiling cauldron, the upturned boats, and the screams of wretched, drowning humanity.

Then, as Peter watched, mesmerised by the holocaust, he was suddenly aware that three destroyers were concentrating for the counter-attack. The boat that had been on his starboard beam had her stern well down, and was churning up the sea so that her wake frothed white. Then she dropped everything she had and Peter could actually see the throwers hitting the water, little white spouts splashing on her quarter. On either side, two more Navigatori were racing in for the kill, their flag-hoists streaming at their yard-arms to make a brave sight and one which always made Peter's heart beat the faster.

"Poor old *Restless* is getting the heat all right, Number One," Peter muttered between clenched teeth. "And there goes the rest of the convoy — emergency turn to starboard — and steering miles away from us as fast as it can go. Down periscope."

Peter's eyes were showing disappointment as he turned to face them: everything had been set dead right. But what did it matter so long as the enemy was sunk? What mattered now was the heat which *Restless* was receiving less than a mile away. Peter couldn't quite understand it, for it was unlike Joe Croxton to be caught napping. Then the first shocks of the exploding depth charges clanged against *Rugged*'s sides, a tattoo of hammer blows.

"They haven't wasted much time, sir," Number One said. "But they've got a job on, to catch Lieutenant-Commander Croxton."

Peter was silent for a moment.

"Up periscope," he said quietly.

His back stiffened when he looked again. The second Navigatori had just run over and, as he watched, the first mountains of water jumped skywards, and from the corner of his eye he could see the third destroyer already racing in.

"Phew!" Peter whispered, "and the other two are joining up — that makes five in all."

The cacophony of the counter-attack was still rattling against *Rugged*'s pressure hull.

"Joe's in trouble, Number One, big trouble, I think," Peter said quietly. "The destroyers were too quick off the mark."

"He may have broken surface."

"Possibly."

Another battery of shocks struck the boat, so that even at this distance, Elliott had to remove his headphones.

"I must create a diversion," Peter said. "I'm going in to attack the nearest destroyer. Perhaps that will draw them off, so watch out for fireworks. Stand by all tubes. Start the attack!"

CHAPTER 7

Black Despair

If Peter had been allowed time, he might have been more prudent. As it was, all he could contemplate was the picture of *Restless* being depth-charged to destruction, and if he could help Joe Croxton there was nothing else to be said. Now that the Captain of *Rugged* had made his decision, his mind was clear. He coolly drove his submarine into the noose, the bevy of circling destroyers his suicidal target. *Rather like prodding a hornets' nest*, thought Peter, *only worse*.

When he last looked he estimated that he was about twelve hundred yards from the Navigatori that had just finished her attack. She waited now, impatiently, for her next run-in.

"I'll have to get a move on," Peter whispered, "or I'll be too late. Joe can't withstand this sort of heat for long," and once more there was a sickening series of explosions, much nearer this time. "I'll take her deep for a minute to speed up and get closer — I'll have more of a chance then."

"Eighty feet, shut off from depth-charging," he ordered.

Peter watched the pointers creep down the gauges; he noticed the bulkhead doors moving silently on their hinges and then he felt the skin prickling up the back of his neck.

"Forty feet, sir," Number One reported.

"Group up, full ahead together. They won't hear us with all this hubbub going on."

While the little submarine shuddered to the new power Peter passed his instructions to Brocklebank at the Fruit Machine.

"I'm going to take the nearest destroyer, Sub, and I hope she'll still be stopped by the time I'm in position. Torpedo depth-setting, eight feet," and then Peter turned towards the Navigating Officer, Sub-Lieutenant Taggart, who was crouching over the chart table.

"Tell me when I'm at eight hundred yards, Pilot. If we're to draw the blighters off *Restless*, I've got to get in close."

Men glanced at each other across the Control Room. *Too bloomin' close for my liking*, was the unanimous opinion of them all. It was like tweaking a cobra's tail.

"Half a minute to go at this speed, sir," Taggart reported, stopwatch in hand.

Peter glanced at Elliott, the imperturbable H.S.D., and the man's eyes held his own.

"If you can manage it, please, Petty Officer Elliot, an all-round H.E. sweep. I'm coming up from deep. Group-down, stop both."

"All tubes ready, sir," the Sub reported, his voice now under control, "depth setting, eight feet." For this inexperienced officer, sensitive and intelligent as he was, this deliberate attack upon five of the most efficient submarine killers, seemed madness. Though he had not known the comradeship of the Fighting Tenth, and in particular that of *Rugged* under Croxton's command, he could just comprehend the loyalty that drove Sinclair at this moment. But the young man's inside heaved when he felt the trembling of the boat cease and knew that the way was coming off her. She was gliding silently through the depths now, waiting to glide up into…?

"I can't give any accurate report, sir," the H.S.D. murmured from the Asdic cabinet. "There's too much destroyer H.E."

"All right, I'll have to risk it," Peter replied. "Take her up, Number One. Slow ahead port. Periscope depth."

"Periscope depth, sir."

"…and Number One."

"Sir?"

"Don't break surface, for Pete's sake. We're coming up under five Navigatoris."

"Yes, sir. I know."

Benson did not take his eyes from his instruments.

Brocklebank shut his eyes. Only perfect teamwork in the Control Room gave them any chance now. Their combined skill was their only chance: Captain to First Lieutenant, Coxswain to the planesmen, the helmsman, the telegraphsman, and, standing by the panel, as unshakable as the Rock of Gibraltar, the last resort in all emergencies, Saunders, the Cornish Outside E.R.A. *This is where the months of training and experience come in*, the Sub thought; *any slip in the drill now and we have not much time left to us.* His vivid imagination painted the picture that lay waiting for them barely thirty feet away now: the stopped destroyers, listening, waiting their turn whilst one of them ran over the stricken *Restless*, Brocklebank clenched his teeth. No dream this, but harsh, brutal fact, with thirty-five Britons being blown to bits less than a thousand yards away — men that he knew, friends of his, with Jack Burnham, their Sub, a fellow crony from his training class. They'd joked about 'the heat' often enough as youths up in Scotland, but this was reality, harsh, final, and unamusing.

"Twenty-eight feet, sir."

In the terrifying silence, Brocklebank heard the snap of the Captain's fingers. Peter Sinclair was working the attack periscope.

I wouldn't like to be in his shoes, the Sub thought. *God give him strength! He's got all our lives in his hands at this moment, to jettison or to save — and not only ours but perhaps those in* Restless *as well.*

Brocklebank glanced round the Control Room: the figures as they stood poised, tensed in expectation, were for a moment frozen motionless in time, like those on a Grecian frieze. There was silence while they waited for the report that would pronounce their fate.

Swish!

The Captain's sandals hissed as they scraped the corticene when he spun round on the periscope.

"Target THAT! I'm sixty degrees on her port bow and she's stopped."

"Red three, sir," Petty Officer Hicks reported from behind Peter's back.

The snap of the periscope handles was like a pistol shot.

"Clear of aircraft!" Peter said. "Ship's head?"

"Three-five-two, sir," Bowles grunted from his wheel.

"Port five, steer three-four-nine. Up periscope."

Slowly the glass drained and the appalling picture flashed before him: and with it came a terror that Peter dared not show. With his face glued to the eyepieces, he pressed his forehead into the soft rubber.

Oh my God, my God! he groaned inwardly, his mind a whirling maelstrom of despair. *I'm too late by a few seconds. God, Joe, I'm sorry*, and he felt like sobbing across the periscope handles.

"*Stand by all tubes!*"

The sharpness of the order jerked men into a sudden awareness of disaster. Never before had they felt such intensity, such hate poured into a commonplace command, and even they were shocked. Each man tried to guess from the face at the eyepieces what disaster lay upon the surface; but there was no clue from their Captain, apart from the pallor of his face. The knuckles on the periscope were white as they gripped the handles in an agony of self-control, and, as Taggart watched, he wondered whether the Old Man had forgotten the length of time he had been showing the periscope. The Navigating Officer was worried, for something terrible must be happening.

"Breaking-up noises, sir. Green four-o."

But the Captain seemed deaf, his only movement being the sudden twisting of the periscope.

Peter barely registered the horror that he saw before his despairing eyes. He knew only that the terrible disaster would be branded into his memory for ever, a scar of infinite depth and pain. He counted four destroyers disposed in a circle, and all with their bows pointing towards the centre. The nearest two were stopped, and Peter remembered being amazed that they wallowed in the sea, even in this flat calm.

She needs a bottom-clean, he thought professionally to himself when he saw the lengths of weed trading from the exposed bilge keel as the nearer of the two listed for a moment. And then he realised why they were rolling: one of them had completed an attack and had just turned sharply, her wash overtaking them both to send them rolling.

But it was the cotton-wool puffs of smoke that wisped from their for'd guns which first caught his attention — black and yellow were the fumes as the cordite streamed stickily along the barrels. He glanced to the left, and over on the far side of the perimeter he saw the smaller silhouette of another Navigatori, pointing directly towards him, stopped and waiting. He continued his sweep and there, less than six hundred yards away, the outline of a powerful destroyer loomed blackly against the sun. At her bows a white gash glanced, while amidships there was a deep depression along her waterline as she raced through the sea. Astern of her, a boiling mass of water kicked and heaved, bubbling and jumping in a frenzy of delight.

Peter gasped as the destroyer, a picture of immense power, swept across his vision. Bunting fluttered from her yard-arms and, as she slid by, a black puff belched from her for'd funnel: *the boiler rooms are having trouble with their fans*, Peter mused grimly. *I bet the Chief'll get hell!*

Then, as Peter suddenly realised the implication of the directions in which all the ships were pointing, the two for'd mountings of the attacking destroyer jerked into life, black puffs spouting from the barrels.

Even before he looked, Peter knew what he was going to see. In that split second, he could foretell the whole horror that he had to witness, the ghastly tragedy that he was now powerless to prevent. The cross-wire of the graticule gently crept up the stern of the nearest stopped destroyer, until it crossed the break in the fo'c'sle.

"Fire one!" Peter croaked.

The boat jumped from the discharge, then shuddered as the air belched back inboard.

"I'm too late," Peter whispered. "Oh God, I'm too late."

There was a gentle pattering on *Rugged*'s pressure hull, like the first drops of a thundershower upon a tin roof. All the destroyers were firing now, machine-guns as well as the heavy stuff. Peter wanted to drag his eyes away, but he could not. He knew only too well what the machine-guns were for and his mesmerised gaze followed the green tracer to where they struck the water.

"Fire by time interval!"

From somewhere far away he heard his own voice giving the order instinctively, like a jabbering sleepwalker. *At least one of them will join* Restless, he thought dispassionately, as he watched the track of the first torpedo go bubbling towards its target.

But there, in the centre of the circle of the pack, a black vee jutted, like the dorsal fin of a shark. All around this object the sea boiled and spouted from the metal that was being flung at the surface, and then suddenly the black fin reared upwards to hang motionless for an instant, and revealing in all its nakedness, the gleaming roundness of *Restless*'s pressure hull. Peter could see the tiny figures of men leaping from the conning tower, jumping into the lashing fury of lead, and then, quite suddenly, an orange flash exploded just abaft the gun at the base of the tower. The world stood still and suddenly, as Peter watched, *Restless* just disintegrated before his horrified eyes, in a terrible sheet of flame and steam.

Then Peter, mesmerised until now by the tragedy, snapped suddenly out of his trance. He swung round on the periscope.

Capitano di Fregata Cesare Ricasoli was tired. He had not even been ashore at La Goulette, for no sooner had he appeared off the jetties than a flashing signal lantern dispatched him again on escort duty with his Division. Then, having taken a north-bound convoy to Marittimo, he was ordered to turn round and escort another south-bound back to Tunis.

"That's two days and three nights on the bridge," he complained to himself as he stifled a yawn and leant over the bridge to watch his Division finish off this British submarine. She had certainly carried out a brilliant attack on the troopship, but, by God, she was paying for it now, and he smiled grimly to himself as he watched his superb team carrying out their counter-attacks. *Zeno* and *Malocello* had just completed their runs-in and now it was *Vivaldi*'s turn, and he smiled proudly as he watched her circle to line up carefully on the trapped submarine.

"It's only a matter of time now," he muttered, more to himself than the blue-jowled Officer of the Watch in the crumpled uniform.

He pricked up his ears when he heard the detonation of gunfire, and he was surprised to see *Malocello* opening up with her four-point-sevens. *Zeno* quickly joined in and Cesare Ricasoli jerked his eyes round to spot the splashes. Ah! there they were — and, *sapristi!* the pointed stern of a submarine's after-ends suddenly bobbed from the sea. Then the whole boat spewed upwards from the depths, the water cascading down her rust-splotched, blue conning tower.

"Tell *Vivaldi* to ram, signalman!" the Capitano di Fregata screamed across the bridge, and he jumped for the radio telephone, tearing the microphone from its socket.

"Commander 'D' calling *Vivaldi*," he blurted. "Commander 'D' calling *Vivaldi*. Go in and ram. Go in and ram," and then, trembling with excitement he waited, a helpless onlooker. But there was no need to give any orders because *Vivaldi* had instinctively read Commander 'D's mind and was already threshing towards the stricken submarine, gouts of smoke belching from her funnels.

"*Guarda! Guarda! Torpedini!*"

The anguished cry came from the young Officer of the Watch. From the terror in his voice Ricasoli knew that the tracks couldn't be so far away, and his eyes followed the outstretched arm which swept towards *Zeno*. As the trained eye of Commander 'D' sighted the torpedo track, he could see that *Malocello* was in mortal danger.

"Sound six blasts on the siren," he shouted above the pandemonium now gathering impetus on the bridge. "And all hands keep your eyes skinned for periscopes — there must be another blighter about!"

Ricasoli started to raise his binoculars, but he could hardly believe his eyes, for there, directly ahead of his *Tarigo*'s bows, the thin pencil of a periscope showed clearly; and what was more extraordinary, remained visible. Ricasoli was aghast, almost speechless.

"Full ahead together!" he screamed as he leapt for the binnacle. "Stand by to ram! Shut all watertight doors!" and he bent low over the compass card to con his ship towards the sliver thrusting itself so brazenly from the sea.

"Only about a hundred yards, I'd say," Ricasoli muttered, and instinctively he remembered his ramming drill. "Stand by depth charges, shallow depth settings!" he yelled as he made his last-second course adjustments.

"Steady! Steer three-one-four ... nothing to starboard, Coxswain!"

Ricasoli's dark eyes were gleaming. There was nothing to do now but wait for the crash. He planted his feet wide and braced himself for the shock of the impact.

Peter thought that his heart had stopped.

"Stop both, flood 'Q', emergency change of depth!" he heard his voice ordering calmly, as if they were out on exercises in Inchmarnock Water.

He was still peering through the periscope when his lips moved, but even as he gave the order he banged shut the handles.

For a moment he closed his eyes to shut out the dreadful picture that had filled the periscope on his last look.

He had been using the attack periscope, and even with its low-power, nearly the whole circle was filled by the bows of a destroyer. Evidently she had moved up astern of him, neither she nor *Rugged* being aware of each other. But she was very conscious of him now, for already a white streak showed at her knife-like bows, while, straining across the port guard rails in the eyes of the ship, three seamen gesticulated wildly, their arms swinging on to his bearing. *If it was not so disastrous*, thought Peter, *their antics would seem ridiculous*, and he glimpsed the clean sheer of the destroyer's bows, scything down upon him.

She'll hit just for'd of the conning tower, Peter mused unfeelingly, shocked into a world of nightmare quality. He even saw 'A' gun depressed on to the safety rails and pointing harmlessly over them; he could only just see the director tower, with the white cross-trees of the fore-mast abaft it, because the flare of the bows swamped all else.

"All torpedoes fired, sir!"

Peter opened his eyes and glanced at Brocklebank. How young he looked as he stood by his Fruit Machine, telephone in hand and peering anxiously at his Captain.

God! How I've failed them, Peter groaned within himself. *I've failed Joe, and now I'm taking* Rugged *to her grave also*. He cocked his head on one side to listen, to catch the first screech of ripping metal as the destroyer's forefoot bit into *Rugged*'s pressure hull, to hear the cascade of the deluge about to engulf them.

Maybe she'll roll us over, he thought. *I've heard of that happening before — but anyway, I've done the only possible thing: I've stopped* Rugged, *and perhaps the destroyer will pass over our fore-ends.* He glanced at the bubble, and already he could feel the beginnings of a bow-down angle.

He glanced at the gauges. Not a movement, not a flicker.

"For Pete's sake get a move on!" the Captain snapped unreasonably. "Get her down, Number One, or we'll be rammed."

The blare of the klaxon had hardly died away when there was a sharp slap on the pressure hull.

"First torpedo hit, sir," Elliott reported quietly. "And loud destroyer H.E. right ahead."

Peter nodded. A cheer rang through the boat, the deep resonance drowning even the second hit, as well as the increasing roar of the advancing propellers. Peter could see them in his mind: great brass blades, swinging more rapidly as the destroyer picked up speed, their oblong shape threshing the water, so that already cavitation must be taking place. With her stern thrust low in the water as she worked up to full speed, these blades would rip *Rugged* wide open.

He tore his eyes from the deckhead. But the pointers on the depth-gauges had only just started to move, slowly, impossibly slowly … twenty-eight, twenty-nine, thirty feet… Peter wanted to shout, holler his lungs out. He could bear this tension no longer — and then, mercifully, she struck.

Although the roar of the destroyer's propellers and the pounding of her engine were overwhelming, Peter hardly noticed the holocaust. He was so engrossed in keeping his submarine reasonably level, so that neither end would present itself as a sitting target, and so lost in concentration from taking *Rugged* down bodily that the terror of the pandemonium affected him not at all. But if the moment had not been desperate, the unconscious attitudes of the men in the Control Room would have seemed grotesque. The sudden realisation that their end had come affected each man in much the same way. In that split second before the sickening crash, each soul had glanced at his Captain. The young man stood there, calm, apparently unaffected by the crisis: but, with a closer scrutiny of his eyes and face, you knew that something terribly swift and ruthless was about to strike — and your inside turned to water. Peter Sinclair's eyes were bright as they watched the planesmen, and the knuckles of his right hand gleamed on the rungs of the ladder. And, by the cast of his head he seemed to be waiting ... waiting...

You couldn't avoid noticing the terror in your neighbour's face. You all knew what was coming next: the death that submariners instinctively refused to contemplate from the moment they joined — death by ramming. How often had we been told of the vulnerability of a dived boat? Of the finality of a gash in the pressure hull? There was nothing, nothing you could do, whatever the drill book said. Shut the doors if you like, trap us all in our own death cell, but once one of the compartments is flooded (and pray God it's not mine, even now), nothing in the world could stop the boat from spiralling down into the depths like an aspen leaf. It was deep here, and you could almost hear the explosions of the tanks as they crumpled, the crackling of the bulkheads as they burst ... and then the water, engulfing, pulverising with its ghastly pressure...

For a second you wondered whether you looked as absurd as the Outside E.R.A., crouching there by his panel, motionless, transfixed in time, wheel spanner poised in mid-air, his other hand gripping a valve wheel for support when the shock came. His mouth hung open slightly, and you could see the tip of his tongue as he slowly licked his lower lip; the whites of his eyes showed, for he was looking upwards at the deckhead, waiting...

And young Henry Keating, the telegraphsman, only eighteen and terrified. He, too, crouched by his handwheel, one hand clutching the handle, ready for an emergency telegraph order, an order which never came. In his dirty blue overalls, his body was twisted half round to watch his Captain's lips, and he could not understand why Sinclair did not speed up — surely he hadn't panicked!

For a moment Keating felt betrayed; but then, as he searched his young Captain's face, he knew that there was no need to lose confidence. He felt certain that all that could have been done had been done, and for a second Keating was content. A half-smile of serenity was frozen on the young face…

The crash went almost unnoticed. The noise was so overwhelming that men's nerves no longer registered fear. A dreadful tearing, ripping shriek — a shattering *clang!* and then the clatter of the propellers as she struck. The holocaust was appalling, a sound that no man who has experienced it can ever forget. The sickening crunching continued for an eternity, and then she listed imperceptibly, as if a giant's hand was rolling her over on to her side. Peter wondered with horror whether she would be rolled over. He braced himself and hung on to the ladder as she went, slowly, gently, until he felt his feet slipping from under him. His mind boggled at the impending disaster. With the submarine rolling over on to her beam-ends, the electrolyte would spill from the batteries, swamping them with acid — and then chlorine, the lethal, writhing, insidious gas that choked you to death.

But suddenly she catapulted upright, swinging for a moment like a pendulum, so that men crashed from side to side, bruising themselves against the myriad protrusions.

Peter held his breath and shut his eyes, the glowing numbers of thirty-two feet burning in his mind — the depth at which the destroyer had hit. Thirty-two feet — and he wondered, with academic interest, whether it was her stern that had struck, low in the water because of her speed, or her knife-like bows that had dealt the blow. Then he listened for the first inrush of water, pattering on to the corticene from the rents in the pressure hull.

She was still wallowing from side to side when Peter gradually realised that there was no cataclysm, no engulfing flood. He opened his eyes ... forty-two feet ... she had begun to move; but was she split wide open in some other compartment, and was this the prelude to her last crazy descent?

"All compartments make your reports."

Peter scarcely heard his own voice. Surely *Rugged* could not have escaped — only the conning tower or the standards were shattered, perhaps? And a shaft of hope pierced his shocked and deadened brain.

With detached interest he watched Brocklebank and Keating as they spun their telephone handles, but, even if a miracle had occurred, the inevitable shallow-setting depth-charge pattern would blow them to smithereens or back on to the surface.

"...Engine Room, all correct ... after-ends, all correct..."

And even if they got away with a savage counter-attack, how on earth could he manage to take his submarine back to Malta, for her periscopes must have gone?

"...fore-ends correct, tube-space correct, sir," and the Sub turned triumphantly towards his Captain to make his report.

No water coming in? It's not possible, Peter's mind protested. And then he watched the pointers sliding across the dials of the depth-gauges ... forty-eight, fifty feet...

"Blow Q!"

Peter watched his imperturbable Number One. Apart from his ashen face, he betrayed no signs of emotion — merely a quieter, more resolute approach to his trimming problems.

And then they realised that the terrifying cacophony had stopped — there was no sound from the surface.

"Well, I'll be…" Peter gasped. "What's happened to the destroyer?" and then he turned towards Elliott who was waiting for orders, his earphones clutched in his hand.

"All-round sweep."

"Aye, aye, sir," and Elliott crouched eagerly over his set, whilst all those in the Control Room waited to know the worst.

"Vent Q inboard."

The roar of the foul air rushing into the boat from Q tank drowned Elliott's report, and Peter had to wait impatiently for a repetition.

"The attacking destroyer has stopped, sir. I can just hear her auxiliaries on green one-six-o. More H.E. on red one-three-o, moving down the port side at slow speed."

Peter scratched his head and then he realised the significance of the sudden silence: perhaps his hunter was damaged, ripped wide open like a sardine tin by *Rugged*'s standards?

Peter's eyes darted to the compass. They would be given no second chance and he had to be quick.

"Port ten, steer o-six-o," he ordered. "Not a tweet from anyone, Number One. Eighty feet and I'll try to wriggle out of this. Petty Officer Elliott, keep me up to date with any information."

"Aye, aye, sir."

And so, silently running deep on 'slow one', *Rugged* slipped out of the noose that so nearly had drawn taut. She gave the enemy no chance, and less than twenty minutes later they had lost contact, the submarine presumed sunk by the Italians.

"Where am I?" the Captain of *Rugged* asked his Navigating Officer, his eyes twinkling. In the long pause that followed his question, Peter ordered the periscopes to be raised gently.

Saunders moved the lever carefully, nursing it with both hands as he watched the steel tube. For a second the periscope bounced, and then the wires twanged taut; the attack periscope was tried, but with the same result — both periscopes were stuck, jammed solid.

"Well, that's that," Peter said. "We're blind."

"You don't need any periscopes, sir," retorted Taggart, the Navigating Officer with a grin, "as long as you've got a navigator. I reckon we're here," and his finger indicated a pencilled D.R. on the chart, four miles north-north-west of Zembra island.

"Thank you, Pilot," Peter replied as he glanced at the chart. "But we may still want air."

"And be able to get out!" Number One added with a chuckle.

"While I drain down the conning tower, Pilot, lay me off a course for a return passage to Malta through the Pantelleria route."

"Aye, aye, sir."

But the conning tower was not flooded, and after dark that night Peter brought *Rugged* to the surface. Without difficulty he opened the upper lid himself, and after a quick all-round look, he set the lookouts. Then he surveyed the damage.

"Phew! We were lucky."

By a miracle the standards seemed to be undamaged, but, drooping over the port side like flaccid lilies, the two periscopes were splayed drunkenly. The for'd jumping wire had come adrift and lay wound round the gun, the insulators caught up in the trainer's handwheel, while, just above the signalman's head, the jagged ends of the bare wire rope gleamed dully.

"Start the generators. First Lieutenant on the bridge," the Captain ordered down the voicepipe.

And then the makeshift repairs were completed, hurriedly and competently. The loose wire was hauled taut and secured by a rope to the gun sponson, and, when it was all over, men breathed freely again. Sub-Lieutenant Taggart obtained a good fix from Zembra, and by dawn Cape Bon was already disappearing on the starboard quarter.

For twelve hours the Captain was remote, alone with his thoughts. The men around him felt his anguish and left him untroubled by the minor details of routine. Number One took good care of the boat, and, after turning over the last dog-watch to Brocklebank, he went quietly into the Ward Room.

"Hullo, Number One."

Benson looked down at his Captain and gasped involuntarily. The man sat along the settee, his legs stretched before him, and the face that looked upwards at his First Lieutenant was almost unrecognisable. In less than twelve hours he had gone grey about the temples, and it was now an old face on a young man's body that gazed upwards, the eyes set deep in their sockets. The cheeks were sunken, and with his growth of several days' beard, the whole impression was one of a haggard and broken man. *Until you look at his eyes though*, thought Benson, and he winced at the pain he saw hiding there.

Peter Sinclair had passed through a terrible crisis. In these few hours his character had changed and from the naive young man had emerged an experienced warrior, ruthless and subtle, with only one ambition. He had but one thought, one overriding aim hammering in his brain now that disaster had struck.

"Sit down, Number One."

The drawn face glanced at the empty bunks. Taggart was working on his D.R. at the chart table, so the two men were alone.

"I haven't told anyone, Number One, but I saw them destroying Joe Croxton and his boat."

Benson slowly looked up from the table, and their eyes met. For an interminable length of time there was no word spoken — just silence between them. Benson dimly registered the distant whine of machines and motors, the faint background hum of activity throughout the boat, but his mind was shocked and numbed. At length he collected himself sufficiently to murmur his sympathy.

And then the floodgates burst. Peter Sinclair started to talk and the words gushed from his mouth as the tension was released. He sat on the settee, his hands motionless on his lap and his legs stretched out horizontally before him. While he talked, his eyes were fixed on the revolver cupboard on the bulkhead, just above the settee, and his words tumbled out dispassionately in a flat monotone.

"Another few minutes earlier with my salvo and we would have saved *Restless*, Number One … only two or three more minutes were needed. They would have sighted my tracks and turned their attention on us."

"She might have been crippled already, sir," and Benson tried to force back the tears that were blinding him.

"And Joe taught us all we know, everything we darned well know."

If Peter had thumped the table it would not have been so unnerving; just a suspicion of emotion and Benson could have borne it. But it was the flat, cold-blooded banality that shocked him so much. He couldn't stand watching his Captain lacerating himself.

"Stop, sir," he whispered. "Stop, for God's sake," and he stood up as if to ward off a swinging blow. "You did all you humanly could. They're in God's hands now…"

The burning eyes from the settee swung across to face Benson and from their dark caverns two coals of fire smouldered, flickering and dancing with intensity.

"You really believe that?"

And then the First Lieutenant did a strange thing. He leant across the table. He put his hands on his Captain's shoulders and deliberately held him rigid so that he could not move.

"Sir, you must never repeat these things … never, never," and Benson fixed his Captain with a calm gaze. "Never, sir, do you understand?"

Then suddenly the First Lieutenant felt the body go limp under the pressure of his hands. Peter Sinclair slumped forward, and the tired head collapsed into the cradle of his crossed arms on the table.

"Come on, sir," Benson said gently. "Get some sleep," and he eased the exhausted man back on to the settee. He reached for his own blanket and, in spite of protests, covered his Captain with it. The despairing man rolled on to his side, turned his face from the light, and before he knew it, merciful oblivion had rolled over him in blessed sleep, sweet nature's balm.

The First Lieutenant did not return at once to the Control Room. For a few moments he stood still, staring down with compassion on his Captain. Scalding tears welled slowly to the surface and rolled through the grime on his face. With a gesture of impatience, he dashed them from his eyes, blew his nose and regained his self-control.

"You poor devil," he whispered. "You'll never forgive yourself for Joe Croxton's death, whatever the rest of us may think. I feel almost scared, he hates the enemy so. Peter Sinclair, you'll never be the same man again," and as Benson turned towards the Control Room he was sad because he knew that he was right.

CHAPTER 8

The American Chooses

"And then you came home?"

Peter nodded at his merciless questioner. For two hours now, he had been alone with Captain 'S' in his room on the balcony of Lazaretto. Those four walls acted as an improvised Conference Room for his Commanding Officers, and screwed on to the white door a wooden tally modestly announced: 'CAPTAIN "S"'. The younger officers passed it with respect as they tiptoed by in their sandals.

The last time that Peter had reported to this Holy of Holies was when he had been interviewed on the occasion of Harry Arkwright's rescue from Castellare Poliano. Joe Croxton had been Captain of *Rugged* then, and, as Staff Officer to the Captain (Submarines), Tenth Submarine Flotilla, he should have been here now. Instead…

"Let's go out on to the balcony."

When the older man had settled himself into one of the chairs on the cool balcony, Peter joined him in the other, half-facing him, yet turned towards the yellow sandstone of the battlements across the water.

Making a factual statement on what one considers to be a grievous dereliction of duty on one's own part is not easy, particularly when the result is the death of a personal friend and the destruction of a submarine and her Company — let alone the wiping off of one's own periscopes through carelessness.

"It might well have been a double tragedy," Captain 'S' said quietly, his gaze still fixed on Sinclair, his youngest and most recent Commanding Officer. Peter was looking across the turquoise of the deep water that separated Manoel Island from the battlements of Valetta opposite; great slabs of vertical sandstone they were, yellow in the hot sun as they reared from the depths of Lazaretto Creek.

As his unseeing eyes gazed across the creek, he propped his head between his hands and rested his elbows on the parapet of the balcony, the better to conceal his anguish from the severe searchings of Captain 'S'. By a single misjudgement Peter had finished his career anyway, he was convinced of that; and, if it had not been for the unspoken sympathy of his friends in the Mess, he would not have known how to carry on as if nothing had happened: a difficult feat in the bare shell of the Ward Room, with four recent gaps in the letter-rack and with four empty chairs at the white-clothed table.

His eyes focused upon a blotch of colour that slid across the elusive blues of the creek: a dhaisa-man was paddling homewards in his dhaisa, gaily painted in its traditional colours. As was the custom, the Maltese was standing up and facing for'd in his dhaisa, and as he plied his oars he leant forwards from the waist in a crouching motion that kept time with his rhythmical strokes. He was singing and the sadness of the refrain floated and echoed across the water.

Down below them and less than thirty yards away, *Rugged* lay alongside the sandstone wall of the building, her conning tower already swarming with the figures of dockyard fitters in their buff overalls as they scrambled over her to remove the periscopes.

"Listen to me, Sinclair."

Peter turned towards the severe voice which beckoned him back to sanity. The rugged face that had been carefully contemplating him was lined, and above the mahogany forehead, creased and lined by years of worry and submarining, a circle of white fringed the huge head. Captain 'S''s hair had turned white overnight, so it was rumoured, in that tragic April of 1942 when half the flotilla had been lost, its most brilliant captains among the casualties. But what was most striking about his leader's face was the intense blue of the eyes, piercingly astute beneath the beetling eyebrows. Captain 'S' did not know quite how to handle his young fire-eater, but decided that severity was the best cure for this black mood of self-pity.

"First of all, Sinclair, the loss of *Restless* and Joe Croxton is no more your fault than it is mine," the older man said firmly. "You might as well say that I should never have sent you all on the Tunis Iron Ring — eh?" he snapped the question at Sinclair.

Peter was stunned. He'd not thought of it in this light.

"And what's more," the quiet voice continued, "I'd send you out there again, you know it, in spite of the risks. That's what we're here for, to take risks," and then Captain 'S''s voice suddenly softened with compassion.

"What do you think it's like for me, my boy?" he asked. "I'm restricted to this blasted island and have to send you chaps out on patrol, time and time again, asking myself every hour of the day if there's anything I can do, any single little thing, that would make your job safer. I just sit and wait, wait, wait…"

Peter looked up. The wise face was looking directly at him, desperately trying to cure him of his depression.

"And what would you say if I drifted around in a frenzy of self-pity every time I'm poleaxed by another loss in the flotilla?" Captain 'S' asked. "I feel it enough, you know, Peter."

The sudden sound of his own Christian name snapped some chord in Peter's nervous system, and to his intense shame he felt hot, scalding tears in his eyes. Blinded by emotion, he could no longer see the creek as he sat upright in his chair, face half-turned from the man whom he would have followed to the end of the world.

Captain 'S' did not attempt to dam the floodgates of pent-up emotion, realising in his wisdom that it was better thus. He waited for Peter to compose himself, and when 'S' spoke it was with understanding and compassion.

"You did all you could and more," he said. "Nothing could have saved Joe, and as for the accident to your periscopes, a few months ought to put *Rugged* back in the fray again."

Peter looked long at the kindly man.

"You really feel that, sir?"

"I do."

"Will you still allow me to command *Rugged*?"

"Yes."

"May I be allowed to fly home in order to break the news myself to Joe Croxton's wife and people?"

"No."

The kindly face was set hard now, and seemed to be weighing up the quality of Peter's fibre. The young man's mouth was a thin line of disappointment, as he bit back the unasked question.

"I want you for a job."

Peter rose from his chair: he leant against the balcony and gazed in bewilderment at the twinkling blue eyes of his chief.

"Of course, if you would rather not take it on, you have only to say so, Sinclair," the voice of cunning continued. "But I dare say the coming three months' wait for your periscopes might be a trifle boring. However, you might like to keep yourself employed during that time by helping me."

Peter groaned inwardly. A shore job and in an office, but he owed it to 'S' and he pulled himself together.

"Of course I will, sir."

Captain 'S' seemed amused, but Peter could not see the joke.

"I'd rather be at sea, sir," he blurted.

'S' laughed, and rising from his chair he slapped an arm about Peter.

"Come into my makeshift office, Sinclair. There's a map there and we can talk without being overheard."

After the glare of the balcony, it was a few minutes before Peter's eyes readjusted themselves to the gloom of 'S''s bedroom. From one side of it there led a small annexe that 'S' had converted into a temporary map room. He stood aside and as his hand swept over the map, he recounted the incidents of the past few months.

"So, you see, we've been having mysterious casualties in the flotilla — there was no accounting for the loss of *Reliant* or *Renegade*, merely the bald announcements on Rome Radio; and, as for *Rigorous*, she has not returned and must be presumed lost, disappearing utterly, no trace whatsoever. And now there's Bill Trowbridge in *Rattler* — she's long overdue…" the voice continued flatly, a voice suddenly old and sick with weariness. "Yes, Bill Trowbridge…"

But as Peter watched, the shoulders suddenly squared themselves and Captain 'S' almost hurled himself at the map.

"But there *is* a clue, and we're not going on like this, sitting back and watching the enemy sink our boats," and he spun round to face Peter.

"You're going out to stop it, Sinclair," he snapped. "Because we have two clues." Captain 'S' was now his old self, and he swung round to address the wall map of the Mediterranean.

"Here, this is where the boats disappear," and the palm of his hand smacked against the area of the Greek Islands. "Here, in the Dodecanese. They've all been on that billet."

Peter stood up to inspect the map more closely. Here were the familiar names: Rhodes, Samos, and the Straits of Scarpanto. He knew them by heart from previous patrols.

"And the other clue lies in Sliema Creek, Sinclair. But I don't suppose you've noticed her."

Peter thought for a moment, then shook his head.

"Apart from the two minesweepers and an old caique, there's nothing there that I have noticed," Peter said. "Jake Hamilton captured the caique on his last patrol, didn't he?"

"Yes, but that rotten old hulk isn't as innocent as she looks. Jake found a false bulkhead in her, and inboard of the high bulwarks are built hidden gun mountings."

"A Q-ship?"

"Yes, you're right, but she's cleverly camouflaged. If Jake hadn't gone aboard himself I doubt whether he would have nobbled her. As it is, I've placed an armed guard aboard her in an effort to keep our knowledge secret."

The glimmer of an idea raced through Peter's mind.

"And the losses are still going on, sir?"

"Yes, dammit. *Rattler*'s not in yet — eight days overdue."

"Maybe the caique in Sliema Creek is not the only one. Perhaps there are two, maybe more, operating in groups," Peter said.

"Maybe."

"And…" Peter continued as the pieces fell into place in his mind.

"Yes, you've got it, Sinclair," the wise face smiled. "Will you take it on?"

Peter smiled. But now the light that sparkled from his grey eyes was one of determination and excitement.

"When do I sail, sir?" he asked.

"Well, Hank, how about it?"

Peter Sinclair sat on the balustrade of the unobtrusive villa which nestled at the foot of the cliff on the eastern shore of St. Paul's Bay. It was cool in the shade, and in the stillness of the moment he could hear the *plop!* of the tiny pieces of masonry, flipped idly by his fingers, as they splashed into the sea a few feet below him. An enormous fig tree spread its leaves across one corner of the house, dappling the balustraded balcony in shadow. "How about it, Hank? Will you come with me?"

Peter repeated the question, for he thought that Lieutenant George Jefferson, U.S. Navy, had not heard him. The tall American was leaning over the balustrade and was watching the ripples gliding their mazy way across the turquoise shallows. He wore only a pair of shorts, and beneath his mahogany shoulders there flowed the perfectly co-ordinated muscles of the athlete. His barrel of a chest was poised delicately upon nimble feet, and it was obvious that he had not won his welterweight at Annapolis for nothing.

Altogether a powerful chap, thought Peter, *but not quite the stuff of which Jan Widdecombe was made. However, it would be giving the American the battle experience he needed and, as Jan trained him, he must be the best available under the circumstances.*

Almost as if reading his thoughts, Hank stood up and turned towards Peter. When he spoke he was looking down at Peter, and their eyes met squarely.

"Well, Peter, I guess I'll string along with you this time, but it's only for one reason."

There was a long pause and then Peter raised his eyebrows imperceptibly.

"Yes, Hank?"

"I'm coming to show you supercilious Limeys that a Yank can compete with the best of you," and though there was a grin on the American's round face, a hard light gleamed in his eyes.

Peter laughed as he shook Hank's hand.

"Okay, Hank, you win! I always thought that Jan Widdecombe was unbeatable. But he trained you, so I reckon you must be the next best. All I ask is for you to come along and not to have a chip on your shoulder: we can't afford bad feeling on this sort of lark."

"Sure, Pete, there's no bad feeling," Hank continued with a grin, the wide mouth creasing the face that still bore traces of puffiness from soft living. "But I just want to prove that we can keep up with you British."

"You don't have to prove anything, Hank. Just be yourself."

"Okay, okay, I get your point, Sinclair. I'd sure love to come, and you're the boss," and the burly American, six feet four in his bare feet, thumped Peter on the back. All trace of resentment had vanished as they shook hands on it, and then in the cool of the evening they laid their plans for the operation. Lists of stores and weapons, ammunition and explosives, charts and disguises; all these were organised, but the most difficult of all was the nominal list of men.

"I'll take them from *Rugged*," Peter said.

"I can't help you there."

"There's the rest of the ship's company to be considered while *Rugged*'s being repaired," Peter continued. "The First Lieutenant and Coxswain better look after them ... and then Number One will need a relief, so we'd better give him Brocklebank."

"That leaves Sub-Lieutenant Taggart for us," Hank added.

"Yes, we'll take Taggart. Then there's the Second Coxswain, we'll take him," and Peter chewed the end of his pencil as it hovered over the piece of paper.

"What about an engineer for those diesels?"

"I think the Outside E.R.A., Saunders — he's dependable; and the Stoker P.O., Hicks. But the Chief will have to stay and look after *Rugged*."

"Signalman?"

"Yes, I reckon so. We'll take Goddard."

"That's four."

"We'll need another four for the guns."

Peter thought carefully. The guns' crews must be seamen, the best and most versatile that *Rugged* could provide.

"Stack, the Gunlayer, for one; then Able Seaman Bowles, he's good. Keating, the youngster, and..."

"... and who else?" Hank asked with a twinkle in his eye.

"All right, Hank, you win. You know I couldn't go without Bill Hawkins."

"I reckon you two can read each other's minds after all you've shared together."

Peter stabbed the paper for the final full stop.

"We've got two days, Hank. Do you think you can have your side of it ready by then?"

"Sure. When do we slip?"

"At dark on Thursday, the day after tomorrow. Get your stores on board tonight and tomorrow night. We mustn't be seen aboard the caique during daylight. Do you still want to come?"

"Sure, Pete, you can't stop me now. I ain't no sailor, you know, but I guess I shan't have much to do," and he laughed.

"You'll get all you need," Peter replied.

He was a better prophet than Hank realised.

CHAPTER 9

The Lull Before the Storm

If any inquisitive German aircraft had been patrolling one hundred and ten miles east-south-east of Malta at dawn on Friday, 13th September, it would have sighted an old Greek caique. She was a strange sight as she rolled to the swell, because she was steaming fast away from the besieged island, as if in terror of being trapped. But, on closer inspection, it would be noticed that her old sails were in tatters, which was hardly surprising, after the violent easterly gales that had been raging for the past few days. She had evidently been blown well to leeward, losing most of her canvas, and now she was desperately trying to avoid capture by the English, and was steaming away at full speed on her twin Mann diesels. She must be in a bad way, though, with most of her crew injured by the gales, or why should she leave her sails brailed up? They flogged themselves into tatters as they streamed in the wind from her own way, the blue cross and bars upon a white ground flapping at the truck of her mainmast.

If the aircraft had dived upon her, the pilot would have smiled to himself as his impressions were confirmed. There seemed to be only a swarthy Greek at the wheel, and the shambles on the upper deck showed plainly the ordeal through which she had recently passed. Gear was littered about the decks, and lengths of rope lay entangled where they were last discarded during the emergency. Wisps of steam and smoke belched from the exhaust on the port quarter, while from her long bowsprit the jib flapped uselessly in her own wind, for her crew were not even capable of lowering this.

Yes, thought her Captain, Lieutenant Peter Sinclair, Royal Navy, *I can't make her look any worse!* He was supporting himself by his arms as he leant across the rails of the ladder which led down into the filthy saloon aft. This companionway was sheltered by a box-like structure that had been fitted on to the upper deck, and which ran from the foremast to the poop. About eight feet high, the Greeks had fitted it to give additional accommodation, and this it certainly did at the expense of working the gear. Except for a small area around the foot of the foremast there was no clear working space the whole length of her upper deck, a disadvantage which Peter, as a seaman, detested.

He smiled to himself as he looked out of the entrance of the companionway. Across the stern the cloudless sky reeled in its immensity, while every now and then the deep blue of the Mediterranean hove into sight for a brief moment as the old caique rolled to the swell.

"How I long to stop these infernal engines," Peter shouted to the man on the wheel. "It will be grand when we set sail!"

Able Seaman Hawkins grinned back at his Captain, but he did not take his eyes from the compass card.

"It will that, sir. She's a proper cow without the canvas on her."

Peter heaved himself upwards a few feet and carefully searched the horizon. Then he emerged on to the upper deck and stretched himself in the sunlight.

"I'm going round the upper deck, Quartermaster. Shout if you want me."

"Aye, aye, sir."

With a feeling of amusement, the young Captain glanced at the older man who wrestled with the wheel abaft the foot of the mainmast. Even here, aboard the deliberately lax schooner, the discipline of the years showed itself naturally and without question. *How wise the whole system is*, thought Peter, *built as it is upon the experience gained since Alfred's day.* He strolled a few paces to the taffrail and for a brief moment he glanced at the wake bubbling astern which left a faint slick in the water. He leant over the taffrail and he caught sight of the transom, the Mediterranean gaiety of the brightly painted name moving his heart with joy.

"*Zephyrus*," he muttered. "The West Wind," and his imagination flashed back to Clovelly Bay which faced the Atlantic and cradled Lundy in its enfolding arms. He closed his eyes and in the happiness of the moment his imagination took him to the cliffs of Cornborough, and he could feel again the soft turf under him as he lay spread-eagled upon the cliff edge. The heady wine of the purple thyme flushed through him and he could see the splash of gold where the gorse bobbed against the embankment of the old railway cutting which had connected Bideford to Westward Ho! so long ago. He heard the roar of the Atlantic as it crashed and surged against the pebble-ridge, the stump of Fanny Bennett Rock ruggedly shooting cascades of spray high into the air as the seas broke upon it. And then gently, caressingly, the West Wind soughed in its sweetness across the clifftop, the sea-pinks nodding and dancing in their happiness, while the rock doves and choughs wheeled overhead.

"Aircraft, sir, red four-o!"

The report rang like a pistol shot, and Peter dragged himself from his reverie. He jumped to the hatchway and pressed the alarm buzzer which nestled by the ladder and which had just been fitted by the dockyard. Crouching at the entrance to the companionway, he could hear the snapping of ammunition drums as they were banged home on to the old Lewis guns. He had scrounged six in all, allowing almost a gun each for the upper deck party, and during the short spell before sailing they had put in hours of Lewis gun drill.

"It looks as if we're going to make use of it," Peter muttered. Sub-Lieutenant Taggart crouched below him, a grin across his open face, the gun wobbling in his inexperienced hands.

"For Pete's sake stop pointing that thing at me," Peter shouted. But after making a cursory circle around the *Zephyrus*, the aircraft made a shallow dive over her, and then disappeared whence she came, Bill Hawkins waving enormous friendliness as she passed over.

"Fall out action stations, Number One!"

Taggart grinned as he clambered past his Captain. It was fun being Mister Mate of this hooker, even though the ship's company totalled but eleven. He moved for'd through the deckhouse to pass the order.

"Fall out action stations, Coxswain!"

Rugged's Second Coxswain, the black-bearded giant, Acting Petty Officer Jack Weston, was enjoying his promotion as Coxswain of *Zephyrus*. Down below there was little room, but he had managed to squeeze his eight men into the fore-peak like sardines. All available space had been taken up by steel buttresses to strengthen the gun-mountings; by racks of ammunition for the two quick-firing three-inch guns; by boxes of machine-gun ammunition, and, right aft, the fireworks locker which also housed the 'sticky' bombs. These last were a recent innovation but their success had been proved by experience. When placed beneath or along the requisite object to be destroyed, they were handy because they needed no securing. They stuck through their adhesive. Sinister in their red paint they protruded egg-like from their boxes.

There was even less space in the deckhouse that stretched from abaft the foremast to the mainmast. The Greek crews of the caiques usually made this their living quarters while the cargo was stowed below. Ventilation and light filtered through the square ports and the doors which were cut into the side of the deckhouse, but these were now replaced by dummy shutters to conceal the two three-inch guns. On pulling a lever, these shutters fell inwards to give the guns their full traverse, and then the shining barrels would protrude wickedly from amidships, able to fire on most bearings, except down the fore-and-aft line because of the masts.

The machine-guns, too, were hidden. There were two mounted on each side, two in the eyes of the ship and able to fire right ahead, and two on either quarter. Their mountings were on the upper deck, and slatted shutters had been cut in the high bulwarks, so that once again on the pull of a lever, the shutters could fall on the instant to allow the guns to fire.

"What a lash-up!" Peter chuckled as he strode for'd. He ran into Able Seaman Stack, the gunlayer, who was oiling the port for'd Lewis gun. Bowles stood by him, clipping up the belts of ammunition.

"One A.P., one tracer, one incendiary?" asked Peter as he glanced at the different markings of the .303 ammunition.

"Yes, sir," Stack replied. "That's what you wanted, wasn't it, sir?"

"Yes. These caiques are pretty inflammable."

Stack grinned.

"The cutlasses are all in their racks now, sir. Almost like the olden times, ain't it?"

"Can you use a cutlass, Bowles?"

"Never tried, sir, but the Coxswain said he'd give us some drill in the 'dogs'."

"Where did he learn how to use one?"

"He was in *Cossack*, sir."

That was enough for Peter. *Cossack* of *Altmark* fame — *Cossack* of 'the Navy's here!' He smiled as he watched his men who looked a bloodthirsty lot, itching for a fight.

Well, it won't be my fault if they don't get one, he mused as he leant against the side on the port quarter, his back to the sea and the sun drenching him with warmth. His arms were stretched along the rails and he looked upwards in contentment at the mastheads. Without topmasts, he mused, a caique was no beauty. Their short masts gave the ship a dumpy appearance, and he viewed the poles with misgiving when he noticed a large scarf in the foremast, just below the hounds.

"How I long to get the sail on her!" he yelled across to Hawkins on the wheel.

"Yes, sir. She'll look better then."

The headsails — a staysail and a large jib set from the squat bowsprit — flapped in tatters, an untidy and horrible sight for any seaman, and Peter groaned as he caught sight of them. *Not a bad idea really*, he thought. *They ought to confuse any reconnaissance aircraft anyway*, and he grimaced as he looked at the tatters. He had found some rotten whalers' sails and had hoisted them, so that the caique looked as if she really had taken a hammering in the gales. With no mainsails or mizzen, and with her headsails in ribbons, she had no option but to flee on her engines.

His eyes followed the ratlines in the shrouds on each mast, and then he noted the footholds which led cross-like from the hounds to the truck.

For the lookouts, I suppose, when they search for the tunny. He looked at his watch — only ten-thirty; then he saw Hawkins eyeing him, a grin on his open face.

"What the dickens are you laughing at?"

There was a pause and the man switched on his I-mustn't-annoy-an-officer face.

"You don't look no good as a Greek, sir."

And then Peter nearly jumped from his skin as a bellow of laughter exploded by his right ear.

"You sure don't, bud! You Limeys always look British, even if you wear funny hats," and Hank thumped Peter on the shoulder.

Peter was annoyed. He had gone to much trouble in trying to achieve a modern-Greek effect. He had allowed his beard to grow, but even that was no great success, for it had emerged as a tri-colour: brown, grey, and, incredibly, a streak of green. But what with his old grey bags, filthy blue shirt, and his *pièce de résistance*, the black beret, he had hoped that he looked the part.

"Well, Hank, you're no great shakes yourself."

Hank was flabbergasted.

"Me? Aw, shucks, you're jealous, that's all."

But darkness fell at last, a comforting mantle. Peter sighed deeply, a prayer of thankfulness from the very depths of him. Unless the aircraft had reported them, they were undiscovered, and now they had the whole night before them.

"All hands on deck!"

The Coxswain's cry brought the motley company tumbling from their hidey-holes. This was the moment they had all been longing for, to set the sail on her.

"Stop main engines."

Peter blew down a whistle-pipe, and, to his surprise and infinite relief, the diesels coughed, spluttered once, then died away.

"Thank heavens for that!"

The silence was exquisite. The slip-slap of the wavelets slopped against the timbers while bare-footed men padded along the planking of the upper deck.

"All ready, sir," Mister Mate Taggart reported.

"D'you mind if I do it?"

"No, sir, of course not. I'm not up in this sort of thing, anyway."

Peter was excited. Now she should come alive and lift naturally to the gentle swell, driven by this southerly wind. A broad reach, he reckoned, with one of the loveliest of sailing breezes.

He had brought her into the wind, and the rotten headrails were already over the side.

"Bend on staysail and jib," the Master ordered quietly.

Weston had anticipated the order and the jib was soon bent on to the outhaul.

"Hoist mainsail: main halliards and peak halliards together!"

There was sudden activity down both sides, and then Peter sighed contentedly.

"Yes, sir, it's music, ain't it?" Hawkins murmured.

Peter nodded as, feet astride, he watched the gaff climb into the night sky. The sheaves squealed merrily in their blocks and then, when the great sail filled and billowed, the deck started sloping under him as the schooner listed.

"'Vast hoisting peak!" he yelled as the luff stiffened and the main halliards took up the slack in the mainsail.

"'Vast hoisting main. Hoist peak."

When he was satisfied with the set of the mainsail, he set up the halliards. "Man mainsheets, stand by to hoist mizzen!"

The evolution was repeated on the mizzen and then the great moment came. With the two spreads of canvas looming above him, there only remained to set the jibs and her billowing sails would fill.

"Hoist jib!"

The hands ran away with it, Bowles manning the out-haul, and, in a trice, the port fore-sheet was hauled taut. The curve of the jib thrilled Peter's heart as it bowed against the eastern horizon, and then he set the staysail.

"Check main halliards, port twenty!"

The little ship slowly paid off and, once she had gathered way, Peter afted the mizzen and mainsheets. An adjustment on the sheets, a squaring-up all round, and then the hands were dismissed to their night watches.

"Course, sir, one-one-o."

"Very good."

Peter stood on the poop, Taggart and Weston beside him.

"She's grand, ain't she, sir?" purred the Coxswain.

A silence descended upon the three men as they listened to the unfamiliar sounds of a sailing vessel. With their knowledge and experience of modern machinery, they lost touch with the sea itself, so it was all the more satisfying to be part of this live thing, this caique which could not have been very different from the most famous ship of all time. It must have been through this water that the Apostle Paul's vessel was driven before the gales. Swamped and overwhelmed, they must have abandoned hope about here, with only a mad passenger to sustain them before being dashed to pieces on the rocks of Malta. As Peter listened, he realised that time leaves no mark upon eternity. Here were the ropes creaking in their blocks to the strain of the tackles and purchases just as they did nine hundred years ago. The jib was not set up correctly, and he could hear from for'd its foot flapping gently. The huge booms of the mizzen and main lifted and dropped with the motion of the ship and he delighted in the enormous spread of canvas, the reefing points dangling in their horizontal lines.

"We'll have sail drill tomorrow, Weston: it may come on to blow, so we ought to know how to reef down."

"Both sails have reefing-down tackles, sir, and the leach is hauled down by means of a rope strop led through the reefing-point cringle."

"Lowering the tack at the same time?"

"Yes, sir, then tying the reef points."

"I reckon we can reef close-hauled, without luffing-up. We don't want these booms thrashing about."

"It will be fun trying tomorrow, sir. The weather's set fair anyhow," Taggart added.

It certainly was a grand night. With a force three breeze broad on her beam, the odd white horse gleamed fitfully upon the black sea, then was gone. The sails strained at their sheets, and Peter was interested to note that they were not loose-footed, but secured to their booms with separate lashings through each eyelet. *Funny*, he thought, *if she were mine I'd change that*. He did not relish a mountainous sea climbing on board and plumping down in the mainsail where it could not drain away. *My old* Waterwitch *was better rigged than that*, he mused, as memories of his schooldays flooded over him. His father had owned a Morecambe Bay prawner and the lovely old boat had been their pride and joy. Peter had learnt the backbone of his seamanship from her, by listening to the unsolicited advice of the fishermen.

The stars shone in the ultramarine of the night sky, and across the immensity of this mysterious bowl the trucks of the two masts curvetted gleefully. For the first time in months, Peter's heart sang with joy and he was happy and content with the beauty and peace of the night.

"Good night, sir," Weston growled as he saluted and strolled for'd.

"Good night, Coxswain."

"Well, I'm going to hit the hay too, sir. Good night," Taggart murmured.

"Good night, Number One. But don't forget to relieve me for the Middle!"

Peter was left alone with his thoughts and in the silence of the watch he strolled around the upper deck. He patted the gleaming barrels of the guns as he went by, and he was amused to see a seaman curled up and asleep at each of the mountings. *They're not going to be caught napping*, he thought; *it won't be their fault if we don't avenge some of the 'boats'*. And then a black cloud of depression swamped him as he remembered the tragedy of his last patrol. But he shook himself and the remorse left him when he remembered the kindly words of Captain 'S'. All that mattered now was the destruction of the flotilla's killers, and all aboard *Zephyrus* shared the same resolution.

"We shall see in a day or two," he said aloud. He was happy again as he listened to the music of the rigging singing in his ears.

The days had started to merge one into the other as they settled to their new routine, when at 0800 on Monday, 16th September, they finally altered course to the northward.

"Course, sir, three-three-o," young Keating reported from the wheel.

"I'll have to send a man aloft soon, Number One. We ought to sight Scarpanto in the afternoon."

"And slip through the Straits tonight?"

"If luck holds. We haven't been sighted yet."

Fortune had certainly been with them for, since that first Friday, the thirteenth, the sky had remained blue and empty of aircraft. They could not have been luckier with the wind, which remained between force three and four, and still blew from the same quarter.

They had continued sailing all day on Saturday, but in order to make maximum speed, Peter had engined all night until he reckoned they were due south of Cape Anemomylos in Crete. He altered course to 050° then, and remained on engines until dawn on Sunday morning.

From then onwards they remained sailing, much to the relief of all aboard. Not only was it more pleasant, but for a caique to be motoring in mid-Mediterranean was unnatural. They passed no nearer to Crete than fifty miles, thereby slipping unnoticed past the air patrols. It was a glorious Sunday morning, the sea sparkling and the sun beating down hotly upon the planking. Men stood bare-headed and bare-footed around their Captain while he pronounced the traditional 'Prayer to be said before a Fight at Sea against any Enemy.' He had brought his old prayer book and these men felt comforted and unselfconscious now that they were about to go into action. There was no cynicism here; there never is when you have to face reality. These men knew that for them the choice was simple: extinction or survival: concentration camps and all that the horrors of a police state imply or freedom in an imperfect democracy.

But now the sun was over the meridian on that Monday, and they all knew that before another day had dawned they would, in all probability, have encountered the enemy. *Zephyrus* was bowling along merrily before the southerly wind. With her great sails out to their limit over the starboard side, and with her headsails curving in billowing crescents, she was a spanking sight.

"She must be making six or seven knots," Peter said to Taggart who was reading the log which gyrated over the port quarter.

"Yes, she's certainly shifting, sir."

Peter's heart sang as he watched the wake curling away under the counter, a mosaic of green and white as she bounced through the seas. The sheets were checked right away, and as the huge booms bucked to the swell, the blocks at the peaks creaked in unison.

"Land-ho! Red one-five!" Goddard hailed joyfully from the masthead at five-thirty in the evening, and by seven o'clock the island was clearly visible from the upper deck. Mauves and blues glowed softly in the setting sun and then twilight was upon them, the cliffs of Scarpanto melting into the western haze. The stars glittered above them and the little caique *Zephyrus* sailed on into the Sea of Crete, the island-studded waterway of ancient time.

CHAPTER 10

Hand-to-Hand

The Captain of the Greek caique *Olympia* had had enough. Seized from her original owners, the Germans had refitted her as a Q-ship to trap British submarines.

"And here I am," muttered Oberleutnant zur See Kurt Holzt, "in command of a filthy old hooker like this when I might be at Kiel," and he spat over the side in disgust.

But nevertheless he was content within himself — had he not sunk one submarine with his own pet device? And he looked over the stern with affection to watch the thin wire that vibrated and hummed as it sliced through the water. There was a thousand kilogram contact charge on the far end of it, and any nosey parker of a submarine who trailed him from astern was in danger of having his pressure hull shattered. He smiled to himself. Perhaps he might earn another Iron Cross, for he had sunk one British submarine; had he not recovered some of the horrible debris to prove it? And he rubbed his hands together with satisfaction.

His second-in-command, Leutnant zur See Johann Prinzel, appeared silently at his side, buttoning up his overalls.

"Sorry I'm a few minutes late, sir!" he said nervously. "I overslept."

Holzt snorted. He wasn't going to stand for lax discipline.

"Not good enough, Leutnant!" he snarled at his junior. "You reservists seem to think that punctuality is unimportant, presumably because you're used to office routine. But, *mein Gott!*" and his fist crashed down upon the taffrail, "in the

Deutsch Marine you have no personal feelings. The Fatherland comes first, d'you understand?" and he shouted at Prinzel, who stood there open-mouthed, waiting for the idiot to stop. *If I try a Hitler salute*, the second-in-command thought slyly, *perhaps it will prick his bubble.* He clicked his heels smartly, at the same time extending his arm in the ludicrous Nazi salute.

"*Heil Hitler!*"

For a second Holzt was beaten, for he had to break his train of thought.

"*Heil Hitler!*" he threw in quickly. "But here you come, a junior…"

"I said I was sorry, *mein Kapitan*. Now please turn over the watch. I think there's fog around," and he shivered as he felt a sudden clammy coldness. He pulled the collar of his overalls tighter about him.

"*Himmel!*" Holzt swore. "Do you think you can manage, *mein* Prinzel?"

"*Ja, mein Kapitan*. But when should we meet *Io*? She's relieving us, isn't she?"

"That Italian fool? About eight o'clock, the orders say. But you must call me if this cursed fog persists after dawn."

"*Ja, mein Kapitan.*"

It was with relief that Johann Prinzel watched his Kapitan squeeze through the hatch-coaming. *What a horror the man is*, he thought, smiling to himself. *These Nazis make you sick; give them half an inch of authority and they are as happy as sandboys, and the more insignificant the authority the more petty the official. But I suppose it's the same the whole world over*, he thought. *I've no doubt the British have their same troubles.*

Then this liberal-minded man glanced at the sails. He'd never understood the sea anyhow, but he'd done his best. He always felt happier when he had two feet on dry land and he sighed for the beauty of his home near Flensburg. The green woods which came down to the edge of the Baltic, the exciting blue of the water with its white dots of canvas upon it; the cool lagers in the underground *bier kellers* in the sweltering Julys, and the strawberries — those luscious strawberries, dunked in profusion into the centre of those round gateaux, the whole covered with jelly and laced with cream. And then he shivered.

He had not dared to ask the Old Man to allow him to return below to fetch a sweater, and now he was feeling the cold of the fog in his bones as it rolled about them. For the last few mornings they had been dogged by this early morning hazard: it was easy to go aground on one of these numerous islands, and even more difficult this morning was the task of keeping a rendezvous with *Io*.

"The Italian is usually late anyhow," Prinzel muttered, and then he raised his voice as he shouted to the lookout in the eyes of the ship.

"Keep a sharp lookout. We're expecting to sight *Io*."

"*Jawohl, mein Leutnant.*"

The man's voice seemed like a ghost's, distant and eerie as the fog rolled round them. The stuff came in patches, and when the sun climbed out of the east at six forty-five, its rays glowed brightly on the far side of the mist so that the fog banks became luminous barriers.

"A glorious sight," Prinzel murmured, as *Olympia* nosed her way through the thick curtain. The mist clung to her in a tenuous embrace, curling along the upper deck and rolling over the stern. Suddenly her bows would cleave through a patch, and then a shining brilliance would burst upon them and the headsails would gleam, white and curved in the clear light of dawn.

"What beauty! Straight from the Odyssey," Prinzel whispered as a circle of blue water spread out before them, free of the constricting fog. The rays of the sun struck the surface obliquely, giving a turquoise translucency to the sea. And then the edge of the next patch of fog would roll upon them, blanking out this miracle of colour.

I'll never get tired of this, Johann mused, *but I suppose* Io *may not have left Erakleion — any excuse is better than none for her*. Then the fog rolled away once again and *Olympia* found herself in another blue world.

"*Io* five degrees on our starboard bow, sir!"

The call was music in Johann Prinzel's ears. Now for home and beauty! He strolled over to the starboard side and there, sure enough, *Io* bore down upon them. She looked trim, better than usual, and he was amused to notice that she was flying a Greek flag from her truck. Better than the green, white and red of the Italian Marine, he supposed, and he grinned because he had little time for his Italian allies.

Io was running before the breeze, the belly of her mainsail filling. She looked weird as she gradually materialised. She was white and shining in this peculiar fight.

"She's coming round into the wind," Leutnant Prinzel muttered. "Perhaps she wants us? I'd better luff up too," and then he moved over to the wheel. "I'll take her, Quartermaster, while you go and report to the Kapitan that *Io*'s in sight."

"Now it's your turn, Hank."

Peter Sinclair spoke softly for he did not want his voice to carry in this fog.

"Hands to boarding stations!"

The whispered summons flickered through the *Zephyrus* like forked lightning. Every soul on board, except for E.R.A.

Saunders and Stoker P.O. Hicks on the engines and for Keating on the wheel, was crouching below the starboard bulwarks within seconds of the alarm, because their Captain had prepared them for this emergency as soon as he saw the fog coming down.

"Number One Lewis manned, sir."

Peter nodded at Stack who crouched by the black snout of the for'd gun on the starboard side. *If I luff up, the starboard side will become my engaged side*, thought Peter, *even though the caique now lies ahead and is broadening on my port bow*.

"Number Three Lewis manned, sir," Bowles whispered hoarsely.

"Stand by to luff up," Peter hissed. "Look out for the booms!"

The tension was now electric. The two caiques approached in silence, the only sound being the creaking of the blocks, the swish of the sea and the gentle soughing of the breeze in the rigging.

The sight of his cut-throat crew made Peter smile as he stood, legs wide apart, upon the poop. He himself carried a .45 Colt, but he didn't expect to use it. He relied upon his boarders who seemed fully equipped.

Hank was in his element, a veritable walking arsenal. A tower of strength, he crept on all fours amongst his waiting men, checking their weapons. A red knitted pom-pom cap graced his shorn head, while through his broad leather belt he had thrust one cutlass, a Colt, one Commando knife and three stick-grenades, and from his right hip hung two red sticky-bombs. Yes, Hank was happy all right, and from the gleam of teeth in blackened faces Peter could see that wide grins belied the boarders' nervousness.

"Port twenty!"

"Port twenty, sir."

The masts creaked as the pressure eased and then all was confusion while the booms threshed.

"Haul taut main and mizzen sheets!" Peter hissed, his eyes flickering across the starboard bow.

There she was, less than half a cable away! He had judged it just right: he could already see their officer waving half-heartedly. Even from here Peter judged him to be German.

"Good-o, lads! You've got your real enemy this time — they're Huns! Stand by grapnels!"

The enemy caique had begun to round up now, and Peter judged they would collide just forward of her mizzen mast. She seemed quite unsuspecting, the officer in the stern standing on the poop, his arms outstretched along the rail.

The distance lessened … fifty feet … forty … thirty…

Peter could now see the look of contempt upon the German's face. The man seemed disgusted at the filthy ship which was coming alongside. Then Peter saw the man glance at the bulwarks, a look of suspicion flickering across his face. Peter waited no longer.

"Let go grapnels!" he shouted at the top of his voice. "Open fire! Saint George for Merry England!"

The ancient battle cry came quite unselfconsciously from his lips and then, like music in his ears, a cheer roared in answer as the White Ensign broke from the masthead to flutter in the breeze. Hank's red top bobbed up, the Lewises stuttered and the grapnels snaked across as the two ships crunched together.

There was a sudden rolling and then the grapnel lines tautened, but Hank and his men were already across the rails. Yelling blood-curdling oaths, they were at the hatchways in one bound. The guns stopped, and in the lull that followed, an unnatural hush fell upon the two ships. Then Jack Weston hurled a grenade down the fore-hatch while Hank lobbed a sticky-bomb down the after companionway. A few seconds later the decks of the *Olympia* jumped twice and it was all over.

"Aw, heck!" said Hank Jefferson, U.S.N., afterwards, "the trouble with you guys," and he twinkled at Peter, "the trouble with you bloodthirsty Limeys is that you won't let a Yank get a proper crack at these squareheads!"

"Nonsense, Hank! They heard you were coming and just gave up."

"Did they, heck! They were beyond caring before we got on board, *sir*," and Hank emphasised the mark of respect. "The guns mowed them all down."

Thirty minutes had elapsed since the engagement and now *Zephyrus* was drawing away from the scene of the action. Apart from the flotsam there was nothing to betray the incident, but Peter decided to put as much distance as possible between themselves and the scene of the crime.

"Well, that's one swine that will sink no more of The Tenth," Hank muttered as he extracted his foul cob pipe.

Peter did not reply at once. They had taken no prisoners, and the realisation of their ruthlessness appalled him even now. In the heat of battle it was different somehow, but now…

"Yep, Hank, that's so. But I reckon we're lost now." Then he yelled down the companionway, "Have you identified that island on the port bow yet, Sub? I can't…"

But a sudden cry drowned Taggart's reply.

"E-boats, red one-five-o, sir!"

Peter spun round to the port quarter and for an instant he was staggered.

"Where in the name of goodness have they come from, Hank?"

But the American had already leapt for'd and had disappeared into the deckhouse to man the three-inch gun. Then Peter's mind cleared.

"Action stations!" he yelled at the top of his voice. "Action stations!"

At the same moment he jumped to the port side and pulled the iron lever; the shuttering fell down with a slam and then the barrel of the three-inch gun began to traverse.

"Hoist topping-lifts!" Peter yelled in order to clear the booms and mainsails from the field of fire. "Start main engines!"

He jerked the starboard lever and the remainder of the shuttering fell outwards, both guns now exposed to view.

"Port ten, steer north. Stand by to open fire! Target — leading E-boat, range one thousand yards."

The booms were now lifted clear, and as *Zephyrus* swung to port, the diesels coughed into life. *Ah, now she's more manoeuvrable*, Peter thought; *now I can keep the masts out of the line of fire*, and he glanced along the decks which were already cleared for action. With three men at each three-inch, that only left Taggart and Hank for the machine-guns — he could just see them there crouching over their sights.

The familiar silhouettes of the E-boats were closing in fast. They creamed straight towards them in line ahead, the Vs of their bow waves foaming whitely.

Maybe they're not sure who we are, Peter wondered, *maybe...* and then his eyes swung to the masthead — the White Ensign was flying defiantly from the truck! *Well, there's nothing for it now but to fight it out — a pity, but there's no alternative.* Peter's mind raced. *Perhaps I can dissuade them if I engage them early...*

"Open fire!"

The crash of the guns drowned the helmsman's report, but *Zephyrus* was now steady on her course and thereby presenting her minimum target. The Lewises stuttered and ribbons of green tracer floated towards their attackers.

Able Seaman George Stack had not earned the reputation of being the best gunlayer in the Tenth Flotilla for nothing. Now he was to prove his skill, and the months of active experience were about to pay off. His shooting was accurate, the first round exploding right ahead of the leading E-boat, while Number One gun, with Hawkins as layer, was a trifle left for line. Then Peter heard above the racket Stack's hoarse voice adjusting the ranges. The gunlayer squinted along his sights. He squeezed the trigger as the cross-wires swung on.

The enemy was retaliating now, and then above the cacophony, there was a peculiar fluttering above him and Peter realised that metal was flying both ways. Pieces of wood flew off the taffrail alongside him and then, higher up in the rigging, tatters of canvas suddenly threshed in the wind.

I hope they stay in line ahead, Peter prayed, *it's our only chance*, and then he groaned as he saw Keating suddenly spin round at Number One gun. The young seaman's hands flew up as if in self-protection and he dropped the shell which he was loading into the gun. He remained motionless for a second and then crumpled to lie where he fell. Peter saw Hank jump from his gun and turn the man over. For a second Hank stood still and then he took the young seaman's place. The gun barked once more.

The E-boats were in to five hundred yards when Stack started hitting. The fifth round was dead right for line, but slightly over. Then Peter could not believe his eyes, for there was a vivid sheet of orange flame abaft the leader. It happened suddenly, a horrifying spectacle of fire and exploding ammunition, and then the last boat hauled suddenly out of line to avoid her stricken companion.

A cheer rang from *Zephyrus* and the breeches slammed home with redoubled fury, a frenzy of desperation adding its impetus. If they were caught now, they were done for…

Suddenly the leading boat sheered off to starboard, for a few seconds a perfect broadside-on target. The other survivor turned hard on her heel to career away on the port quarter. Then, once out of range, they turned together, to point once more towards *Zephyrus*.

"Well done!" Peter yelled. "Stand by for round two! They're licking their wounds. They'll attack from different bearings this time." And as the young Captain watched, the two sleek silhouettes slowly gained bearing as they slid up on either side of the caique.

"They're going to attack on either bow!" Peter yelled, "or at least try to. But I'll alter course when they start their run-in. Are you all ready, Number One?"

"Yes, sir, there's plenty of ammo, left."

"You'd better take Lieutenant Jefferson's gun."

"Aye, aye, sir."

"Lieutenant Jefferson!" Peter shouted.

The long American left his gun and, though he hardly appeared to move, he reached his Captain's side in a few seconds.

"Is Keating…?"

"Yeah, but by God, these Heinies are going to pay for it," and Peter watched the fury burning in the pale eyes.

"Right, Hank — it's up to you now — only the for'd gun will be able to bear. If they attack from ahead, our firepower will be halved."

"Aye, aye, sir," and the American slid off to Number One gun.

"Here they come, sir!" Taggart's voice floated aft from the eyes of the ship. "On either bow!"

Well, Peter thought grimly, *this is our last chance. We haven't a hope, and though I daren't let the others know, I'm sure the Huns will remain outside my effective range to use their torpedoes. They'll fire when I turn to bring my guns to bear.*

"Stand by!"

From the starboard rail, he could just see the leader of the E-boats. A white mountain built up astern of her as she gave her engines full throttle. An awesome sight she was, tearing straight for them, her guns spitting and the green tracer swinging low in a gentle arc towards them.

They're trying to keep our heads down, I reckon, so I'll hold my fire a little longer… I'll turn now to throw them off balance and that will bring Number Two gun on…

"Starboard twenty!"

The caique answered to her helm quickly and, from his position by the quartermaster, Peter saw Stack swing the barrel of Number Two gun on to the left-hand E-boat.

"Target for Number One gun — right-hand E-boat! Number Two gun, target, left-hand boat! Stand by!"

Peter felt oddly sad at the way things had gone. Although they had avenged some of the losses, what was the sinking of one caique compared to the submarines? And now to be finished off by two prowling E-boats… What a way to end the war, either by a bullet or being put in the 'bag'. He looked up and groaned as he saw the E-boats lunging towards them, weaving from side to side in an effort to throw off the guns. Dare he wait any longer…? The enemy's shooting was more accurate now and the bullets whocked into the caique's timbers. Keating had been killed already, and they had a long way to go yet. A small fire had started at the foot of the mainmast, so they must be using incendiaries... *It's now or never*, Peter decided. The swing of the ship had stopped, and he was vaguely aware of the unidentified island which seemed to be much nearer now — half a mile, perhaps.

Oh, God, this is the end! He could see the bunting streaming from the cross-trees of the leader, and even her torpedoes were visible, sprouting from their bow tubes. *I must watch those like a lynx*, he thought, and he whistled as he saw the mountainous bow waves. *Now's the moment, now ... point-blank range...!*

"Open fire!"

Peter opened his lips to yell the vital order, but as he did so there occurred an amazing incident and he could not believe his eyes. He glanced at his guns — they had not opened fire yet... But directly across the path of the E-boat leader a line of shell splashes suddenly burst, great gouts of black water, orange flashes at the bases of the leaping cones. The target disappeared behind the screen of spray and flying metal, and then, as she emerged, another salvo dropped from nowhere, bracketing her this time and barely two cables from *Zephyrus*.

The caique's gunlayers were bewildered, for not only were they unable to sight the target, but spotting their own fall of shot was an impossibility. Peter glimpsed their frustration, as he saw the drawn faces of the gunlayers when they turned towards him in bewilderment.

The next salvo was the last straw for the leading E-boat, and at three hundred yards she lost her nerve and swung on her heel, followed smartly by her consort.

"Check! Check! Check! Cease firing!"

As the mist of spray and the cordite fumes drifted away, the island came into view. Gone was the fog now, lifted from the vivid cobalt sea, and from these depths there jutted this small summit of a submarine mountain, brown, green and shining in the morning sun. And there, slightly to the right, motionless and silent was the explanation for their deliverance.

She was less than a mile away, and she was still rolling from the recoil of her broadsides. Lean and powerful in her brown silhouette, she exhibited the familiar lines of a destroyer, an old 'V-and-W', but at her stumpy mainmast there fluttered an ensign that Peter did not recognise immediately.

From the eyes of the little caique a bellow came from Hank and then a great cheer rang from the remainder of the gallant company, the echoes rolling across the intervening water. A wisp of steam streamed from the destroyer's foremost funnel, the notes of her siren wailing in joyful answer. Then the white crescent and star upon the red background of her ensign clicked in Peter's brain.

"She's a Turk!" he yelled. "We must be inside Turkish territorial waters!"

"Just as well, sir," Taggart shouted from his Lewis gun, and he stretched his arm out to port. "Look at those devils out there!"

Peter swung round. Two grey shapes lay low in the water, biding their time while they waited for the caique to emerge from the shelter of the Turk's guns and from the protection of the three-mile limit.

The destroyer was nosing towards *Zephyrus* now and, as she turned, Peter could see lines of sailors upon her fo'c'sle.

"The decision is not difficult," Peter muttered, "in fact I have no choice," and he turned to face his men.

"Train fore-and-aft. Secure all guns. I'm going to accept the protection of our Turkish friend."

CHAPTER 11

Incident in Istanbul

"There are friendly neutrals, neutral neutrals," and here the British chargé d'affaires smiled — "but no unfriendly neutrals."

Chuckling at his own sally, the grey-haired diplomat moved across his high-ceilinged office to close the door. "Yes," he went on, "we ought to be able to get you out all right."

"All of us?" Peter asked.

"Yes, through Asia Minor, then down to Beirut."

"When do we start?"

The chargé smiled condescendingly.

"All in good time, my dear boy, all in good time." Then he added reprovingly, "Don't forget that you and your men were languishing in the waterfront jail until today. Only two days ago you came in as a prize of war, for infringing Turkish territorial waters."

"I know, sir, and I really am grateful to you for getting us all out of clink. But how did you do it?"

"Even the Ataturk administration is not beyond the odd itchy palm, and the British Government allow me funds for just such contingencies. The Turks will take over the caique themselves."

"But you can't have many escaping prisoners of war through this way?"

"You'd be surprised, young man. Istanbul is an eastern Lisbon — a clearing house for the spies of all the warring nations. Here, come and have a look!" The chargé moved to the spacious, bow-fronted window and, with the thumb of one slender hand crooked into the waistcoat of his immaculate grey suit, stood astride the marble floor, his other hand sweeping across the panorama of the city which spread-eagled below them.

"Yonder lies the Bosphorus." His hand stretched to the left towards what appeared to be a wide river. "While beneath us, over there, is the Sea of Marmora."

The expanse of blue water made a fine background to the city which sprawled over the sides of the hills below them. The rays of the mid-morning sun glinted off the gilded minarets of the mosques which studded the motley of sandstone buildings — the jigsaw that pieced together dwelling to dwelling and hovel to hovel, and which compounded the mysterious city of Istanbul, the gateway to the Bosphorus.

"What's that smudge on the horizon, sir?"

"The island of Marmora. Beyond lies Gallipoli and the Dardanelles," and the older man sighed wistfully.

"You were in the Dardanelles, sir?"

"Yes, but it's a long time ago now. You youngsters would know little about it — it's forgotten, back in the limbo of the history books already."

"Not quite, sir. I recognised the Anzac memorial as we passed through in *Zephyrus*. We learnt of the campaign at Dartmouth, and, after seeing those exposed beaches, I now realise what a ghastly business it must have been."

The older man was silent for a while and he continued to gaze out of the window.

"Yes," he replied, "I became a cynic until three years ago. I thought of the men who had died on those yellow beaches, who had been torn to shreds in the shallows by the crossfire of Johnny Turk in the cliffs. I thought that my friends who had lain slumped across the barbed wire had been betrayed by your generation, by young men like yourself," and then he turned towards Peter.

"But I know better now." His eyes with their faraway look turned again towards the horizon. "That memorial to the Anzacs which overlooks the long spur of Gallipoli should have reminded you that we never finished the job properly — and now it's up to you and your kind, my boy. I'm sorry we failed."

"You didn't fail, sir. The politicians couldn't cope."

"It'll be the same this time, if you don't watch out. For God's sake see that the men who fought the war are allowed to run the country — then perhaps this will be the last of all wars."

"This really is the war to end wars, sir. We've had just about enough," said Peter with a sigh.

"You really think that?"

The grey-headed man stretched out his arm and placed it upon Peter's shoulder.

"Bear with me for a moment, and I'll drop you a few hints: I can do no more than that. Light up your pipe and listen for a few minutes." He indicated a chair and his voice dropped so that Peter had to strain to catch his words.

"My dear boy, if we don't look out we're going to lose this war, and lose it at any moment."

"Surely not, sir — the blasted Hun is just beginning to feel the pinch, isn't he? We've got over the worst — Crete — Singapore — Norway — all that's behind us, and now the stuff's rolling out of the factories. Remember the days of rifles against Stukas? Those days are past now."

"Fiddlesticks!"

Peter's eyebrows lifted. It was an odd remark from a staid diplomat.

"Look here, Sinclair, you keep your eyes open while we wait for a reply from Malta and London. I've booked rooms for all of you in the Hotel Kemal — a seedy, second-rate boarding house, because you would have attracted too much attention anywhere else. Wander around the city, particularly the German colony, and keep your eyes open. Enjoy yourselves, but report to me before you go."

"Certainly, sir. Thank you for all you've done."

"Well, during your enforced stay here, you might as well have a rest. But, for God's sake, be careful! This cosmopolitan city boasts more cut-throats to the square yard than any other — and I'm certain there's something big going on in this corner of Europe. The Hun is up to something in the Balkans, I'm sure of it."

"Are there many Huns in Istanbul, sir?"

"The place is stiff with them. Merchants, shopkeepers, the whole outfit. That's what worries me — that, and the smiles upon their Teuton faces!" He crashed one fist into the palm of the other hand. "So long, my boy. Enjoy yourself." He pushed Peter out of the room. "Come back and see me next week."

The chargé's description of the Hotel Kemal was certainly apt. Seedy and dirty, the Britons from *Zephyrus* were glad to get out of the place during the day.

"Keep in twos or threes," Peter told his sailors after lunch. "Stay together and keep your mouths shut. Watch out, because the place is stiff with spies, I believe," and he laughed as he glanced at his motley crew. In spite of the light tropical clothes that the Consulate had found for them, they were obviously British.

"Better be in by ten, Coxswain. Then we can foregather in my room here for briefing."

"Aye, aye, sir. But where are you going, in case I want to contact you?"

"To the races. Lieutenant Jefferson and Sub-Lieutenant Taggart are coming with me."

Weston laughed. "Don't lose all your money, sir!"

"Plenty more where it comes from, Coxswain. This is on His Majesty's Government!"

The men left the bedroom in high spirits at the prospect of a 'run' ashore. Peter, Hank and Taggart unpacked their communal suitcase and stowed away their gear. The room was made more dingy by an acacia in the courtyard and the tree was so close that the branches touched the window.

The three friends were glad to leave, and they deliberately chose to stretch their legs by walking to the racecourse which lay on the south-western side of the city. It was fascinating exploring this Turkish metropolis, the meeting place of East and West. As in all cosmopolitan ports — Cristobal, Cairo, Marseilles and even London — the riff-raff of the world tended to congregate there, but somehow Istanbul possessed an enchantment absent in the others.

"It's the minarets, I reckon," Taggart volunteered. "The sun on them adds the final touch."

"Nonsense, boy. They've nothing on Manhattan's skyscrapers."

Peter and Taggart grinned. When would the American learn?

"Let's eat," Hank continued.

"The first race starts in twenty minutes," Taggart said. "We'll get something there."

They were walking down the centre of a crowded street and on all sides the bustling humanity rubbed shoulders with them. Women in yashmaks still abounded, their eyes furtively curious from behind their black veils. Over all hung the aromatic smells of sweet tobacco, thick black coffee and the all-pervading stench of poverty. Ragged little urchins scampered about them, wheedling for alms, while from the doorsteps old men in red fezzes squatted on their haunches and looked on in amusement.

The racecourse nestled in a shallow basin in the hills outside the city, and now the street narrowed to little more than an alleyway, the balconies of the hovels nearly meeting overhead. The crowd had thinned out and the three men could see the beginnings of vegetation ahead of them.

"It's odd, sir," Taggart said quietly, "don't look now, but I reckon we're being followed."

Peter laughed. "You're not serious?"

"Don't look round, but I'm certain we have company."

Peter nudged Hank.

"The Sub's got the jitters — he reckons we're being followed!"

Hank suddenly stopped and peered into a dingy shop window, where he took an inordinately long time admiring some shoddy jewellery. The other two walked on, but swung round when they heard the American shout.

"Hey, you guys! Come and take a look at these…" Peter and the Sub retraced their steps to the engrossed Hank.

"See those three scallywags, sir?" Taggart whispered.

"Those men lighting each other's cigarettes, about fifty yards away?"

"Yes — they were outside our hotel when we left."

Peter joined Hank at the shop window.

"O.K., Hank," he murmured, "we've seen all we want." Then he added loudly, "Come on, for Pete's sake, Jefferson — we'll be late for the first race," and he dragged the American away. They quickened their pace and were glad to enter the tree-lined avenue that led to the entrance of the racecourse.

"You're right, Sub."

"You know," said Hank, "I had a nasty feeling myself. I had a hunch we were being followed."

"And now we're certain," Peter added. "Let's see if they stick around at the races. What do they want with us?"

Taggart laughed shortly.

"It's all part of the German espionage machine, I'll bet. Their usual damnable efficiency."

"Well, we'd better stick together anyway," Peter said. "Watch out in the crowds and keep your eyes skinned. I don't like the look of these dagoes."

Then the clamour of the race-meeting hit them. They rounded the corner and the entrance to the course blocked the road. The turnstiles clicked merrily and it looked as if the whole of Istanbul was squeezing in to watch their beloved sport.

Peter bought three entrance tickets and they were soon inside the enclosure.

"Let's look around for a bit before placing our bets," Hank suggested, and, elbowing his way through the excited crowd, his huge frame made a passage for Peter and Ian Taggart.

They dodged the professional beggars who were doing a roaring trade, and then wandered towards the rows of bookies around whose stalls half the population of Istanbul seemed to be clustered. Squawking fowls added their quota to the noise of the vendors of Turkish delight whose success in the selling of their wares was in proportion to the loudness of their cries.

"What a ghastly din!" Taggart shouted above the racket.

"Half the fun of the fair!" Peter yelled above the heads of the crowd. "Come on, let's have a look at the nags!"

The saddling enclosure was the usual ring, and Peter was nostalgically reminded of the point-to-points on Dartmoor — clouds sweeping across the tops, the tors black and menacing from the flying shadows; and then, as the sun wins through, the blaze of the gorse, its scent heady on the wind, dancing in golden glory on the turf-lined tops of stone walls.

The ring was where the comparison ended, however, and Peter gazed at the horses with distaste. The wretched beasts needed food for they were appallingly thin, their skin stretched tautly against their ribs.

"Look across to the other side of the ring, sir."

Peter caught Taggart's whisper and there, sure enough, were their three shadows, leaning across the rails on the other side, and pretending to judge the horses.

"Our friends are still with us, Hank."

"Damn good filly, that," Hank yelled. "Come on, you guys, let's go place our bets." Then he started to mutter to himself.

Hank's getting angry, Peter thought with amusement. *I hope our shadows don't irritate him too far. But why in the devil are they so interested?*

They had to fight their way towards the bookies. The crowd was thick and Peter was amused to see how every type of performer was busy trying to increase his earnings. There were jugglers, tumblers, barrel-organ grinders with monkeys perched on their shoulders, yes, and even the gulli-gulli men.

"Watch me, fellers," Hank grinned. "Give me your piastres and I'll place the bets."

Meekly and with relief Peter parted with his money.

"Hundred piastres on Yawuz Sultan, please, Hank."

"Same for me, Hank," Taggart yelled. "But don't spend it all at once."

The bookies were taking the money as fast as they could, for the 'off' was any minute now. Peter put his hands in his pockets and waited for Hank to complete his bartering. He realised with a pang of uneasiness that a fight was developing between a gang of ruffians and that the struggle was beginning to separate him from Ian Taggart. He found himself nearly swept off his feet as the knot of brawling men surged towards him. Peter stepped back to try to keep out of the way and when he did so he kept his back towards the bookies' stalls.

He suddenly lost sight of Taggart's small figure in the press, and for a moment he was uneasy as the crowd pushed against him, increasing the distance between himself and his two friends.

Could this be intentional? Is this all a put-up show, and is someone deliberately trying to separate us? he wondered.

The blaring of a barrel-organ deafened him, and he looked quickly whence the noise came. A tall beggar was churning the handle of a portable organ — a box-like affair on the top of a staff. A marmoset crouched on the lid, busily scratching itself. Across the top of the instrument was a letterbox slit, and into this one was hopefully expected to place one's piastres.

The noise was deafening and Peter longed to tell the beggar to stop his infernal grinding. The man's face suggested a picture of poverty and debauchery, for he was obviously a confirmed dope addict with his sallow skin and slack lips. Peter shivered. It was an evil face. Then, for an instant, the man's eyes met his.

Later, when Peter described the incident to Hank and Taggart, he was still uncertain how the spark of recognition had first kindled, or whether he or the beggar had first recognised the other. But in that split second Peter could have sworn that the beggar was mocking him.

Peter was amazed by the eyes of the giant Turk which had now become suddenly intense. Instead of the drug addict's listless hopelessness, they glittered with a smouldering fire. The pinpoints of the sunken brown eyes flickered as they held Peter's gaze for an instant, and then — and this was what completed the circuit in Peter's memory — the man's eyelids dropped, like those of a snake, over the eyeballs.

Peter shivered momentarily, mesmerised by the reptilian evil of the man. Surely he couldn't be that swine Kramer, Kapitan Ulrich von Kramer, the S.S. agent? Peter's eyes flew to the beggar's hands for confirmation, for twice before the German had betrayed himself by his own uncontrollable idiosyncrasy. And now, too, Peter knew that this man must be that dangerous German agent, von Kramer, for the Hun's knuckles were white as they twisted the handle of the barrel-organ. Although Peter could not hear the revolting crackling of the tendons, he recognised the flexing of the fingers as they fought for control on the upright stand of the instrument. It was von Kramer, he was certain.

Suddenly the beggar let fall the organ, cutting short the tinny refrain. The monkey was flung from his shoulder and the mite chattered with fright as it landed at the feet of the crowd. Kramer's huge hands clawed towards his young enemy, but recognition had flashed its danger signal and Peter had dived into the mob.

Now that action was demanded of him, Peter lost his momentary uneasiness. *I've got to get away quickly*, he thought, *and there's no use in trying to escape on my own — they'll head me off in no time. I must find Hank and the Sub.*

"*Rugged ... Rugged!*" he yelled above the hubbub, as he jumped on to an upturned cask. "*Rugged!*"

There was a roar not far away and he saw Hank's flailing arms come battering towards him, the crowd falling back angrily on either side. Kramer was struggling too but, as he gained on Peter, he stumbled, tripped by Taggart's hands.

"Come on, sir," the tense face of Ian Taggart shouted in his ear. "I wasn't the Blundell's scrum-half for nothing. Let's get out of here quickly — the crowd's turned nasty."

Peter fought his way towards the gates, while he heard Hank and Taggart panting behind him as they brought up the rear, their fists and elbows working like pistons.

"Taxi!"

Peter reached the pavement outside the gates, and a smiling, dark-skinned face welcomed him into a bug-ridden cab. There was a patter of feet and then Hank leapt into the back seat, followed rapidly by the Sub. Peter slammed the door and jumped up beside the driver.

"Hotel Kemal!" he shouted. "Pronto!"

As the ramshackle cab gathered speed, Peter looked back. There was a scuffle at the gate and then the mob broke through like a river bursting its dam. In the forefront was a filthy beggar, and for a second he halted to gaze after the receding taxi. Then he turned about and was swallowed up by the crowd.

They paid off the taxi when they reached their hotel and Peter was glad when the front door slammed behind them.

"Phew!" Taggart exclaimed when they stood in the hall grinning sheepishly. "Not exactly a friendly reception from the natives, was it?"

"They were hired thugs," Peter replied quietly as he slowly climbed the stairs.

"How d'you figure that out, Pete?" Hank asked. "The only three guys to take an interest in us were our three shadowers and the big beggar."

Peter had reached the landing and was approaching their bedroom door when he turned to face his friends.

"You won't believe me, I know, Hank, but there's been an extraordinary coincidence this afternoon — darned sight stranger than fiction. I bumped into one of Himmler's agents: the beggar with the barrel organ."

"How d'you know?" Hank asked incredulously.

"I'd met him before, Hank. He's Ulrich von Kramer, and wherever there's trouble, he'll be in the thick of it. He's ruthless and clever, and the last time we met he swore he'd have my life."

"He didn't seem keen on you today," Taggart replied, lowering his voice. "But hadn't we better go inside or the whole pub will hear us."

There was a pattering of feet from the stone-paved hall below and then they heard the proprietor struggling up the stairs. He was a fat man and was puffing when he reached the landing. He seemed startled and his hands gesticulated nervously. He could barely be heard when he spoke at first. Then he beat his breast and threw his hands up in despair. Finally he struck his forehead and pointed to the door.

"Sair have quit my 'otel? You quit, huh, this afternoon?"

Peter shook his head.

"Been out all the afternoon, Johnny."

"At the races," said Taggart.

"Lost all our dough," Hank added sadly.

Peter was puzzled.

"What's up, Johnny? Did you think we stayed in?"

For a moment the rotund Turk stood still. But, taking courage, he went to the bedroom door and turned the handle, rattling it. Finally he knelt down and peered through the keyhole, but he was defeated because the key was in the lock, turned from the inside. He faced the foreigners in bewilderment.

"Sorry, Johnny, but we'll have to break your door down because the key's jamming it," Peter said. There was a crash as Hank's shoulder thudded against the flimsy door. Peter pushed his way past the protesting proprietor and rushed into the room.

CHAPTER 12

The Friendless One

After the glare from outside, the comparative darkness of the bedroom was momentarily unsettling. It took a few seconds for Peter to adapt himself to the gloom. His eyes were riveted upon the only light source, a slit that streamed between the two curtains because the right-hand one was not drawn completely.

Peter heard the others stumbling behind him as he gingerly felt his way towards the window. His hand stretched out to draw back the right-hand curtain when he felt his feet prodding something soft. He threw back the curtain.

For a few seconds there was silence as the light streamed into the room and then he heard Taggart gasp. Peter felt his scalp prickling as he stared at the object at his feet.

"Don't draw the other curtain! Get down, sir!" he heard Hank shout.

Peter ducked. He found himself crouching over the crumpled body of a man. Then he crawled back behind the protective screen of the curtain which remained drawn. When he stood up he heard the Turk moaning softly from somewhere in the centre of the room.

"Keep out of the light, everybody," Peter said quietly. "The poor chap's been shot by someone outside. Look at the window."

Beneath the sill was a small window seat, half-hidden by the left-hand curtain, and upon this ledge splinters of shattered glass were sprinkled. Peter saw Hank moving to the back of the room. The American wriggled on his stomach into the light where, from beneath the bed, he could see through the window to the world outside.

"There's a house less than fifty yards away. Its windows are overlooking our courtyard," Hank said. "The murderer can draw a bead on anyone in this room."

"Come back out of it, Hank," Peter snapped.

Ian Taggart was propping up the Turk who was paralysed by fear and for a moment the Sub lost his patience.

"Shut up, for God's sake." He shook the terrified man until his teeth rattled. "Pull yourself together, man. Did anyone come into your hotel this afternoon?"

The Turk eventually understood but he shook his head vigorously.

"No man come — no one, sair. No one."

"The poor chap must have climbed up the tree and got in through the window," Peter said. "Give me a hand, Hank. Let's pull him out of the line of fire so we can have a look at him."

The body was dressed in simple stevedore's clothes, threadbare and dirty. They dragged the corpse gently along the floor until it was shielded by the drawn curtain. A dark stain trailed along the boards.

"He didn't stand a chance, sir," said Hank quietly. "They drilled him with a heavy calibre bullet, just as he was drawing the last curtain. He fell where he stood."

"He must have climbed in and gone straight to the door, locking it before going back to draw the curtains," Taggart suggested.

"Yes, and been hit as he was drawing the last one," Peter said. "But why was he calling on us at all?"

"He couldn't be one of Kramer's men or he wouldn't have been shot," Hank said.

"Look!" Peter snapped. "There's something scrawled on the paint of the window seat."

Hank was peering over Peter's shoulder.

"It's written in blood. He scribbled it as he was dying."

"He must be one of *our* agents," Taggart said. "Perhaps he came to warn us."

"Or give us information," Hank added.

Peter could just decipher the dead man's message.

"It looks like a numeral four and a little two, but I can't make out the line underneath."

"It's a capital U, a small v, and another capital which I can't make out. His hand seems to have smeared the last letter," said Taggart.

"He was a brave man," Peter remarked. "I reckon he realised he hadn't much time because he knew he was being followed, or he wouldn't have tried to draw the curtains. He locked the door, so that he couldn't be surprised that way."

"But what does 4^2 mean?" Hank asked irritably. "And what's this 'U' 'v' something?"

Peter was copying the message on to the back of an old envelope.

"We'll try to decipher it later," he answered briskly. "There's nothing we can do for this poor chap now. I reckon he's one of MI5's boys," and he stretched the dead man out upon the floor.

They heard a commotion downstairs, a slamming of doors, and then the laughter of British sailors.

"Well, the troops are back," Peter said, and his chuckle broke the tension in the room. "We're getting out of here, troops as well." He turned to the proprietor. "How much do we owe you, Johnny? We're leaving."

The man's eyes glinted at the sight of money and when he started haggling, Peter thrust a handful of notes into the Turk's hands.

"It'll help to pay for the door," Peter said.

The proprietor salaamed with surprise and gratitude.

"Get the troops going, Sub," Peter snapped. "This place is being watched by Kramer and I want to clear out. We'll all leave in force. Get cracking and let me know when you've got them mustered in the hall."

"Aye, aye, sir."

Taggart left the room, followed by the Turk. The evening was now well upon them and the light was fading. Hank was throwing their gear into their grip and he was taking good care not to cross the line of fire.

Peter knelt by the murdered man. *The chap's obviously an Englishman*, he thought — *probably been out here for years by the tan on his face*. The man's mouth was parted and his eyes were open, an expression of pleading upon his face as if he were trying desperately to tell them something. There was blood on the index finger which had scribbled his last warning. *The message must be vital*, Peter thought, *or he wouldn't have risked his life to reach us. He probably knew he'd never reach the Consulate alive, so he tried to get to us. He must have seen us leave the caique when we arrived and decided to try and reach us with his information. But the waterfront is notorious for its grapevine intelligence and Kramer's boys also must have seen us arrive.* As Peter went through the man's pockets, he found himself wrestling with the mystery, trying to solve the riddle. But there was no clue as to the man's identity, except for a small colt automatic in his hip pocket. Peter removed it and handed it to the American.

"Shove it in the grip, Hank."

Peter gently closed the man's eyes and crossed the arms over the mutilated chest.

"God rest his soul," Peter murmured.

"Amen," Hank added quietly. "And now let's get out of here."

The motley collection of stranded sailors reached the British Consulate as darkness was falling. Apart from two characters who were watching the house from the pavement opposite the hotel, and who followed them at a respectful distance until they were chased off by Weston and three seamen, they all reached the Consulate without incident. But they felt happier when the porter closed the massive door behind them.

"Back again," said Peter with a smile, and then he asked to see the diplomat who had undertaken to arrange their escape from Turkey.

"He's at dinner, sir. Whom shall I say?"

"Lieutenant Sinclair and his party. We're not expected."

"Very good, sir. Would you mind waiting here a moment?" and the imperturbable man slid off in the direction of the dining room.

Half an hour later, Peter, Hank and Taggart were enjoying coffee with the chargé d'affaires in his study. The kitchen staff had rallied round and given everyone a meal, and now Weston was organising sleeping arrangements in the cellars.

"It's very good of you, sir, and I must apologise for being such a nuisance. But you see now why I decided to return here."

"Yes, my boy, but I don't like it," the older man replied gravely as he flicked cigar ash from his jacket. "The whole sequence of events confirms my worst suspicions."

"How d'you mean, sir?"

"You must bear with me for a few moments while I put you in the picture. Please relax, gentlemen, while I tell you the story so far. You see I've already reported your arrival, in cipher, to Malta and to the Foreign Office. I'm now awaiting instructions from London."

"When do you expect a reply, sir?"

"At about two-thirty this morning."

Peter smiled.

"You haven't wasted much time, sir."

"The F.O. can get a hustle on when it wants to, you know," and the eyes twinkled from beneath the wrinkled forehead.

"Where do you keep your wireless, sir?" Hank asked.

"In the attic. It's only manned at routine times, because I've only got a small wireless and cipher staff."

"And the next routine's not until two-thirty a.m., sir?" said Taggart impatiently.

"Yes. I'm afraid I can't be any quicker. After all, your Captain 'S' in Malta, who controls you, has got to contact the Foreign Office through the Admiralty. Their Lordships and my bosses have got to have a chinwag before they make a decision. It all takes time. And you may be surprised when the signal comes in."

"I know, sir," Peter said apologetically. "We realise you're doing all you can. But we want to get on our way."

"That's how it is, sir," Hank added.

"But please go on and put us in the picture, sir. Sorry we interrupted," Peter said.

The older man extracted his pocket watch from the waistcoat of his old-fashioned dinner jacket. He glanced at the time; deliberately flicked some fluff from his trousers, then drew deeply upon his cigar until the end glowed.

"You know, Sinclair," he began, "the riddle of the murdered agent is quite possibly the one missing link in the chain."

"You mean his bloodstained scrawl, sir?"

"Yes." The charge drew from his jacket pocket the crumpled envelope upon which Peter had copied the message. "I think I've got the second part of the message, but it's only a guess, mind you."

The three friends stiffened in their chairs.

"The fact that you recognised the S.S. agent in Istanbul helps a lot. He's a high-up in the German Intelligence and I knew from my men that he was in the Balkan area. He sometimes comes down here to check up on his cells. What did you say his name was?"

"Kramer, sir."

"His rank and full name?"

"Kapitan Ulrich von Kramer, sir. I think I told you we'd run across each other before."

The chargé paused for a moment and then his eyebrows raised imperceptibly as he posed the question:

"*Ulrich von Kramer?*"

For a second there was silence and then Peter and Hank both tumbled to it together.

"Of course, sir, the second clue!" Peter cried, slapping his knee.

"'U' 'v' and the smeared capital must have been a 'K'," Hank blurted out.

"Could be, couldn't it, gentlemen? But what about the 'four squared'. The 4^2, eh?"

Peter was grinning. He was beginning to enjoy this. *It's too like a Buchan story to be true*, he thought, and then he heard the chargé continuing quietly:

"All the evidence of the last six months suggests that the Hun is up to something really big in the Balkans, but we can't put the jigsaw together yet. He's been pouring technicians through from Germany, and the S.S. seem to be here in a high proportion. We keep coming across the word — *Vernichtungswaffe* — can any of you translate it?"

Peter thought for a moment.

"War-winning 'something', sir?" he volunteered.

"Literally it means, 'war-winning weapon', but that hasn't helped us much so far. The Hun is harassing the partisans so energetically that we can't get hold of much information. If it wasn't for their leader, an able man who goes by the name of Stefan, their guerrillas would be swept out of central Yugoslavia."

The chargé paused and again looked at his watch. Peter took the hint.

"Well, sir, we'd better let you get some sleep. But we'd like to be around when the signal comes through."

"I'll arrange to have you woken. But I wish we could unravel the riddle of the first part of the murdered man's message."

"The 4^2, sir?"

"Yes, but no doubt we'll know one day."

Hank laughed shortly.

"Not much chance of that, sir, as far as we're concerned. We'll be on our way back to Malta soon."

They rose from their chairs and the chargé left the room to show them to their beds.

"Two-thirty, sir."

Peter felt the pressure on his shoulder and from habit he leapt out of bed. He roused Hank and the Sub, and five minutes later they were taken to the top floor. A spiral staircase led to an open steel door in the attic, and from inside the room Peter could hear the familiar piping of Morse.

The chargé was already there, clad in an old dressing-gown. A middle-aged man sat at the receiver, earphones on his head, while from a loudspeaker above the set came the usual cracklings of wireless signals. The Morse was pouring in now and the operator's pencil flew along the pad as it jotted down the enciphered groups. Suddenly Peter recognised the message-ending group and the transmission stopped. The pencil hovered a moment above the pad while the operator glanced at the clock, and then the time of receipt was filled in: two fifty-eight.

"Come and help me decipher it, will you, Sinclair?" the chargé asked.

They followed him down to his office where, after locking the door behind them, he opened the safe and extracted the cipher books. Hank prowled backwards and forwards while Peter helped the chargé to decipher, Taggart writing up the signal. The message slowly took shape and finally it stared boldly up at them in black and white:

IMMEDIATE. To Chargé d'Affaires, Istanbul, repeated to Captain 'S', Tenth Submarine Flotilla, Malta, from Admiralty.

TOP SECRET. Confirmed that KRAMER operating in Balkans area between Belgrade and Istanbul, as Officer Commanding security of enemy project and of espionage ring attached thereto.

Established that enemy attaches utmost importance to security of production area, having 1,000-plus S.S. security guards in vicinity, believed to be Montenegro.

Caique party under command of Sub-Lieutenant Taggart is to return by quickest route to Beirut where Fourth Submarine Flotilla will arrange passages to Malta.

Lieutenant P. Sinclair is to contact STEFAN, Partisan Leader in Montenegro, for further orders. Chargé is requested to arrange with local agents for Sinclair's safe conduct to area.

Enemy suspected to be manufacturing 'heavy water' for war-winning explosive. Vital, repeat vital, that production be destroyed.

Lieutenant Sinclair is to locate partisans and destroy this plant.

Submarine Rapid *will rendezvous off Dubrovnik on night of 20/21 October to evacuate Sinclair. Acknowledge. 020139/10.*

For a while nothing was said between the four men. Peter stared at the curtains, while the green shade of the chargé's desk lamp threw a weird light across the message.

"I'll take Hank and Bill Hawkins," Peter Sinclair said calmly. "When do we start?"

"Can you be ready within the hour?" the older man asked. "I knew this was coming because I requested it. There's another caique waiting on the waterfront to take you to Salonika. I'll give you a good meal before you leave, even though it's a quarter to four!"

"Thanks. But will you come, Hank? You know what the risks are?"

"I said I'd come with you on this jaunt, Pete. And I'm not figuring on letting you down now. Guess I'll string along."

Peter grinned and then turned towards Taggart.

"So long, Sub. Good luck to you on your trip back with the troops. It ought to be fun."

"Thanks a lot, sir, but I wish I was coming with you. You'll probably be in Malta before me," and the two men shook hands.

"Hope so, Ian," the American added. But in their hearts they knew that the chances of their returning alive weren't very bright.

"You haven't asked Hawkins yet, sir."

Peter looked hard at the American.

"There's no need to ask him. His family was killed in his home by a German bomb."

The schooner slipped before dawn and, on the short sea passage across the Aegean, Peter found it impossible to shake the memory of the murdered agent from his mind. 4^2 ... 4^2 ... 4^2, the message hammered away inside Peter's brain. Both Jefferson and Hawkins craved alike for sleep and solitude, so by mutual consent they all left each other alone on these last few days of relative comfort. Four squared ... the square of four ... four multiplied by four ... his mind wrestled continuously with the dead man's message.

They had been entrusted to the capable hands of Georges Sulieman, an inconspicuous man who passed very well as a minor Turkish merchant. Bundled into this schooner, which was even more filthy and cramped than the *Zephyrus*, it took over a day and night to reach the entrance to the Dardanelles. At dawn on the next day they cleared Gallipoli, yellow and hot in the glistening sunshine, and by nightfall they had passed the memorial to that dreadful campaign: the proud pinnacle to remind the world of the Australian and New Zealand dead.

But with the riddle of the unknown man's message unsolved, Peter could not sleep. Instead he prowled the length of the upper deck during the two nights' passage across the ancient sea.

The caique altered course to the westward and the Island of Lemnos shrank away to the southward during the early afternoon. It was soon swallowed up in the blue mistiness of the horizon and then, broad on the starboard bow, Mount Athos rose from the ultramarine deeps.

The outline of Cape Drepanon was difficult to see in the moonlight, but by midnight the caique had rounded the Cape and was hurriedly waddling up the Gulf of Salonika, Mount Olympus looking down on them from the western shore. The low-lying marshlands fell away below the horizon and then, in the blaze of dawn, the port of Salonika hove into sight.

Peter leaned across the rail while he watched the port coming nearer. Hank Jefferson sprawled to his left, Bill Hawkins on his right and all three were dressed disreputably in tattered shirts that had rotted along the neckband, and in patched and greasy homespun trousers of neutral colours; but they all had solid boots. They had not shaved for the past few days, and now they could not be distinguished from the natives.

The crew of the caique was not overfond of the Salonika Greeks. Memories of the Armenian massacres were still too vivid to allow for much mutual trust, so the crew did not go ashore, Peter, Hank and Hawkins remaining below all day. But before the moon rose on that night, Georges Sulieman slipped across the brow with his three disreputable protégés.

They walked fast, and on the far side of the town they emerged suddenly into a poverty-stricken country landscape of almost barren fields. The shadow of a man slid out from the depths of a pantiled farm building and then Georges took his leave as silently as he had come.

"This is dangerous work, my friends," he whispered in the darkness. "Trust no one. Everyone is against you, and until you reach the partisans, the Germans and fifth-columnists are all around you. If the enemy don't get you, the Communists will, if it suits them, so, in the name of Allah, be careful." His little eyes glistened for a second and then he was gone.

"*Kom!*"

The shadow detached itself from its surroundings and soon they were slinking in single file across the fields, while to the westward a background of Lombardy poplars swayed in the night. It was towards this group of trees that their guide seemed to be making, and then, quite suddenly, they came upon the river Vardar, shimmering in the moonlight. The moon was rising as they reached the bank and there, just below them, ran the single-line railway, its rails gleaming in the light of the moon.

Their guide dropped on all fours and then, without a word, slithered down the embankment. He was very cautious now and, after some minutes, he beckoned them over the rails. Then, at the foot of the tall poplars whispering above them, they waited by the banks of the river. The huge Greek lay still, his head cocked above the grass, alert and listening. Then from far away down the line in the direction of Salonika came the signal he had been waiting for — the toot-tooting of a locomotive. Shortly afterwards, above the gentle rustling of the heart-shaped leaves, the clang of approaching wagons broke the silence of the night. The Greek grinned in the shadows and indicated by signs that they should stand by for action.

The earth below them started to tremble and then the rumble of the iron wheels on the rails became louder. The engine belched past them, showers of sparks leaping from the funnel, and the driver's cab glowing red. The smoke from the wood-firing streamed across the tracks, then curled away along the embankment to hang heavily above the waters of the Vardar. Suddenly a bell jangled, followed by the screech of steel biting into steel, and then the long line of wagons clattered to a halt. A red lantern bobbed in the darkness near the engine, and when Peter looked at the Greek he saw he was smiling.

"*Vache — lina — lina…*" and his hand swung up and down the lines.

"Cow on the lines," Hank whispered.

"Organised by the Resistance, I expect. Stand by! Our friend is moving."

They slithered after him, and when he reached the shadows of the wagons he bent double and loped down the track, away from the engine. He bent to peer at the numbers on each wagon. After three attempts he found the wagon he wanted — a large wooden affair with metal stringers over which was spread a heavy tarpaulin. Their saviour lifted the corner of this and then, to Peter's surprise, a bony hand showed momentarily.

The clanging of the bell drifted down from ahead and then the whistle blew. Steam escaped with a roar from the leaking cylinders, and the train shuddered, clanked and moved.

Peter clambered up the sides of the truck, and, as he slipped his legs over the side and under the tarpaulin, he felt someone lean out to help him and his companions. Hank and Bill Hawkins followed him, and five seconds later the tarpaulin flounced back on top of them. The train jerked then gathered speed.

In the darkness they slowly recovered their breath, and then, "Welcome to Montenegro, my friend," a deep voice said in perfect English. "I apologise for the conditions."

"Thanks, chum, but who are you?" Peter asked.

"They call me Stefan," the man in the darkness replied.

CHAPTER 13

Vernichtungswaffe

"*Heil Hitler!* All S.S. officers mustered in the Assembly Hall, *Herr Kommandant.*"

Kommandant Ulrich von Kramer did not rise from his desk. He was weary after his overland journey from Istanbul and he felt in no mood to harangue his officers. But alert them he must, because they were becoming slack. He also felt that the British were on the scent of something, but he supposed it was inevitable after all these months.

Besides, it was over six months ago that the Engineers had finished their tunnelling. The Citadel had taken a year to construct and with the effort involved it would have been a miracle if nothing had leaked out, surrounded as the Germans were by the guerrilla forces of the partisans.

The Kommandant's eyes lifted momentarily from the sheet of paper, and for a second he deigned to notice the presence of an officer standing to attention on the far side of his desk.

"*Jawohl.* Wait outside."

The leutnant was not surprised at the curtness of his superior officer, and he saluted, clicked his heels and left the office.

These youngsters need disciplining, Kramer thought, *and* mein Gott! *they were going to get it.* The Kommandant was putting the final touches to his speech, and he had no qualms about keeping his officers waiting. The delay would impress upon them the importance of their Kommandant. Surely they all knew that Himmler himself had chosen Kramer? The appointment of Kommandant of the Security force at the

Citadel was a key one. The responsibility for the security of all the scientists and technicians; for maintaining complete secrecy about the purpose of the Citadel; for clearing the area of the Yugoslav partisans and for the safety of the *Vernichtungswaffe* project itself — all this rested upon the broad shoulders of the S.S. Kommandant.

Ulrich von Kramer rose from his chair. He picked up his cap from the corner of his desk and placed it squarely upon his head. He stood in front of a mirror, checking his appearance, and he was satisfied with the image: a tough body, six feet tall, with a chest almost as deep as it was broad and he adjusted the Iron Cross on his tunic which General von Speidel had presented to him in North Africa before the retreat. The face which stared back from the mirror was wearing well, the Kommandant thought. It was a mobile face, yet expressionless, the intelligent eyes steel-grey and sunk deep in their sockets. "The ideal face for a spy," Himmler had once said, before the contretemps that had spoilt their relationship: Kramer's appointment at Castellare Poliano had been the result of that — and Kramer smiled as he remembered the incident. But this job showed that Himmler had relented — he couldn't afford to keep a good man down. The Kommandant set his cap squarely upon his bullet-shaped head, picked up his gloves and flung open the door. He heard the leutnant clicking his heels and then falling into step behind him. Their footsteps echoed as they strode down the long corridor. At the end was the Assembly Hall, and Kramer still marvelled at this amazing engineering feat for the *Vernichtungswaffe*.

Even after all these months the Citadel still astonished him. Up here in the foothills, the natural hillock which formed the roof of the Citadel was hidden from the outside world by the encircling forests. The Citadel covered a square kilometre, the whole project being over thirty metres below ground and tunnelled into the rock. Inside this impenetrable fortress the scientists, with over a thousand technicians, were working night and day upon the weapon that would end the war in a few hours. He'd heard that less than a kilogram of the stuff could reduce London to ashes, and it was his job, yes, Ulrich von Kramer's job, to see that all this was safeguarded. The Kommandant was secretly content as the swing doors of the Assembly Hall opened in front of him, held by one of his junior officers. He heard the rumble in the hall as the assembly rose to its feet, and then he mounted the steps leading to the stage. The lights went out in the auditorium as he reached the rostrum which was spotlighted from either side. For several seconds he stood motionless, silhouetted against the huge photograph of 'The Führer' on the backcloth behind him. Then he removed his cap, handing it to an aide standing on one side.

"Sit down, gentlemen."

The hall rumbled again and the Kommandant stared into the blackness in front of him. Apart from the blurred front row of the more senior officers, it was impossible to distinguish the sea of faces of his audience.

The silence was complete. None of the coughing that precedes most lectures, no throat clearing or subdued buzzing of conversations. They were afraid of their Kommandant. The eyes that flashed in the inscrutable face appeared to search out each individual in the audience. Each officer felt uncomfortably insecure as he waited for the worst. Then the Kommandant began, the monotone rustling through the hall, each syllable loaded with menace.

"You must remind yourselves, gentlemen, why you are here. You have grown somewhat slack," said the man on the dais, and the hush deepened. "And inefficiency I shall not tolerate. You are here to safeguard the Citadel, the *Vernichtungswaffe*, and its inmates. Any officer failing in this duty will answer to me for his dereliction of duty."

The powerful man on the rostrum stood motionless, like a waxen effigy. His mouth barely moved, his words issuing silkily from between the thin lips. Every officer in the hall felt the cruelty that lay beneath the suave exterior, yet they knew he would never order them to attempt anything that he would not do himself. And in the matter of espionage and disguise there was nothing that he could not achieve. He commanded respect as well as fear.

"You may be interested to know, gentlemen," the monotone continued, "that there has been a new development. The enemy appear to have got wind of our activities in these parts, so we must assume that sooner or later they will pinpoint this area. When I was in Istanbul last week, I ran across one of their agents," and then for the first time his voice betrayed a trace of emotion. "I have met him before on two occasions, and I would like to give you a word of warning. Never, my friends, underestimate your opponent — and this one in particular."

The huge fist enveloped the glass of water from which he drank, and a sigh rustled through the assembly.

"He is from the Royal Navy, a Briton named Sinclair. Unfortunately he recognised me in Istanbul, and knowing the fellow as well as I do, I can promise you he will try to find us if he's given the chance. He did not arrive in Istanbul intentionally, but I had him shadowed. He left with two others in a fishing schooner, bound for Salonika."

The Kommandant looked up from the rostrum, and those that knew him best noticed that his hands were beginning to twitch spasmodically at his sides, the only idiosyncrasy that he ever betrayed, and that only when he was under stress.

"They landed in Salonika yesterday."

A low murmur ran through the hall and then suddenly ceased as the speaker continued:

"The railways are being watched and we expect him in Skopje at any time. I am waiting for him."

He paused expectantly.

"Have you any questions, gentlemen?"

There was an awkward silence, then a brave soul spoke up from the back of the audience.

"*Herr Kommandant*, should he slip through our men in Skopje, do you expect him to make for the Citadel?"

"Almost certainly. But if he slips through the outer perimeter of your patrols, I will have the offending officer shot. Any further questions?"

The Kommandant looked innocently towards his invisible questioner, and a smile twisted the corners of his mouth.

"But he will not get through Skopje alive, gentlemen. I have made certain of that."

Ulrich von Kramer turned about and faced the portrait on the wall. This was the signal for the whole audience to rise to its feet, and when he raised his arm in the Nazi salute, a deafening shout rang through the hall:

"*Heil Hitler! Sieg Heil! Sieg Heil!*"

The Kommandant descended from the rostrum, but while he was doing so an agitated aide rushed in through the swing doors. He clicked his heels, saluted and tentatively held out a message pad. Kramer glanced at it, muttered something to the aide, and strode quickly from the hall.

In the silence that followed, only the clatter of the aide's feet could be heard as he scrambled on to the stage. Then his high-pitched voice shrilled through the assembly:

"All Heads of Departments," he piped, "are to report to the Kommandant's office immediately."

It must have been about eleven-thirty when their journey started but, cramped in the darkness of the jerking wagon, Peter had lost all sense of time. He awoke fully when the train trundled to a standstill, clanking and hissing. He felt their unknown companion rise from his knees and then a wedge of pale light startled them as Stefan's knife slit the tarpaulin to give him a peephole.

"The town of Veles," he whispered in perfect English. "I have a man in the signal box. He will warn us if all is not well."

The trucks jerked across some points before banging and jolting to a halt.

"I feared so," the man at the peephole muttered. "There is danger ahead, or Petrovitch would not have moved the kerosene lantern." He cocked his head on one side and then, even above the hiss of escaping steam, Peter heard the guttural shouts of German troops.

"Come, my friends! Clear out and follow me! They'll be searching the train before we reach Skopje."

He lifted the corner of the tarpaulin cautiously, then wriggled out over the back of the wagon so that he was straddled across the couplings. Bill, Hank and Peter followed while Stefan held up the tarpaulin, all the while muttering politely, as if he were in a London drawing room, "Come, my friends, we must hurry, we must make haste."

Then, swift and silent as a shadow he dropped to the track and disappeared down the embankment where he crouched, waiting for the others. Peter followed Hank's example and leapt into the night, but then he found himself rolling down the steep embankment, the wind knocked from him. Dimly he remembered the mysterious Stefan waving to the signalman in the signal box above them, and then he felt himself being dragged along by Hank. Vaguely he registered the cries of angry Germans behind him and the sound of rifle-butts knocking against the wooden sides of the wagons. And then, as the jack-booted Huns worked down the line of trucks, there was a commotion and the blowing of whistles.

"Hurry, my friends! We must cross the Vardar here. It would not be safe by the bridge. Follow me!"

Stefan was like a shadow in the moonlight. He suddenly disappeared ahead of them and then, once again, Peter found his feet slipping from under him. Footsteps splashed in front of him, and he clutched at Hank's supporting arm while they floundered across this cattle ford of the broad Vardar. At no time did the water come above his thighs, but, above the panting of his lungs which were beginning to function properly again, Peter was grateful for the infernal din of the train winch was starting again. The splashing of their strides across the river was drowned by the bustling wagons whose clatter was already fading into the distance.

Stefan was waiting for them, concealed behind a clump of withies, and Peter could see by the moonlight that he was smiling as he welcomed the three foreigners.

"Welcome to my country," he smiled. "The Vardar is our boundary and we are safer now, though, until we reach the Gostivar country, we shall travel by night only. Then we shall be among my people," and a note of pride crept into his voice. "Come, let us walk until twilight and lie up in the barns of a good patriot. We will talk then."

Peter laid a hand upon the arm of the lithe figure.

"You're Stefan, leader of the partisans?"

"That is so. I am so called after our first king who was crowned in Siberia seven hundred years ago."

"We are honoured, sir," Peter replied quietly.

"You are important guests and we have much work to do against the German butchers. We have so little time."

"You speak good English," Peter said.

"I was up at Oxford in thirty-eight. I learnt to love the English." He looked at Peter, and even in the half-light Peter discovered a restless fire flickering in the leader's jet-black eyes. "Come. We must go."

The partisan leader, whose name was already a legend in the Balkans, swung off across the meadows at a steady pace, putting as much distance as possible between themselves and the Vardar. He loped along soundlessly, effortlessly, and from time to time he would halt suddenly, holding up his hand. He would sniff the air like a setter pointing, and then move on again, certain of his bearings. By no means frail, he seemed lightly built. Slightly stooping about the shoulders, his bird-like head was tilted forward from the neck, and the eyes that peered sharply from beneath his craggy brows suggested a wild restlessness. About forty years old, he had been educated in England before the war and had made it his second home, having mastered the language which he now spoke so fluently. He was a born leader and loved his Yugoslavia passionately.

Stefan travelled by the stars, keeping clear of the roads and hamlets. Occasionally a dog barked, awakened by the scent of humans and then, as the first streak of dawn broke in the east, a cockerel crowed not far away on their right. He changed direction and made towards a farmstead nestling by a group of cypresses which seemed to be in the foothills leading up to the distant mountains, black against the night-clouds.

A light shone in the only room and Peter, looking at his watch, saw that it was four-thirty. A dog barked, and the lowing of cattle waiting to be milked broke the stillness. A lamp moved across the window three times, and Stefan halted. He put his hands to his mouth, and the shrill cry of a night-bird — some sort of owl, Peter thought — shrilled through the dawn. Stefan waited, and then the door opened, a lantern being placed outside.

"Our friend expects us," he said. "He will give us plain food and be glad to do so. Come, let us feed and rest."

The journey to the partisans' stronghold in the mountains took three nights of hard slogging, and by the end of the trek Peter and Bill Hawkins were beginning to feel fit. Apart from blisters on their feet, they found that they could just manage to keep up with Stefan's pace. They travelled during darkness only until the morning of the third night when they were met by an escort of six partisans at the approaches of a stone bridge.

Dawn was breaking, and the pleasure of the rendezvous was no one-sided affair. With wild whoops, the stocky patriots bounded towards their leader, their bearded faces grinning with delight. Peter wondered how they would salute their leader, and he nearly jumped out of his skin as they pounced upon Stefan and lifted him shoulder-high. When once on the ground again, Stefan gabbled an introduction and the three friends had their hands nearly wrenched from their arms by the enthusiastic escort. As cut-throat a band of brigands Peter had never seen. In sheepskin jackets and trousers, their feet well shod in their national *opanka*, with round black *kapas* upon their heads, it was obvious that these men lived rough. It would take more than a few divisions of German troops to subdue these warriors who had resisted all attempts at subjugation for so many centuries.

Then they all went on together and presently came upon the swirling waters of a dark mountain river.

"The Crni Drim," Stefan said proudly. "We call it the Black Devil, for it forms a natural boundary between us and the enemy. The Germans don't like crossing it."

Neither did Peter, and he was glad when he had negotiated the two tree trunks that spanned the torrent. They all crossed safely, but their progress grew slower as they climbed higher into the mountains. They struggled up the savage gorge of the Crni Drim which slashed its way between the forests. Though the first nip of autumn was in the air, Peter felt himself giddy from the heat and the height when he glanced down at the rushing torrent below them. Lower down, where they had crossed the river, the topsoil of the banks had given it an unpleasant chocolate colour. But now, as the river snaked out of the gorges, the countryside gradually changed its character. Spruce and pines were sprouting in the crevices of the gorge, but most amazing of all was the dramatic change in the soil structure. Instead of the brown earth, quartz-like rocks and boulders now glittered in the clear atmosphere which was sparkling mauve and violet in the sunshine. The gorge suddenly opened out ahead of them and there, purple with distance, the mountains brooded in detached grandeur.

The higher the appalling track snaked, the more remarkable the country became, so that Peter marvelled at the change. The red ochres of the rock strata mingled with the greens and blues of the vegetation, and even the granite sparkled with the fantastic hues of its hidden treasures. Like the jewels of the Orient, the crystals flashed: turquoise, amber, topaz, emerald, and deep coral pink, the colours refused to mingle together, each retaining its own vivid hue. The Black Devil responded also, leaving its muddiness to the valleys below; aquamarine and turquoise, its course carved out of the solid granite, it now flowed serenely in the most transparent liquid that Peter had ever seen. *Clearer even than the chalk streams*, Peter thought, and he wondered where the source could be.

Then they left the river and continued up towards the forests at the foot of the mountains. But by the evening they could see the township of Gostivar below them in the valley, while Debar to the westward, now occupied by Mussolini's troops, was given a wide berth.

"We are entering Albania," Stefan said as they crossed a high ridge. "But, up here in the forests, they leave this country to us," and he smiled as his arm swept across the panorama which stretched before them. To the north westward, mountain ranges stretched into the distance in long spurs, while ahead of them the granite peaks reared from the pine forests.

"What are those scorched trees in the foothills ahead of us?" Peter asked, when he saw the charred patches at the edges of the forests.

"That?" Stefan replied contemptuously. "The Germans tried to flush us out by firing the forests, but it didn't pay them. We came up behind them and picked them off until they stopped."

As dusk was falling, Peter was pleased to see a group of partisans waiting ahead of them with four mules. They mounted wearily and continued on their way, but for some time now Peter had felt that unseen eyes were watching from the forests. They passed several outposts but the men melted like shadows into the gloom as soon as they had greeted their leader. Then, just as darkness fell, Stefan called a halt as a patriot stepped out from a gash in the mountainside. The big man took his leader's mule, and then willing hands helped the three foreigners to dismount. And so, footsore, weary, but very much tougher, Peter, Bill and Hank reached the partisans' headquarters, which was a large cave in the side of the mountain.

A group of boulders concealed the tortuous entrance and the three strangers followed Stefan until he reached the cave. A fire blazed in the centre and from the pot simmering over it there wafted the most delicious smell.

"Come, my friends, we eat now," Stefan smiled. "Tomorrow I show you my country."

After gorging themselves on mutton broth, Stefan and his lieutenants formed a circle round the fire, and there they quietly reported the happenings of the last few days to their leader. Stefan invited Peter and his friends to join them, and a feeling of contentment came over them as they lolled by the warm embers, the glow of the dying fire reflected in their faces. Stefan occasionally interrupted his men's accounts to explain some detail to his guests, and then the situation reports would continue.

It appeared from these that something unusual was going on amongst the Germans. The young men around their leader were grave and kept their voices low, but when they had finished, Stefan explained their anxieties.

"For a long time now, about eight months to be exact, we have noticed an increase in the German forces." The leader passed some black cheroots to his guests, and, puffing away at these special luxuries, Peter relaxed in this atmosphere of comradeship to learn all that he could.

"The Germans have thrown out a strong force around Lake Mavrovo, a small lake which was intended eventually to become a reservoir. Do you realise," Stefan continued incredulously, "that they maintain half a division of troops to throw a cordon around this area?"

Peter whistled, and then Stefan asked him sharply, and directly, "What's your conclusion?"

"They're keen to keep out intruders. They must have some vital secret."

"That's how I figure it too," Hank added. "But what's in this Mavrovo lake?"

"Not so fast, my friend! Listen to this. This cordon encircles the lakes that lie a thousand feet below Mavrovo, but inside this ring there is another security screen around the Sixteen Lakes."

Peter slowly felt something tugging at the drowsiness swamping his thoughts, and then he raised himself on one elbow.

"Did you say the *Sixteen* Lakes, Stefan?"

Stefan looked up.

"Yes, sixteen. The locals say they're accursed. They won't go near them."

"Go on with your story, please," Peter asked, now fully alert.

"The Crni Drim, or the Black Devil as we call it, has its source in Lake Mavrovo, and it cascades down in a series of waterfalls to a patchwork of small lakes a thousand feet below," Stefan continued as he twirled his cheroot. "They are known as the Sixteen Lakes, but now they are cut off completely by the enemy. There's something going on there, my friend, which is big, so vast that the enemy are not even allowed into Skopje for recreation." Stefan was now sitting upright and in his intensity his eyes flashed in the firelight.

"The Germans run a special train which comes to Skopje from Belgrade, direct from Germany. It is sealed and is manned by the Gestapo."

"And after Skopje, where to?" asked Peter.

"That's part of the mystery. The train disappears into the foothills of the mountains and once inside the outer cordon of security troops, no one really knows where it terminates. You see, they've even sent out diesel engines to haul the wagons up from Skopje, so that no one can trace the destination because there's no smoke."

"But you say it disappears in the general direction of the Sixteen Lakes?" Peter insisted.

"Yes, that is so, my friend. Why do you ask?"

Peter hesitated for a moment and then he decided to tell the partisan leader all that had happened to them in Istanbul.

"I knew you were coming," Stefan added when Peter had finished. "I had a message from London on our wireless," and he smiled ruefully as he added, "but it is not a very good set!"

"Good enough," Peter laughed, "for you to know why we've come to help. Intelligence in London believes that the Germans are concocting a war-winning explosive by using a substance called 'heavy water'. And they think the Germans have this plant somewhere in your country."

"But could it be here, my friend?"

Then Peter told the partisan leader about the murdered man's message in the hotel.

"Four squared, you say?" Stefan asked. "Surely that's sixteen, isn't it, if I learnt anything at school? And von Kramer — he's the S.S. Kommandant."

Peter smiled. Stefan was alert now and had jumped to his feet. He stood staring down at Peter, his eyes gleaming.

"And I'll bet you, my good Stefan," Peter replied, "that the German project is between number 4 and number 2 lake."

"Could be. But the third lake's invisible from here. It's surrounded by hillocks and pines."

Peter rose from the floor and looked directly at Stefan.

"Take me to the third lake tomorrow, Stefan," he said. "I have little time."

Another six days were to elapse, however, before Stefan and Peter were convinced that they were on the right trail, and, by then, they were certain. Stefan had sent out his best patrols for six nights running, and on this, the sixth night, the last piece of information locked the jigsaw together.

The shadows of the pines were lengthening across the boulders when Stefan and Peter lay crouched on a ledge some three hundred feet above Lake Mavrovo. Below them lay the deepest part of the lake, and over the ledge that stretched directly beneath them, the black water cascaded into space. Clouds of spray billowed upwards from the eight-hundred-foot drop, and around them the vegetation grew lush and green from the perpetual moisture.

Along the track that ran round the perimeter of the lake, Peter could just see the movement of German sentries, their carbines slung across their shoulders, the square helmets on their heads. By the near side of the falls, fresh concrete works were visible: four gigantic grilles, set in fresh cement, and behind the grilles the gaping mouths of enormous pipes. A pier had been constructed to funnel off the water supply for these monsters, and the current swirled towards the grilles.

Stefan and Peter talked in low voices, but they were safe from detection because the roar of the falls was deafening, while less than a hundred yards above them, a party of twenty partisans kept guard for their leader.

"Jovan's patrol got right inside the inner cordon, Peter," Stefan said. "Right by the falls."

"What did he find?"

"Where the railway disappears. The track leads into the rock, half a mile from the falls." Stefan pointed to a circle of pines a thousand feet below them. Around this wooded island a necklace of lakes, shining blue in the dusk, strung out down the valley.

"There's your secret, Peter. There's the third lake, and inside those trees is a plateau about a mile square. You can't see it from here because of its pine trees."

"How do you know this?"

"Look!"

Stefan's hand stretched towards the east, and there, low in the valley so that they were actually looking down on it, a black speck grew larger as it flew towards them.

"Watch carefully."

Peter's eyes ached as he watched the tiny dot enlarge to a low-winged monoplane. It flew silently towards them and the mountain, the drone of its engines muffled by the roar of the falls. It slowly circled until it disappeared, hidden by the wall of rock beneath them.

"Keep looking!" Stefan murmured.

Out to the right the monoplane flew, still circling until it was over the ring of pines by the third lake. Then it vanished.

Stefan smiled.

"There's a small airstrip on top of that plateau, but below it the Germans have burrowed for nine months to make a small underground city. The Citadel, they call it."

"Out of the bare rock?"

"Yes, with their usual efficiency. They have workshops, factories, everything. And that's where they are making their *Vernichtungswaffe*."

"Their what?"

"*Vernichtungswaffe*: their war-winning weapon, a weapon to end all wars."

"How do they get the power?"

Stefan nodded towards the four grilles by the falls.

"Hydroelectric. The water plunges down those pipes to the underground turbines in the citadel."

"What about air ventilation?"

"All along the edge of the airstrip, they have sunk huge ventilation shafts — mushroom-topped pipes, some supply, some exhaust."

Peter gazed downwards. What an enormous project! The enemy must be confident of success if they were investing so much effort in such a colossal scheme.

"And that explains Kramer's presence," he added as an afterthought. "He must be in charge of all the security."

Stefan was backing into the undergrowth.

"Come, my friend," he said. "We have seen enough. Let us go and make our plans."

He rose and Peter followed the lithe figure as it slithered through the scrub.

But in the Citadel, the Kommandant was also deploying his forces. He sat in his office, a circle of his officers around him, their caps across their knees or placed on the floor by their chairs. They watched von Kramer in silence, for he was in his most dangerous mood: quiet, sinister and under perfect control. His close-set eyes flickered from face to face, but not many of his staff cared to meet his glance.

The contents of von Kramer's office were in startling contrast to his manner. On the wall behind him was plastered an enormous photograph of Adolf Hitler, but Kramer had not cared to add that of his chief, the Gestapo Head, Himmler. Ever since Castellare Poliano, Kramer had lost faith in his chief, but although the Kommandant was fast regaining favour in Berlin, he still resented Himmler, the two-faced butcher. On Kramer's desk was an enormous box of chocolates, a vivid pink ribbon glaring harshly under the subdued electric lighting. He munched these sweets continuously, the stubby fingers lingering in the chocolate wrappers from time to time. He chewed while he gazed upon his cowering colleagues who were sitting so comfortably in his cretonned chairs. The pink walls of his room were decorated in heavy Teutonic taste: gilt-framed mirrors predominated, and in between were black wooden carvings from Bavaria, boars' tusks from past hunting glories and, in the corner, a motley collection of whips and repeating rifles. Yes, altogether a strange contrast, thought his officers, but then the Kommandant was a strange man.

"You must not assume that the English swine are coming this way," Kramer said quietly, "but, just in case, alert your sentries. Double the watches until further orders."

"*Jawohl, mein Kommandant*," his second-in-command murmured.

"You see, my friends, if you allow this Sinclair to get so far as inside the outer perimeter, I will have the officer responsible shot for dereliction of duty. At this stage of the programme, when we are just about to complete the *Vernichtungswaffe*, dereliction of duty is tantamount to treason to the Fatherland." He banged his fist on his desk, shaking the chocolates from their box.

"He cannot get through, *mein Kommandant*."

Kramer glared at the speaker and spat his contempt.

"He escaped me at Castellare Poliano; he got away at Sidi Barrani, so don't be so cocksure. Don't, my boy, ever underestimate your opponent."

"*Nein, mein Kommandant.*" The unfortunate fellow shrivelled into his chair, determined to hold his tongue.

Kramer was seething inside himself at the thought of the empty wagon trucks on the Skopje goods train. But he betrayed no emotion.

"If by chance he should slip through," he continued, "I want him brought straight to me. I want to know what he knows and what he is after."

"You think he may know of the 'heavy water'?"

"Possibly."

"How will you find out, *mein Kommandant?*"

"You know, my friend, I have my methods," and then he laughed. "They always squeal in the end. Yes, they always squeal," and his eyes glinted as they stole to the bunch of weapons stacked in the corner.

CHAPTER 14

The Price is Paid

Stefan had been adamant: he could offer no chance of success while there was a moon. So they waited another week for a moonless night, and now the moment had arrived.

Peter and Stefan had left their mountain headquarters at dusk and now they stood together in the fading light, looking down upon the Sixteen Lakes. Their eyes were glued upon the tree-ringed hillock that they knew to be the Citadel, and then Stefan looked at the Briton.

"God be with you, my friend."

Peter smiled and took the outstretched hand. During the past week these two men had discovered each other's measure, and now they felt a comradeship between them that men only find in action. For the past five nights, Peter and Stefan had been reconnoitring right up to the perimeter of the Citadel, and on Wednesday fortune had favoured them. One of Stefan's patrols had captured an S.S. officer on the outer defensive cordon and they had brought him back to their mountain headquarters.

The German had taken one look at his captors, who were surrounding him in the cave, before blurting out what he knew of the Citadel, and this was recorded. Stefan had a model of the Citadel fashioned out of stones and mud, and when the S.S. officer had approved it, the partisans took their prisoner outside. Peter did not see him again.

But after sleeping during the mornings, the guerrilla leaders and their three guests would pore over the model until they had memorised it perfectly. Lake Mavrovo lay over a thousand feet above the Citadel, due north of it, but less than a mile away; and the falls which cascaded over the containing precipice spilled out into the valley below to form the Sixteen Lakes. At the side of the third lake was a small hillock, thickly ringed by pines, and the Germans had levelled off the top for a landing strip where they kept their small reconnaissance aircraft. Below this mound lay the Citadel, tunnelled out of the rock and invisible to the casual observer.

At the northern end of the Citadel was the Power House. Here the piped water-power which plunged down from Lake Mavrovo was funnelled directly into the four gigantic turbines. Separated from the Power House by a massive floodgate was the next section, the Gearing House, where the high speed from the spinning turbine rotors was reduced into controlled power. The four revolving shafts then ran through thick concrete into a larger compartment, the Dynamo House. The Citadel widened at this point and at the far end of the Dynamo House was the huge switchboard which distributed the electricity supply to the underground fortress.

The *Vernichtungswaffe* itself was being processed in the heart of the Citadel, in three separate factories known as Blocks Number One, Two and Three. It was said that a thousand kilometres of piping ran through Numbers One and Two Blocks, but little was known about Number Three, because only the scientists and a few picked technicians were permitted entry; here it was that the end product was being manufactured.

On the western side of the three blocks ran the accommodation for the scientific staff and technicians. On the eastern boundary lay the administrative section, and on the southern was the entrance to the Citadel. This was a huge tunnel hacked out of the granite face at the southern end of the hillock, and into this cavern ran the single railway track which ended alongside the unloading bays, a hundred metres inside the entrance.

The opening was guarded day and night by the *élite* of the S.S. garrison; on the western side of the tunnel and on the southern flank of Number Three Block was the officer accommodation for the S.S. On the opposite side of the entrance, and extending until it met the administrative section on the eastern side of the Citadel, were the barracks for the S.S. troops. Each section was self-contained, but honeycombed by corridors and passages which connected one area to another.

Stefan, Peter and his two comrades had rehearsed the operation until they each knew by heart the part they had to play. And now the night of decision was upon them — at last it was time for action.

"Good luck, Stefan," Peter said quietly. "It's good to know that you and your boys will be covering me."

"Let's go, my friend. It will be zero hour by the time we reach our positions," and the partisan leader loped off down the hill into the darkness.

It was one-thirty in the morning and it was drizzling when they left the shelter of the pines surrounding the Citadel. Stefan had brought a strong force of his guerrillas, and these had silently dispatched nineteen of the unsuspecting enemy guards on the outer perimeter, with no one the wiser. That had taken care of the cordon from the cliff of Mavrovo to the third lake, so the Hun should remain quiet until the watch was relieved in the morning. When they were close to the inner line of sentries, Stefan stopped to wait for Peter and his friends.

"God speed," he whispered. "The tunnel of the Fire Exit is directly ahead. I'll keep you covered."

Peter grunted and edged forward, Hank and Bill following. Stefan melted into the darkness and they were alone.

Back in the headquarters of the cave the operation had not seemed too difficult. It had seemed simple to locate the small tunnel which ran out like a rabbit hole from the hillock and which served as an emergency Fire Exit on the northern side of the Citadel. The plan was for Hank to deal with the sentry guarding the exit and then Hawkins would cover Peter and Hank while they approached the sides of the hillock. Peter was to slip down the tunnel of the Fire Exit and gain an entry, while Hank climbed the sides of the mound to find the two mushroom heads which were the supply and exhaust ventilators to the Power House.

Yes, it had seemed easy, back in the cave, but now Peter felt his heart pounding. He glanced quickly at Hank and Bill, and he was reassured when he felt them near him. Hank's lithe figure had been festooned with hardware — grenades, coils of fuse, sticks of dynamite; Commando knife, cheese wire and .45 Colt, but in spite of this armament he moved silently in his rubber-soled boots, swiftly and like a shadow, his balaclava cap rolled down over his forehead. Bill Hawkins' stocky shape had been amusing by contrast. Not to be outdone, he carried a vast armoury, including a quick-firing weapon. With his Sten he could cover both Peter and Hank.

The American had to find the supply ventilator, then thread the fuse cable down the thirty-foot length of trunking. Peter had to reach the Power House, and somehow grab the fuse which Hank had passed down from above. The cable was slow-burning, and had been accurately measured to consume its length in sixty minutes.

On feeling three tugs from Peter, Hank was to light the fuse. But first, Peter had to place his detonators at the points where the four huge pipes entered the turbines in the Power House. If these focal points could be destroyed the avalanche of water would be catastrophic: the Citadel would be deluged by millions of tons of unleashed water. But what was he to encounter if he ever reached the Power House?

He shivered as he felt the drizzle driving against his face, and then a helpless futility swamped him. How could they possibly succeed? But, with only two days left before the intended rendezvous with *Rapid* off Dubrovnik, he had to strike now, for he could no longer postpone the attack. He was convinced that this was indeed the enemy's heavy water project. The very nature and colouring of the river known as the Black Devil showed that there was something exceptional in the substance of these waters, surely? Yes, this *must* be the project, for why should the Hun place such importance upon the vast scheme?

Suddenly Hank stiffened beside him. Peter could not see a yard before his face, but he reached out to check Bill. And there they waited while Hank crept forward, their faces slashed by the drizzle in the wind. Peter counted the seconds which soon turned to minutes, and then he found his teeth chattering, as the rain ran from his lips, nose and chin. Bill nudged him and he thought he heard a muffled groan. Then there was complete silence in the mizzling wetness.

With nothing but his thoughts to pass the agony of waiting, the delay was unbearable, but suddenly the darkness seemed more dense ahead, and then he felt the heavy breathing of Hank in front of him. A hand clawed out of the murk and he heard a hoarse whisper.

"Okay. I've fixed the sentry. Come on."

Peter's doubts vanished as he moved forward. To have with you a man of Hank's competence was in itself a stroke of luck and he gladly followed the tall shadow, Bill bringing up the rear.

A great mass suddenly loomed above them as they reached the last row of pines. It was the sloping bank of the hillock and directly ahead of them was an even deeper blackness.

"There's the Fire Exit, Pete, and my two ventilators are twenty yards in from the bank. Good luck, bud."

"So long, Hank. Give me fifteen minutes before threading the fuse."

"Okay. It's a quarter to two now."

"Bill, stay in the trees here and cover the exit," Peter said as he checked his watch. "Three shots will bring Stefan and his boys straight in. But don't summon them unless things become desperate."

Bill's grin gleamed even in this darkness and then he whispered hoarsely:

"I'll be here waiting for you, sir. Never fear, I'll be here. But I don't like your going down that there tunnel without me. Sure I can't come with you, are you, sir?"

"Sorry, Bill. This is a one-man job and I'd better get on with it."

Bill shook his head, and the water dripped from him as he slipped the German cape over his head.

"Good luck, sir."

Peter nodded and without a word strode towards the entrance of the Fire Exit tunnel, Hank scrambling up the side of the mound as he did so. Peter did not care to look back. Seldom had he a duty less to his liking and he felt the back of his neck prickling as he reached the entrance. The roof of his mouth had gone dry and his heart raced as he loosened the

Luger in its holster. *It's as well that Stefan captured these uniforms for us*, he thought, *even though they are a rotten fit*. Hank's Gestapo outfit had been too short in the sleeves, whereas Bill's was bursting at the seams across the shoulders. Peter's, in fact, was a reasonably good fit, and as he was the one who had to penetrate the Citadel, he was allowed to keep it. But three Huns had been killed by the partisans to provide these disguises.

Peter slid a step into the tunnel. He stopped. Nothing, not a sound, except … above the thumping of his heart a steady *drip! drip!* echoing at the end of the passage. Then, as his eyes grew accustomed to the deeper gloom, a dim blue light slowly became visible at the far end.

"Here goes," Peter whispered to himself. "Only a lunatic would take this on. Thank heavens I've been using my German recently!" and he settled the Gestapo cap squarely upon his head, pulled down his tunic and strode forward, as silently and as confidently as he was able.

The blue lamp shone over a steel door, 'EMERGENCY FIRE EXIT, DO NOT LOCK' the red capitals announced in German. A pencil of light streamed through the keyhole, and from somewhere Peter could hear the faint whining of machinery. He crouched down guiltily and peeped through the keyhole. He could see nothing but the opposite wall of a white corridor. He withdrew his head as a shadow crossed the aperture and he heard the sound of voices.

Must be a busy passage, but I wonder whether it's right or left to the Power House, he thought as he squared off the pack on his back.

He turned the handle of the door. He pushed, but nothing happened. He pulled gently and the steel door swung noiselessly towards him. Then he blinked in the brightness of the lights.

The sudden warmth and light snapped some hidden spring in Peter's consciousness, and he remembered Jan Widdecombe's words when they had landed in North Africa. "Once you are committed," he had said, "your only chance lies in you yourself believing that you are a German. Live the part for every second of the twenty-four hours and then you may have a chance."

Peter deliberately slammed the door behind him and he shuddered as the noise reverberated down the corridor. He saw two figures come striding towards him; an officer and a trooper, he thought. Peter stamped his feet and started to flap his arms about to shake off the water that had settled on his uniform. As the oncomers reached him, he bent down to brush the drops from his trousers.

"Filthy night!" the officer remarked.

"Foul," Peter grunted.

And then, mercifully, the two passed on down the corridor. Peter's hands were, he was pleased to note, quite steady. He straightened himself and turned right to follow the two men down the long passage. At the end a noticeboard faced him, and even from here he could see an arrow pointing to the left, and above it the words in German, 'POWER AND GEARING HOUSES.'

Peter strode forward. So far, so good. *It's been too easy*, he thought. *I hope they are not expecting me. Anyway, it's too late now*, and he walked on boldly, turning left at the end of the passage. As he turned the corner, he nearly knocked down a soldier. The man apologised and saluted quickly. Peter swore before returning the mark of respect.

"Be more careful, can't you?" he snapped.

"*Jawohl, mein Leutnant*," and the man stood back, waiting for Peter to proceed.

Peter chuckled. He was beginning to enjoy himself. And then at the end of the next corridor was a red door, over it the German inscription: 'DANGER, AIRLOCK TO POWER AND GEARING HOUSES.'

Peter slid towards it, his nerves tingling and alert. *Just like a destroyer's boiler room and airlock*, he thought, as he peered through the spyglass to see if anyone else was inside. It was empty, so he entered, shutting the outer door behind him.

Once inside he had time to collect his thoughts, for no one could enter when he was in the airlock. He kept his back to the outer door, for anyone wishing to enter would only see the cloth of his tunic through the peephole. And, if Peter stooped, he would be able to spy through the peephole of the inner door, so giving him an opportunity to prepare for whatever lay ahead.

Inside this steel box he had a moment in which to pull himself together. So far everything had been too easy. The partisans' successful coup against the string of sentries and the capturing of the three uniforms; the silencing of the sentry outside the little-used Fire Exit, and Hank's finding of the ventilation mushroom-heads; and, a few seconds ago, the meeting with the two Germans. He must have convinced them, or else... The horrible suspicion grew in his mind. Was von Kramer baiting a trap, as he had done at Castellare Poliano? Why had everything been so ridiculously simple? Were they waiting for him to strike? Or perhaps Kramer thought he was in the area only to collect information so that the R.A.F. could deal with the Citadel and its *Vernichtungswaffe*. Anyway, there was no retreat now. He must open this steel door in front of him and take charge of events, even though they might engulf him. His own life seemed of little consequence at this moment of unreality. What of it if, by his actions, he should destroy this devilish project but lose his own life? He shook himself and crouched down to peep through the spyhole.

It took him some time to recognise clearly what was visible to him through the aperture, but slowly he recognised a steel handrail, gleaming under the bright lights; then part of an instrument panel and the large curve of a turbine casing, black and shining with its sheen of oil. Suddenly a man's back moved across the steel plating and he could just hear him shouting above the hum of the turbines. "Well, that's one, anyway!" Peter murmured. "But there must be more than that — two or three at least. If there are half a dozen or so, I'll just have to shoot them out of hand, or perhaps use my grenade," and he slid the chunky metal sphere from his belt, its stick into his left hand. With his right, he drew the Luger and snapped off the safety catch.

"Here goes!"

He flicked back the lever of the door and quietly strode into the Power House.

It's good to feel that Bill Hawkins is covering us, thought Lieutenant Jefferson, U.S.N., as he slithered upon his stomach to the two ventilation shafts which poked starkly from the turfed roof of the Citadel. *He's a good man that — no nonsense about him.*

Hank slipped the stormcape over himself as he lay in the wet undergrowth, waiting for a quarter of an hour to pass before starting to unwind the length of fuse which lay coiled by his side. *Peter will be ready in ten minutes*, he thought, *and then I can start threading this goddarned fuse. He's a good Limey, though, that Sinclair, even though he got under my skin. Thought I couldn't match up to Widdecombe, did he? Well, I'll show him. The Yanks can do just as well, but I want a chance to prove it!* He fingered the blade of the knife at his side and for the third time that night patted his gun. This was his first big job on his own, and he knew much depended on it.

He looked at his watch. Five and a half minutes to go before doing his stuff. It seemed odd to think that less than five months ago he had been with his parents in Philadelphia. Less than five months! He'd had seven days furlough, and then came the shock and thrill of his first posting to a battle area. "You're to get your training with the British before going out to the Pacific," the Naval Captain had told him. Hank had unintentionally snorted as he looked out at the black, smelly waters of the Delaware, flowing below the Captain's office.

"There's no need to complain, Jefferson," the Captain had said. "You're going to a tough assignment."

And how right that Captain had been! Hank shivered as the water seeped through the rough serge of his German uniform, but the drizzle had eased when he again looked at his watch. Two o'clock. He wriggled to the right-hand ventilator and slowly stood up. He put his hand to the lip of the mushroom head and felt the suction of air. *This is it*, he rejoiced, and he bent down to reach for the coil of fuse wire.

But as he started threading the fuse he jumped backwards. Five pistol shots rang dully from down below — three in quick succession, followed by two separately, slowly and deliberately.

Peter had no time to think, and what he did, he realised later, he had loathed doing. But the three engineers in the Power House had been brave men. "I had no option," he whispered to himself as he reloaded, the barrel of the Luger still hot in his hand. "When they rushed me, I had to fire." Looking at the three bodies that now lay sprawled on the steel plating, he hated this business of war. But there was no time for sentiment now for, at any moment, the airlock might open, and more Germans would enter. He moved over and stuffed a crumpled piece of paper across the spyhole. Then he threw the locking-bar of the inner door across, so that no one could break in upon him.

Suddenly he realised that he was alone in this huge room and his eyes took in the astonishing scene. Four enormous turbine rotor cases, control panels, and, at the far end, four huge ducts where the water must be plunging down from Lake Mavrovo above. "That's it," he whispered, "that's the place for the charges! But where's the Gearing House?"

And then he noticed that the third wall was made of steel, and, when he moved over to inspect it, he saw that it would open horizontally, probably operated hydraulically. There was a control switch at the side of the door with two buttons, one green, the other red. Over the door was a small siren, and by it a brass tally announcing in German: 'GEARING HOUSE.'

I must get in there after laying the charge, he thought. *If there is an exit, I can escape that way. But I'll lay the charge first and then see if I can get out. I can hear Hank's fuse cable scrabbling about already*, and he smiled as he listened by the huge opening of the supply ventilator. There was a grille in front of the aperture and behind this a green coil of fuse cable was already bunching. Peter prised the grille away with his Commando knife, grabbed the wire, and, taking up the slack, gave it a sharp tug. His heart leapt when there was an answering pull. He glanced at his watch: five minutes past two. Then Peter hauled out enough cable to reach the duct boxes. He dropped his haversack to the floor, removed the dynamite and worked rapidly. Ten minutes later the charges were laid up in parallel inside the inspection boxes at the base of the ducts. If the charges exploded as planned, the four ducts would shatter at identical moments and the inrush of water would be catastrophic.

That's the purpose of this steel door, I suppose, thought Peter: *a flood safety door to hold back the waters in case of an emergency in the Power House. Well, I must make certain that the flood door is open and then nothing can prevent the whole Citadel from being overwhelmed* — and he pressed the green push-button of the flood door. The klaxon blared as he drew his Luger.

He waited while the door slid silently upwards, as if moved by unseen hands. He ducked under the steel door as soon as he was able, his Luger at the ready. But to his amazement the Gearing House was empty, and, apart from the smooth churning of the enormous reduction gearing, sheathed in its safety shields, there was a strange silence about the compartment.

"I suppose the third Hun in the Power House must have been the watch-keeper here," he murmured to reassure himself. But he felt uneasy — things were going too well. Kramer could have laid this trap for him and be forecasting his every move. Peter turned quickly to look over his shoulder, expecting to see his enemy's face leering down at him. The stubble on the back of his neck prickled — but the room was deserted.

There was another airlock exit for the Gearing House and Peter tried it. He entered the steel box and felt the outer door. It opened to his push, and, through the slit in the airlock he could see a passage stretching before him. Certain that his luck could not hold out much longer, he slammed the door shut, opened the inner, and regained the Gearing House. *I must work fast now, whether I'm spotted or not, for I haven't much time,* and he looked at the electric clock over the watch-keeper's desk: it was twelve minutes past two. He moved through the opened flood door and regained the Power House. He checked his detonator connections. He went to the air supply ventilator and took sharp hold of the fuse cable.

For a brief second he paused. This was his moment of decision. Three tugs on the cable and Hank would ignite the fuse: then no power on earth could stop the train of events, except by wrenching the detonators clear before the spark arrived. "And I can prevent that," Peter whispered to himself, "by partially shutting the flood doors after I've left this Power House. Then no one can get in, either through the airlock in the Power House or by the flood door." He glanced at his watch: two-fifteen exactly. He took a deep breath and gave three deliberate tugs. Then, a second later, his hand jerked three times as it grasped the cable. Hank had received the signal and he was igniting the fuse at this very moment.

"Sixty minutes and the whole shebang will go up! I'd better quit!" Peter murmured, as he gave a last glance at his detonators. They were fine! Then he cut back into the Gearing House. He pressed the green button of the flood door switch. The warning klaxon blared; there was an immediate hissing and the massive door, some six inches thick, slowly slid downwards, silently, remorselessly ... six inches from the floor, Peter pressed the red button and the door stopped. He drew his Luger and fired once into the switch mechanism. There was a flash and the smell of burning insulations, and then, as the report of the shot died away, he thought he heard the distant tinkling of a bell.

In the sudden silence, the insistent summons of a telephone made his heart miss a beat. The sound came, not from the Gearing House in which he was, but through the six-inch gap left open by the flood door. The phone was ringing in the Power House.

"Oh God!" Peter whispered, "and I can't get back to answer it!"

He looked round and saw a large handwheel which obviously worked the toothed gearing for operating the flood door by hand in emergency. The phone was still ringing when Peter dashed for the handwheel.

"Keep on ringing…" he prayed, "keep on ringing till I get to you."

But as his hand touched the wheel, there was a sudden silence. The phone had stopped.

Peter was nonplussed. Surely someone would become suspicious now? No reply from the Power House … there'd be hell to pay!

He dashed to the airlock, opened the inner door, and covered the peephole of the outer door with his handkerchief.

I'll leave the inner door open. Then the interlock will stop intruders opening the outer door, he thought. *But I've got to get a hustle on — they'll be coming to see what's up.* And then he heard the phone ringing again, impatiently, urgently.

"Let it ring," he murmured savagely. "There's nothing I can do about it now! I'll fix the emergency gear and then no one can get back into the Power House."

He wrenched a stick of dynamite from his pack, tied a short length of fuse cable to the detonator, and then lashed the explosive charge to the geared teeth of the handwheel. He lit the fuse and glanced at the sparks fizzing down the cable. He looked at the clock: two thirty-five…

Then he rushed for the airlock, slamming the inner door behind him. *Get me out of here!* he prayed, as he pulled out his Luger, and he wrenched at the handle of the outer door. The dazzling lights of the corridor blinded him as he gently closed the door behind him. He looked up … into the black snouts of half-a-dozen tommy guns.

"Ah, Sinclair!" a familiar voice mocked. "Why in such a hurry? We've been expecting you."

The Luger was knocked from Peter's hand and it fell clattering to the floor. The shock loosed off one round and the report echoed distantly down the corridor.

CHAPTER 15

The Master Race

Hank Jefferson and Bill Hawkins were invisible where they stood on each side of the Emergency Fire Exit. The drizzle had stopped and a slight breeze was blowing through the tops of the pines which were swaying in the darkness.

"Twenty minutes have gone, sir," Bill Hawkins whispered fretfully, "since you lit the fuse. And the Captain hasn't come out yet."

Hank was well aware of this, and a dreadful doubt began to gnaw at the back of his mind. He visualised the red sparks of the fuse spluttering their way towards the detonators, and there was no way of stopping it now, for he had pushed the last end down the ventilator. Then the most appalling catastrophe would engulf them all — and Peter was still inside! The American looked at his watch: two thirty-five. His heart was hammering as he poked his head into the dark entrance of the Fire Exit.

"Cover me, Bill. I'm going to see if there's anything going on. The Captain will be returning this way if all is well." Then he slid down the passage to the first door where a sliver of light pierced the gloom through the keyhole. He pressed his ear to the aperture. He could hear nothing ... and then he jumped back as the blast of a shot struck his eardrum. He turned to listen with the other ear, but all he could hear was the distant hubbub of shouting men.

He hesitated for a second. *Shall I barge in*, he wondered, *or shall I go back to Bill? But whatever I do I must be quick for this whole*

Citadel will be a mass of rubble by three-fifteen. He rushed back to the entrance of the tunnel.

"What's up, sir? It's twenty to three!"

There was a catch in the American's voice as he spoke:

"Something's fouled up, Bill. I reckon the Captain's in trouble. I heard a shot."

Bill Hawkins's voice was harsh in the darkness.

"Let's go get him. We ain't got much time."

"Good for you, boy. It's now or never."

"We daren't shoot our way in. Even if we reach him, we'd never get out alive," Bill said.

"Unless..." Hank whispered.

"What?"

"Unless we bluffed our way in and came out with this guy Kramer as hostage."

"Our only chance, sir," Bill replied as he glanced at their uniforms. "If we keep these capes on they'll hide our scruffiness."

"Can you speak German, Bill?"

"No."

"Leave the lingo to me, then. I reckon our best chance is to gatecrash the main entrance. Agree?"

"Right, sir. I'd rather shoot it out than leave the Captain behind. We got nothing to lose."

"You die only once, Bill."

"Yes, sir. You die only once," Bill replied quietly. He looked at his watch. "Two forty-two, sir. We've only got thirty-five minutes left. I'll follow you."

But Hank had already moved off in the direction of the main entrance, which lay four hundred yards away, a huge cavity in the rockface. The single rail track ran alongside the metalled road which disappeared into the darkness of the entrance.

All caution thrown to the winds now, Hank plunged through the undergrowth, Bill floundering at his heels. Then a dim red light appeared ahead of them and Hank halted in his tracks.

"The sentry box, Bill."

Beyond lay the bright lights of the interior of the Citadel, and then, just as the allies paused, a distant jangling and throbbing pulsed in their ears.

"The diesel train!" Hank whispered. "Let's wait. It may help us."

They shrank back into the shadows and suddenly the whistle of a diesel engine shrilled close to them. Then, less than a minute later, the train clanked past them, barely ten yards away, the drivers leaning out of the cab and waving at the sentry as they slowed down by the white wooden barrier.

"Now, Bill! Kick up as much din as you can. I'm going to raise hell. Come on!"

The Leutnant of the Watch was always glad to see the arrival of the nightly train. It broke the monotony of the night watches, and tonight it was more than welcome for it had been a long and miserable watch, cold, wet and dreary. He felt the approach of the diesel long before it gave its customary whistle, for the rails trembled some time before its arrival.

"Lift the barrier!" he shouted to the young soldier in the sentry box. "I'll take his papers," and the Leutnant moved up to the tracks as the engine clanked to a stop beside him.

He held up his hand to the engine driver who was grinning down at him, his shining face moist with drizzle.

"*Himmel*, what a night!" the driver complained. "It's all right for you chaps in this snuggery!"

The Leutnant opened his mouth to reply, but suddenly the doleful wails of an army whistle drifted down on the wind.

Then he heard excited voices rushing towards him and, before he knew what had happened, the frantic notes of a whistle shrilled about him, and two men rushed at him from out of the night. The tall one was an officer, he could see that, and the Leutnant clicked his heels, saluting as he did so.

"*Achtung! Achtung!*" the wild officer shouted breathlessly. "Raise the alarm, Leutnant of the Watch! Raise the alarm, for God's sake! We're surrounded, I tell you, raise the alarm!"

For a split second the Leutnent hesitated. He had his orders. No one to be allowed to enter the Citadel without showing his pass. "No one,' his Kapitan had said, "no one, unless you want to be shot." Yes, the Leutnant had reason to hesitate as he looked at this crazy-eyed officer in the dripping cape whom he did not recognise. But then, there were so many comings and goings amongst the officers, that he only knew a handful of them amongst these hundreds.

"Your pass, please, *Herr Major*?"

Anger flashed in the officer's eyes and the Leutnant cringed back for the expected blow. "I have to do my duty, *Herr Major*," he shouted apologetically.

The tall officer's eyes were blazing.

"Take me to the Kommandant, you fool! Can't you see this is an emergency?" and the officer's hand shot out to grasp the Leutnant roughly by the shoulder. "Take me to the Kommandant at once, or I'll have you court-martialled for failing in your duty."

The name of the Kommandant was enough for the Leutnant. "*Jawohl, Herr Major*. The sentry will take you," and he shouted to the soldier:

"Escort the officer to the Kommandant!"

The soldier clicked his heels, grounded his rifle by his box, and started running on ahead. The Leutnant saluted, then dashed into his office. The wail of a siren howled about them as Hank and Bill rushed past the office of the Leutnant of the Watch. On the wall outside, the dial of a clock glowed. It was ten minutes to three.

As the S.S. guard opened the outer door of the airlock to the Gearing House, there was a dull thud from inside. The inner door jumped towards him and he leapt backwards.

"*Himmel!* What's that?" the Kommandant snapped.

"Better go and find out," Peter grinned.

A swinging blow across the face sent Peter reeling backwards. He staggered to the floor, and when he looked up he saw Kramer staring down at him, his eyes blazing.

"Get on your feet, Englishman. I've a few questions to ask you," and the Kommandant turned to the escort. "Break into the Gearing House. I'll question him in there."

As Peter watched the Leutnant re-enter the airlock, he tried to collect his reeling thoughts. *Only another half hour, and then it'll be all over. I must stall for time; every second I win means a second nearer the explosion* — and he smiled as he watched the junior officer emerge from the airlock.

"The inner door's jammed, *Herr Kommandant*. I can't open it."

"Break it down."

The Leutnant paused. Then he looked fearfully at Kramer.

"What about the forced draught, sir?"

Peter saw Kramer's face muscles working, then the German said:

"Send for the engineers. Tell them to get the door open immediately, then make your report to me. I'm returning to my office," and he turned on his heel. "Follow me and bring the prisoner with you, Sergeant."

They started to frogmarch Peter down the corridor, but his mind was now clear. *If I'm knocked out*, he thought, *they can't get anything out of me. I'll make myself an infernal nuisance...*

He dragged his feet until the guards had to half carry him. He shook himself free and struggled desperately, putting up a mock show of resistance. But they refused to hit him; instead, they threw him on his back and dragged him along the floor by the legs. Peter felt his tunic ripping under him and by the time he had been dragged two hundred yards along the concrete, his shoulders were bleeding. He shouted with the pain but the guards did not stop until they reached the door of the Kommandant's office. Then they yanked their prisoner to his feet.

"What the devil d'you think you're doing?" Peter gasped.

For answer he heard laughter behind him and then the door closed. He looked round and there was his detested enemy, the man he feared above all others.

"If you really want to know, Sinclair, I propose interrogating you," and the huge man plucked a cigarette from his case. "I think I've a right to know how you got in here, don't you? Have you any objections?" he asked suavely.

"Name, rank and number is all you're entitled to ask, Kramer."

The Kommandant rose from his desk. As he strolled round towards Peter he dismissed all the escort except the Leutnant.

"Sound the alarm, Sergeant."

"*Jawohl, Herr Kommandant*," and the man clicked his heels, saluted and turned about. Peter heard the door opening and shutting behind him, but he was aware of nothing except the hands on the face of the small travelling-clock which was half turned towards him on Kramer's desk. It was ten minutes to three — only another twenty minutes now! He tore his eyes away and looked with unconcern at his adversary.

"I said, name, rank, and number is all you're getting out of me."

Kramer stopped directly in front of the Briton. He drew at his cigarette and flicked the ash nonchalantly upon the carpet.

"But you're a spy, Sinclair. Had you thought of that?"

Peter was silent. The eyes that flickered before him were like a snake's, cold and evil. He shuddered and looked away, before the German mesmerised him.

"So what, Kramer?"

Kramer's arm swung and another back-hand blow stung Peter's face. He reeled and slowly rubbed his cheek.

"Don't do that again."

But Kramer was chuckling quietly:

"*Das ist gut!* Did you hear that, *Herr Leutnant*? We mustn't do that again!" and the Kommandant grinned at his junior officer.

"*Ja, Herr Kommandant.* But a spy should be shot."

"But we have to ask our friend a few questions first. Tell me, Sinclair, how did you get into the Citadel?"

So this is it, thought Peter. *Now Kramer's getting down to brass tacks*, and he allowed his gaze to steal towards the clock: two minutes to three! Only seventeen minutes to go, but he didn't welcome death, although, now that it had come to him, he felt strangely at peace. He'd done his best and, after all, drowning in this hellhole was little different to disaster in a submarine.

"How did you get in here?" he heard Kramer repeating.

"By the entrance."

"Which entrance?" the Kommandant insisted.

"Is there another entrance, Kramer?"

"Which entrance?"

Peter refused to answer. Instead he laughed in the German's face.

"I give you until three twenty to answer me. If you don't co-operate by then I'll shoot you myself," and the Kommandant peered at his clock. "You have nineteen minutes."

Peter's heart sang within him — he'd won, yes, he'd won, and he smiled to himself. But this was too much for Kramer.

Peter saw the German's shoulders twitch, and then a sharp pain seared across his temples. The ceiling whirled about him and he knew no more.

A voice he dimly recognised was calling to him from a long way away. Then he realised that his head ached and that his face was wet.

"You're all right, sir … come on…" the voice of a friend he had once known long ago struck a chord in his consciousness. Then the voice pleaded, much nearer now:

"*Come on*, sir … it's me, Able Seaman Hawkins, sir."

Peter felt his mind clearing, and he opened his eyes. Then he sat up suddenly.

"Good lord!" he gasped. "How long have we?" and he grabbed at Hawkins's sturdy frame, hauling himself to his feet.

"Thirteen minutes, sir. We shan't get out if you can't walk by yourself, sir."

Peter glanced about him. Hank stood in the middle of the room, his pistol covering the two Germans who were facing the wall, their hands above their heads.

"Come on, Pete!" he exhorted. "You're doing fine," and his taut face cracked into a smile. "Bill, cover this Kraut while I get the Captain out of here. Then follow me."

Hank lunged at the largest of the two Germans and dug his gun into the man's back.

"Hey, you! You're coming with me!"

The pain of the sudden jab made Kramer fling round. For a moment he thought of grappling with the ice-cool American, but then he noticed the steady eyes.

"Get going, Kramer, and get us out of here. One slip and I pull this trigger. Now *move*!"

Hank opened the door, Peter leaning on one shoulder. There was no one outside the Kommandant's office.

"Take us to the Fire Exit by the Power House — and hurry!" Hank snapped at the Kommandant. "Get going, mister."

Kramer turned left outside his office and hurried down the corridor. Hank looked at his watch: three minutes past three. "Twelve minutes to go," he breathed. "It's going to be close!"

Then Peter heard the office door slam behind him and the scurry of footsteps. A few seconds later there was a dull *crrump!* and a blast of air thumped against his eardrums. No doubt Bill Hawkins had dealt with the S.S. leutnant...

Three minutes later they had all gained the tunnel of the Fire Exit, and now they could smell the resin of the pines and see the first light of dawn breaking behind the blackness of the forest. Hank fired three shots into the air with his pistol and the cracks echoed in the still of the morning.

He waited, and a moment later a shadow detached itself from the gloom of the pines, sliding silently in the night.

"Stefan!" Peter gasped. "Get your troops off the Citadel. The whole lot's going up in less than five minutes."

"The plane is ready and ticking over, Peter. Come with me," Stefan said, ignoring Peter's warning. "We'll look after ourselves."

They scrambled up the slopes of the mound, and there, in the first light of dawn, Peter saw the glint of a revolving propeller. They ran to the little four-seater, Hank forcing the protesting German in front of him. Peter floundered to the side of the aircraft, in time to see a group of partisan soldiers bundling the struggling Kramer inside. Hank was given a leg-up into the pilot's cockpit, and then Peter felt Bill's kindly hands lifting him too and he flopped on to the floor of the plane, Hawkins following after.

"Hold tight, you guys!" Hank yelled as he opened up the throttle. "It's lucky I used to fly the mail back home!"

As the plane gathered speed, Peter saw spurts of red flame from the eastern end of the Citadel. Then figures started running towards them, green tracer spitting from their guns.

"We'll never make it!" Hank yelled. "Those Krauts are too close," and there was a sudden flutter as a line of bullets ripped the fuselage above Peter's head.

"Look, sir!" Bill shouted. "Look at Stefan's boys!" and he pointed excitedly out to the right.

A semicircle of dark shadows was closing in upon the Huns, and suddenly the green tracer started to curve towards the forests.

"Stefan has drawn their fire," Peter yelled, "and we never even said 'goodbye'! Look out, Bill!"

But Hawkins had seen the danger. Kramer was struggling desperately, but a revolver butt put an end to his worries.

The plane was airborne now, hauled into the sky by Hank's skilful hands. Already the trees were a dark mass below them, and, as they climbed still higher, the surface of Lake Mavrovo gleamed in the first light.

"Hey, you guys!" yelled Hank, glancing downwards over his right shoulder. "Look at that!"

Down below, at the corner of the lake where the ducts for the hydroelectric supply had been, there now boiled a terrifying sight. Seas were breaking against the rocks at the side of the lake and a seething mass of water boiled and broke upon the dam. A whirlpool was spreading across the end of the lake, and even at this height they could guess that the holocaust must be breaking upon the Citadel, a thousand feet below the dam. Higher and higher the aircraft circled while green streaks of dawn lightened the eastern horizon.

Peter looked down, his heart missing a beat as he watched the catastrophe overtaking the Citadel. A white mist had begun to spread outwards in concentric circles from the third lake, and at intervals great gouts of steam and debris were flung upwards in superhuman fury. The miasma spread slowly down the valley and, while Lake Mavrovo boiled and surged above, a sheet of silver water began to merge into the landscape where the Citadel had been. Aghast at the catastrophe, Peter let his eyes wander back to Lake Mavrovo and then, as they watched from the plane, the dam started to crumble.

"Pray God that Stefan and his men have got clear!" Peter muttered.

From four thousand feet, the disaster looked like a miniature cascade, like a child's dam on a sandy beach overwhelmed by the oncoming tide. First a small gap, then the tunnel of streaming water, and finally the deluge overwhelming the whole countryside.

"Get going for Dubrovnik, Hank," Peter yelled into the intercom. "There's no point in sticking around here."

Peter had the maps spread across his knees and soon gave Hank a course. The little aircraft pointed its nose across the mountains and towards the Dalmatian coast. It was grand to feel that they might yet make their rendezvous with *Rapid*, now only thirty-six hours away. But they were not there yet.

Bill had been casting around the sky and suddenly his eyes distended with fear.

"Look, sir!" he cried in warning as he pointed to the north-east. "Enemy aircraft!"

Peter turned his head. A speck was fast gaining upon them. By its silhouette Peter knew it of old and his heart sank.

"Get down, Hank!" he yelled. "There's an ME109 on our tail!"

CHAPTER 16

A Slim Chance

At five o'clock on the evening of the nineteenth of October, the Captain of His Majesty's Submarine *Rapid*, Lieutenant John Easton, D.S.C., Royal Navy, was peering through the periscope of his small submarine.

"Well, Pilot," he said, without removing his eyes from the face-piece, "I reckon that's Dubrovnik all right." He snapped shut the handles of the periscope, and the steel tube slid downwards into the well.

"Yes, sir, it certainly ought to be. The battlements at the harbour entrance are very like Valetta, aren't they?"

John Easton bent over to study the chart.

"Where are we now?"

"Here, sir," and the Navigating Officer indicated their last fix.

"Umm … I think I'll go straight in and bottom half a mile from shore. There seems to be the right amount of water."

"About fifteen fathoms, sir."

"Good. Give me a course that will take me within a thousand yards of the fortress at the entrance."

"Aye, aye, sir."

And so, just as the light was beginning to fade, John Easton took a bearing of the Croatian port. The last rays of the sun were falling obliquely across the massive stone buildings, and he could just see where the square battlements cast their lengthening shadows across the more humble dwellings of the town. It was a typical Mediterranean sunset, all golds, reds and bronzes, breathtakingly beautiful. The turquoise of the shadows in the harbour contrasted vividly with the deeper blue of the harbour entrance, and in the stillness of the placid sea was reflected the violet and blues of the stone, softened by the setting sun. The roofs of the houses glowed with velvety purples and mauves, the tiles possessing the magic lustre of time, for they had been fired originally in Roman kilns.

"Take her down slowly, Number One. Silent Routine."

A few minutes later there was a gentle grating sound, and *Rapid* bottomed in ninety feet of water. But by midnight the boat started pounding and it was obvious that a sudden Mediterranean gale had developed. Easton was worried.

"I'll have to make to seaward, Number One. Take her to eighty feet and steer south."

Half an hour later *Rapid* was brought up from deep, and all that could be seen through the periscope was the whiteness of breaking seas.

"Surface!" Easton snapped, and five minutes later *Rapid* was wallowing in the teeth of a gale.

"Start the generators, slow ahead together."

The conning tower was the only part of the submarine which was visible above the curling seas, and John Easton felt relaxed and free from the worry of discovery by the enemy. But, as for the rendezvous with Peter Sinclair's party tomorrow night, he was becoming anxious. If this gale persisted there was no hope of bringing them off, and he dodged below the bridge rail for the hundredth time to avoid the 'green' sea which plumped on board. In the darkness, the water swirled at his feet as it drained through the free-flood holes, and he stood up to peer into the flying spray. Ahead of them was a line of breakers, white and angry as they curled down upon the boat. Easton yelled to his Third Hand above the snarling of the wind: "Send the lookouts below. There's no point in their staying up here."

The Captain was worried. How on earth could he pick up Sinclair in this sort of weather? His last memory of Peter flashed across his mind. Sinclair had taken over as First Lieutenant of *Rugged* from him, when he had been sent home for his 'perisher'. Easton remembered the grey eyes, flecks of blue and brown twinkling from the irises, as they looked him squarely in the face. "Thanks a lot, Number One, for such a good 'handover'," Sinclair had said, and Easton knew that he had meant it. *That's what I like about the chap*, thought John Easton, *he's genuine*.

A sea crashed over the bridge, and the two officers had to hold on tightly to prevent their being washed over the side. Easton could see nothing but blackness above him and he gasped for air as the submarine lunged through the swell. Her bows poised for a moment above the next trough and then crashed down into the sea that galloped towards them. A sheet of flying water spurted upwards and then the boat lumbered through the advancing swell, deluging the bridge once again.

"I've had enough of this, Sub. Go below and tell the First Lieutenant I'm diving the boat."

"Aye, aye, sir."

Ten minutes later, *Rapid* forced her way down to eighty feet, but even at that depth she rolled appreciably.

"Anyway we've got in a good charge, Number One. Let's hope the gale will have moderated by this afternoon."

"It ought to, sir. The barometer is still high."

"Perhaps the weather will ease down; you never can tell in the Mediterranean. But if it doesn't…" and John Easton's voice trailed off with the unspoken realisation of the impending tragedy. *Even supposing that Sinclair is waiting for us, we can never take him off in this*, he thought, and he strolled forward to have his breakfast.

But by two in the afternoon the gale blew itself out as quickly as it had arrived. The sky took on a brassy transparency; the seas disappeared to leave a long, undulating swell, and the barometer remained high.

Easton took *Rapid* up to periscope depth and set course to close the rendezvous, but it was four in the afternoon before they were once again off Dubrovnik. After fixing their position, they took her down slowly to ground on the bottom, half a mile from the entrance to the harbour.

"Silent Routine, Number One. Tell the hands to get their heads down: this should be a busy night."

It was the twentieth of October, the eve of Trafalgar Day.

Twilight was ending when all hands in *Rapid* were jerked awake by a sudden rattling and rumbling which echoed dully against the pressure hull.

"What do you make of it, H.S.D.?" John Easton asked the Asdic Operator, as he stumbled into the Control Room.

"Sounds like a ship anchoring, sir."

"Any H.E.?"

"No H.E., sir."

Easton was puzzled; he wished now that he had set a listening watch, but then the Asdic operators would have been 'watch on — stop on' all night. He glanced at the clock: eighteen minutes past nine — still ten minutes of twilight left.

"Diving Stations!" he snapped. "Keep Silent Routine, Number One. I want to have a look up top."

Four minutes later, *Rapid* was drifting up to periscope depth, her bows pointing seawards as she went ahead on 'slow one'.

"Twenty-eight feet, sir."

"Up periscope."

John Easton found it difficult to see anything. As soon as the glass of the periscope cleared, he could just distinguish the horizon line. He searched towards the harbour entrance — he could pick out the battlements at the entrance; he swung round to seawards…

And then his heart leapt with dismay.

Less than five hundred yards away and blocking his escape route to seaward, a Navigatori-class destroyer lay at anchor, her darkened silhouette sinister in the night.

"Down periscope. Starboard ten. Ninety feet and bottom her."

Easton turned towards his First Lieutenant.

"Well, Number One, this looks like 'the curtain' for Sinclair's shore party. There's a destroyer less than three cables away."

Nobody moved in the Control Room, even the planesmen steadying their wheels momentarily while the awful truth struck home. Sinclair, Jefferson and Hawkins were to be left to die…

"But, sir—" the fair-haired First Lieutenant muttered.

"I'll surface as soon as we hear Sinclair's signal," the Captain interrupted, "and I'll go to Night Alarm when you send the hands to Diving Stations. It's too dark to see her properly through the periscope, so I'll try to catch her by surprise and torpedo her as soon as I surface."

"At least we're inshore of her, sir," Number One suggested hopefully. "She shouldn't sight us against the land."

"I hope you're right, Number One. We shall soon see."

CHAPTER 17

"Greater Love hath no man..."

"You know, of course, what day it is, don't you, Hank?"

There was a long pause over the intercom of the little monoplane. Hank was relaxed again over the controls. He had spent a ghastly hour eluding the Messerschmitt 109 by dodging in and out of the mountain ranges and valleys. By keeping close to the sheer sides of the mountains, just far enough out to enable him to pull the monoplane in a tight turn towards the rock, he had prevented the German fighter from coming too close. The enemy pilot wished to live another day, and so, after shadowing the monoplane for over an hour, he returned to base, having called up reinforcements. The monoplane would fly straight into a hornets' nest as soon as it reached the coast.

"Why no, sir. What day is it?" the American voice at the other end of the wire chuckled. The sun was now a dull red orb above the eastern horizon, and already it was climbing fast into the sky, swiftly transmuting itself into the white-hot source of life-giving heat.

"The twentieth of October," Peter yelled.

"Well?" drawled Hank. "What of it? It sure can't be Thanksgiving Day, so you better ask your Heinie friend there." But before Peter could reply, the Kommandant's earphones were crackling:

"Say, Kramer, what's so special about this day, huh?"

The enormous bulk in front of Peter stirred in anger, having now regained consciousness, and then he ripped the earphones from his head. Above the engine noise, Peter could see the

Kommandant's teeth gleaming white, the thin lips curled back viciously, while the bull neck flushed above his tunic collar.

"So you ain't talking, Heinie?" Hank's voice chided. "That's too bad. I kinda thought you'd like to talk after failing to make our Captain squeal," and Hank half-turned to let Peter see he was laughing.

"Trafalgar Day tomorrow, ain't it, sir?" Bill's voice chipped in proudly. "Glad I ain't in Pompey barracks!"

"Why?" asked Peter above the whine of the wind.

"There's more 'bull' than that on this 'ere day," and Bill settled down happily again, curled up on the floor of the aircraft. Strangely happy at four thousand feet in the heart of enemy-occupied territory, he felt he had a pull for once on the 'barrack-stanchions'.

Hank's eye was on the fuel indicator, and he was glad when he could see the last crests coming up at him, for the gauge showed only a quarter full. *The Adriatic can't be far away*, he thought, and, sure enough, out to the southward the distant haziness of the blue sea showed.

"I'll hit the coast," Hank yelled, "and then fly up it until we make Dubrovnik. Is that okay?"

Peter checked the course on the maps.

"We ought to be about fifty miles below the port, if you're flying straight," and he looked over the side of the aircraft. "We should make the coast in twenty minutes. That looks like Lake Scutari, out to starboard!"

A pale sheet of grey water stretched like a finger away to the north-westward, and already the long shadows from the first rays of the sun were falling across the valleys.

Peter's heart sang for joy when the little machine finally crossed the coast at a quarter to nine. The sun was now well into the heavens and, cooped up in the restricted space of the plane, he began to feel the heat. The Adriatic looked deliciously cool, a deep blue to seaward and turquoise along the coast, inside the ten-fathom line.

"That's Budva ahead!" Peter yelled exultantly. "The next port should be Dubrovnik."

Hank lifted his right hand in acknowledgement and then he shouted over the intercom:

"Hold your hats on, you guys! I'm taking her down to sea level after passing Budva: we'll stand a better chance there if the Krauts come after us."

"You may depend upon them," Peter replied. "We've got their beloved Kommandant, and they'll be out looking for us. They love him dearly."

Bill could be heard chuckling, and then Peter saw him lean back to yell into Kramer's ear:

"They do, don't they, *Herr Kommandant?*"

But Hank's sharp tones put a stop to this badinage.

"Listen, you critters! If we are shot up by enemy fighters, we don't stand a dog's chance. Keep a sharp lookout up-sun, will you, please, sir? And you, Bill," he went on, "keep your eyes skinned to starboard."

The pilot's voice was steady now, calm and matter-of-fact when crisis loomed.

"And the quicker you spot 'em, the longer I'll have to ditch this crate."

Hank's meaning was clear to them all.

Their only chance lay in landing on some strip, or in the water maybe, before any fighters pounced.

"You better all turn round, with your backs to the engine," Hank continued. "But I ain't so fussy about the Kraut!"

But Kramer did turn round eventually, though it was a tight squeeze. Peter was conscious of the skin prickling along the back of his head when he felt the breath of his detested enemy on his neck. Then Peter heard Bill shouting above the roar of the wind:

"I'm longing to stick this knife into your back, Kommandant, so don't lay a finger on my Captain."

Peter could just see below him the miniature houses of the port of Budva, the white roads, and the cypresses green behind them. A fisherman waved from one of the boats drawn up on the beach, and then the town slipped away.

"I'm going down now."

Peter heard the throttle being eased back and then he felt his stomach coming up to meet his chin as Hank levelled her off to a hundred feet above the sea. She was so close to the water that her speed seemed frightening. He could see plainly the darker patches of seaweed, the rock formations under the water and the surf breaking lazily along the beaches. To starboard, the cliffs seemed but a few feet away, and Peter shivered as they flashed past. He never did like flying. The whole business seemed too insecure.

But then he remembered Hank's warning and forced himself to look towards the blistering sun. Shading his eyes with his right hand, he shut his left eye and swept his gaze to and fro across the glare.

"Just like my 'chaser' days," he murmured to himself. "But I'm not looking for dive-bombers now," and he started humming to himself at the prospect of making the rendezvous. He might even be able to glimpse *Rapid* lying bottomed in the water, he thought, but John Easton's too fly for that. *Anyway, there's only another twenty miles to the village of Cavtat, and once that's past we could almost walk the rest of the way.* The sun made them drowsy after their hectic night and Peter felt his senses slipping. It was with a jolt that he just glimpsed the little village slipping past them.

"Cavtat!" he yelled to Hank.

"What?"

"Cavtat!" Peter repeated. "Dubrovnik next, ten miles."

"Yippee, we'll make it yet!"

Peter felt the engine shuddering as Hank gave her all he knew. So near now, so near, and Peter searched with redoubled concentration. Another eight minutes flying time … seven…

"There she is, bless her goddarned soul — Dubrovnik ahead!" and Peter's heart leapt as he heard Hank's exultant call.

"*Achtung, Messerschmitt!*"

The warning came from their prisoner, Kapitan Ulrich von Kramer, and Peter flung himself round towards the Kommandant.

"*Achtung, Luftwaffe!*" The German's restricted arm pointed over their tail. The man betrayed no emotion, but his face had turned parchment grey.

Peter looked up and, sure enough, three black dots were circling high above them, forming up for the kill.

"He's right, Hank! Alarm astern! Three MEs about to attack!"

"Okay, you guys. Hold your hats on!"

Peter felt the nose go down and then the throttle suddenly eased.

"I'll try to make that small strip of sand," Hank shouted. "Run for shelter in the cliffs when we hit. Here we go!"

Hank yanked back on the stick and suddenly the water was no longer rushing at them. Peter felt the plane standing on its tail and then he glimpsed the first fighter, no longer a distant speck but a hurtling hunk of engine with sprouting wings.

"About a thousand yards I should say," Peter remembered murmuring to himself, and then he heard Hank yelling:

"My port wing's going to hit that rock in the sea. Brace yourselves!"

There was a sickening jolt, a tearing noise like linen being ripped apart, and Peter stiffened his whole body. Suddenly he felt himself being spun round in space and hurled upside down; the shock squeezed against his ribs and he was pinned in the fuselage, unable to move, his head less than a foot from the sea.

It took some seconds before he realised that the aircraft had stopped and that he was about to drown. He heard the engine cough, splutter into silence, and then the propeller thrashing the deeper water.

At least I shan't be grilled to death, he gasped to himself. *But I'm going to drown*, and in this last second of life he struggled like a madman before he lost consciousness.

"Bill!" Hank shouted as he clambered from the wrecked cockpit. "Hey, Bill, where are you?"

As the first bullets whocked into the water, the American floundered knee-deep through the shallows towards the group of rocks that had caught his port wingtip. "For God's sake, Bill, where are you? The Captain's drowning."

"'Ere, sir!" The burly seaman's head bobbed up from beneath the stranded plane. "My Gawd, we gotta be quick!" Ignoring the scream of diving fighters, he hurled himself at the shattered tail of the aircraft from where the legs of his Captain dangled lifelessly. With complete disregard for his own safety, the American Commando added his frenzied strength to that of Bill, and while the seaman hacked with his knife, Hank tore at the fabric with his bare hands until they ran red with blood.

"Heave — now, sir!"

While Bill edged his shoulder through the gash, Hank grasped Peter Sinclair's legs and pulled as the weight gave. Suddenly the limp body came with a rush, and, as Hank staggered backwards into the water, Bill rose from underneath to help take the weight of the body that slumped so lifelessly.

"Against the rock there! Quick!" Hank gasped. "The next swine's diving now."

Then the roar of a plunging fighter, the racket as it pulled out of its dive and the whine of the bullets as they sang overhead.

"They can't get us while we're behind this rock, sir," Bill panted.

The tail of the last fighter was still shuddering above their heads, when they saw the first Messerschmitt make a tight turn to port.

"Come on, sir. Let's scarper for that cave in the cliff. It's our only chance."

The dark cleft in the cliff was barely twenty yards away, yet the distance was the longest they had ever endured. Floundering through the water, slipping in the sand, one moment on their knees, the next struggling up the shingle, the limp body slumped between them as they battled to safety, they reached the shelter of the crevice as the leader screamed down upon them. They collapsed in the darkness as the first bullets plumped into the rocks. Then the fighter shuddered as it swept over them in a crazy climb to clear the cliff.

As they lay gasping for breath, they counted three more runs before the avengers made off to the north-westward. All they heard then was the sea, lapping gently on the sand.

"Where's Kramer?" Hank asked the question. He was crouched astride the back of Peter Sinclair, giving him artificial respiration. Bill Hawkins knelt by him, anxiously watching his Captain's ashen face.

"I dunno where the perisher is, sir, and I don't bloomin' well care so long as the Captain's still all right."

"He's all right, Bill. Look, he's coming to!" Sure enough Peter's eyes began to flicker.

"Thank Gawd! Oh, thank Gawd, sir," and Bill Hawkins slipped out into the daylight. "I'll see if Kramer's alive." In the crisis of the moment they had forgotten their prisoner.

But three minutes later, Hawkins was back.

"He's out, sir, clean out."

Hank had propped up Peter against the rock. Their Captain was breathing again, a horrible choking sound, but nevertheless he was alive and gaining strength with every minute.

"He's been sick, Bill, and he's okay. Kramer unconscious?"

"Yes, but he's just coming round."

Hank whistled.

"We must get him on his feet or he'll make trouble, Bill. He'll rouse the whole neighbourhood if he escapes. We'd better quit fast."

"I concur, as the officers say, sir," Bill replied. "But we've got to get the Captain on his feet first."

However, Peter was sitting up by now and taking notice.

"Sorry," he gasped. "Where are we?"

Then, ten minutes later, the pathetic quartet staggered to the clifftop, the groggy Hun amongst them. From there they could see the harbour fortress of Dubrovnik, some four miles away.

"What time is it?" Peter asked wearily. "We've got to be off the harbour mouth by nightfall."

"Only ten-thirty," Hank replied. "That gives us time to reach Dubrovnik before dark."

"The news will have reached there by now, thanks to the Messerschmitts," Bill Hawkins volunteered pessimistically.

"Well, let's get going and lie up before the patrols are organised," Hank suggested. "We'll have to risk the coast road. Can you manage walking now, sir?"

Peter struggled to his feet.

"If Kramer can, then so can I. Come on," he said. "Let's go," and he started reeling across the scrub towards a line of telegraph poles which stretched into the distance. "There's the road."

And before the sun was at its zenith, the four men were within a mile of the outskirts of Dubrovnik.

"Look out, sir. There's troops coming down the road!"

The warning cry came from Bill who was in the lead some ten yards ahead. "They're coming round the corner."

This was Kramer's chance and he took it. He lashed out at Bill with his left. But the ex-Mediterranean champion was expecting trouble, and, sidestepping neatly, the blow whistled over his head. The seaman's right flashed in a beautifully timed uppercut to the jaw. The German tottered for a moment, his knees buckled, and then he fell poleaxed to the ground. It was all over in a second, and Bill rolled him into the ditch that ran by the side of the road. Then he leapt on top of his adversary.

"Quick! Into the ditch!" Peter hissed.

They hurled themselves into the deep ditch and, as they rolled over, they pulled the grass over themselves. Peter held his breath, his heart pumping like an express train. Then in the silence he heard the footsteps of marching men. There was guttural speech, laughter, and then one of the soldiers broke into the first bars of the 'Horst Wessel'. With a crash the others joined in, and the footsteps stamped with the Teutonic swing of the Nazi marching song.

Peter felt the ground tremble with the shock of heavy boots and, as the soldiers passed by in jovial unison, he shut his eyes. If they sighted Bill or Hank, or if Bill allowed Kramer to squeal...

But the danger soon passed and then Hank was by his side.

"We'd better lie up till dark, sir. Let's get into that hayrick over there." He pointed across the road to where a rick stood in the corner of a smallholding. They waited for Kramer to come round and then Hank moved first. Bill and Peter saw his arm waving and they darted across separately, Bill driving Kramer ahead of him. Hank hoisted them up and they collapsed on the top of the musty hayrick.

"Last year's hay," grumbled Peter disgustedly. "Look, they haven't harvested yet," and he nodded towards the corn still stacked in sentinel rows across the field.

But the American was chuckling quietly to himself.

"Our former messmate is too one-track, Able Seaman Hawkins," he chided. "Pray observe the Technicolor panorama, as the sun sinks slowly in the west."

"Of what?"

"Of this goddarned harbour."

Peter sat up and looked towards the curve of the bay, and then his heart missed a beat.

A destroyer lay at anchor within half a mile of the breakwater.

At dusk, the three fugitives with their dejected prisoner slithered like shadows down to the shore. It was very dark, and Peter and Bill had difficulty in following the elusive spectre that flitted before them. Leading the way, Hank was in his element, trained as he was in Commando technique. But all the time Peter felt that Death was breathing down his neck, its cold breath dank upon his shoulders. All the afternoon, patrols of fully armed Germans had passed along the roads and, less than ten minutes ago, Bill thought he had heard the blood-chilling baying of hounds. Peter could not banish from his mind the fear of their running into a baited trap. *The Hun must know we've got to find a boat*, Peter kept repeating to himself for the hundredth time — *the devils must know we're being taken off by submarine or why's that destroyer there?*

"Beach ahead!"

Peter and Bill, with Kramer between them, lowered themselves softly down to the sandy beach to join Hank who was merged into the harsh curve of a rock's promontory.

"There are your boats, you guys. All you gotta do now is to borrow one."

A line of fishing boats bobbed peacefully at their moorings, not more than fifty feet away.

Peter spoke quietly in the darkness. He found it difficult to control the trembling of his voice, now that they had reached the rendezvous, only to find their escape cut off.

"You've got your infrared glass, Bill?"

"Never without it, sir," and he fished a broken piece of dark red glass from his breast pocket. "'Ere 'tis."

"Two grenades will tell *Rapid* we're here," Peter continued. "How many have we got?"

"I've only one, sir," Bill whispered wickedly. "I used me other."

"I've got some, sir," Hank said. "You're welcome to one of mine," and he handed Peter a grenade.

"But how are you going to throw those darned things into the water without waking up the whole town?" Hank asked quietly.

"We'll chuck 'em over once we're in a boat," Peter replied. "We'll have to chance it. Come on, let's swim for it."

Forcing the protesting Kramer ahead of him at pistol point, Peter waded quietly into the placid water, and when he heard the German swimming ahead of him, he struck out silently with a forceful breaststroke. Ahead of him he could see a boat, a dhaisa-type of craft, probably driven by a couple of oars. Through the periscope, he'd often seen the Italians fishing off Palermo in boats like these. They were within ten yards of it now and Peter could see the outline of the destroyer, low in the water, dark and vicious. He heard splashing behind him and he wished the others wouldn't make so much noise.

Kramer gasped as he grabbed the sides of the boat, and then he flopped over the side. Peter cocked his pistol and clambered aboard, but there was no need to worry; the German lay floundering on the bottom-boards like a gasping fish. He did not care for the water.

Peter slid the long oars out from under the thwarts and shipped them between their thole pins. He struggled with Bill and heaved him into the boat. "Cast off," he ordered and turned to drag Hank from the water.

But there was no sign of the American, nobody in the black water, nothing but the ripples.

"Where's Hank?"

"Dunno, sir. Ain't he there?"

As if in answer, there was a sudden staccato firing from the beach, some hundred yards from their point of departure.

Peter's heart stopped still as he slowly eased himself down on the thwart. A line of vivid yellow flashes was stabbing the darkness on the clifftop from whence came a pandemonium of German shouts. The stutter and green tracer from the beach — silence, and another volley from the cliff. Then another burst from the Sten on the beach, but nearer to the town this time.

"That goddarned Yank," Peter whispered. "The crazy, pig-headed, gallant fool. He's drawing them away from us."

He turned towards Bill and the seaman saw in the glare of the fire ashore that his Captain was weeping.

"Hurl the grenades overboard, Bill," he whispered. "There's nothing we can do for him now."

CHAPTER 18

The Scales are Balanced

The tension in *Rapid* was electric. Since twilight they had been at diving stations and had endured Silent Routine all day. Lying bottomed within a thousand yards of an enemy destroyer was no picnic.

John Easton had visited all the compartments and quietly explained their predicament. Never had a submarine been in such a state of readiness. With all tubes blown up and torpedoes set to twelve feet, and with her firing course calculated, she only had to…

Crack! … Crack!

The small explosions clicked against the pressure hull.

The Captain smiled. "They've made it," he whispered as he moved to the ladder.

"Surface! Half-ahead together, steer two-one-three!"

"Blow one, blow six!" the First Lieutenant snapped. There was a roaring all about them, and ninety seconds later the hatch opened, the water draining from the voicepipe.

"Port ten," came the Captain's distant order from the bridge. "Steady!"

"Steady, sir," sang the helmsman up the pipe. "Course two-one-five."

There was a slight pause and the silence was unbearable — at any moment they would be blown out of the water.

"Fire one!"

The boat trembled, and the air whooshed backwards.

"Fire two!"

Phumph!

"Fire three — fire four!"

Phumph! Phumph!

"Hard-a-port! Group up! Full ahead together; dive, dive, dive!"

The hatch clanged above them and then the Captain's voice cut decisively through the pandemonium.

"Twenty-eight feet, Number One. I'm not going down. Signalman in the tower with the infrared Aldis."

A shattering roar clanged against the boat, blasting every man's eardrums.

"Steady!"

"Course one-seven-three, sir."

"Give me two minutes on this course, Number One, then surface," the Captain's deliberate commands continued from the tower.

"Aye, aye, sir."

The boat shook when another torpedo struck home, and a long cheer echoed through *Rapid*, snapping the pent-up emotion. There was a chance now, a faint chance of picking up the beach party if they could only get themselves off the shore.

"Surface! Blow one, blow six. Group down, slow ahead together, both planes hard-a-rise," the First Lieutenant rapped, and then, as the boat swooped upwards he yelled up the conning tower:

"Eighteen feet, sir."

The clips clattered and then the hatch sprung open.

John Easton clambered to the voicepipe cock and opened it. Though his heart was pounding at the risks he was running, he need not have worried for the scene that met his eyes was chaotic. The destroyer was already on her way to the bottom with her back broken, and her bows rearing into the air until they were almost vertical. There was no sign of her after half. Instead, there bubbled and hissed a seething mass of water from which came tormented shrieks. It was a horrible sight and he looked away towards the land, now glowing red along the cliffs from the light of the burning destroyer. As he glanced at the sinister beauty of Dubrovnik, the battlements and housetops flickering with the dancing reflections of the flames from the stricken ship, he heard the signalman behind him already flashing on his infrared Aldis.

"Stop the blowers," he shouted above the noise of the disintegrating ship. *Rapid* had enough buoyancy and, if he kept to the eastward and trimmed well down, she should remain invisible from the enemy ashore who were completely demoralised by the tragedy being enacted on their front doorstep. Easton noticed desultory firing in the corner where the foreshore joined the harbour, but apart from that, the torpedoed destroyer overshadowed everything.

"There they are, sir!" the signalman yelled, pointing with his left hand over the port quarter, while still flashing on his Aldis with his right. "About fifty yards away and going like bats out of hell!"

Easton hesitated a moment and then picked up the frantic rowers through his glasses.

"Stop both, port twenty," he shouted down the voicepipe. "Recovery party on deck — and look slippy!"

It seemed an eternity before the boat bumped alongside. At any moment, guns might open up from ashore and blast the defenceless submarine out of the water. With each minute that ticked by, John Easton liked it less. Then he looked over the side and saw three men being hoisted over the gun sponson. There was a pattering up the bridge-side and then Peter Sinclair stumbled in front of him.

"You're punctual, Peter."

"Thanks. Never keep a senior officer waiting."

Easton was not surprised to see that Sinclair's face was grim and expressionless: he must certainly have been through something.

"Better get below, Peter. This place isn't too healthy."

"I've got one prisoner and Bill Hawkins."

Easton paused a moment as the huge German clambered over the side of the bridge.

"Is this him?" he asked.

"Yes."

"But where's the American?"

For a second no one spoke.

"Over there, John. Throwing his life away so that we could get off."

"Where the small-arms fire is concentrated?"

"That's right."

The barrel of a revolver poked over the side of the bridge rail, followed by Able Seaman Bill Hawkins. He saluted when he saw his ex-First Lieutenant.

"You're adrift, Hawkins," Easton smiled, "but it's good to have you back."

The recovery party were already clambering up the bridge.

"Clear the bridge," the Captain ordered. "Dive, dive, dive!"

It was a perfect autumnal dawn when *Rapid* eventually surfaced off Filfla, the islet at the south-eastern extremity of Malta. She reared from the sea abreast the small minesweeper which had come out to escort her up the swept channel. There was a freshness in the glittering morning and Peter was glad of the white woollen submariner's sweater which John Easton had lent him. White fingers of cumulus were curling from the horizon line in rows of innumerable galleons, sailing across the blue sky.

Valetta slowly drew abeam, its sandstone fortress glaring white in the sunlight. Defiant she stood there, mocking all attempts of the Luftwaffe to reduce her to her knees. The scars of the bombs showed plainly, mere pimples upon the flat surfaces of the battlements. Past the Grand Harbour entrance and on to the small gap which led into Lazaretto creek, the little submarine steamed, no Jolly Roger flying at her periscopes. Her White Ensign flapped bravely in the breeze, and she altered up to pass through the black necklace of buoys which formed the protective boom.

The minesweeper stood off to allow her charge to slip by, and *Rapid* slid into the sheltered waters of the creek. On her main motors now, she circled silently to come to her mooring buoys.

Peter stood at the back of the bridge while her wires were secured, and then he leant over the side with John Easton. Captain 'S' was grinning up at them.

"Welcome home, both of you," he shouted. "The Hun has taken a hammering this time."

"We lost Jefferson, sir," Peter replied quietly. "It's only through him that we are here at all. He's dead."

"But you have this von Kramer, I hope," 'S' asked dispassionately.

"Yes, sir. We've got him down below. Why?"

Captain 'S' stretched his arm across the brow and handed a signal to a rating who passed it up the conning tower side.

Peter opened the pink paper and read:

To Captain 'S', Tenth Submarine Flotilla from Admiralty. Request confirmation that you hold German prisoner of war, Kapitan Ulrich von Kramer. Italian authorities suggest exchange with American Commando taken prisoner by them at Dubrovnik. American's name is Lieutenant Jefferson, U.S.N.

Peter Sinclair handed the signal to Easton, then he turned to look down at his senior officer. His eyes were blurred and he could barely distinguish the burly figure of Captain 'S' when he spoke.

"The best bargain we could ever make," he said.

EPILOGUE

The following announcements appeared in the *London Gazette* of December 16th, 1943:

Upon the advice of the First Lord, the King has been graciously pleased to award the Distinguished Service Cross to Lieutenant P. Sinclair, Royal Navy, and the Distinguished Service Medal to Able Seaman W. Hawkins for courage and outstanding zeal and devotion to duty while serving on special operations in the Mediterranean.

The King has also been graciously pleased to award the Distinguished Service Cross to Lieutenant George Jefferson, United States Navy, for his total disregard of his own safety whilst rescuing Lieutenant Sinclair and Able Seaman Hawkins in the above operations.

GLOSSARY

A.M.C. — Armed Merchant Carrier.
A.P. — Armour Piercing.
ASDIC — The device by which submarines are detected. Submarines are also fitted with this device, when it is used as a hydrophone.
BAG — Slang for a prisoner-of-war camp.
BARRACK-STANCHION — A man who manages to secure for himself a permanent appointment in a shore station.
BEARING — The direction of an object.
BLOWERS — Machines with which to blow out the water in the tanks by using low-pressure air.
BOX — The main batteries.
CARLEY FLOATS — Life-saving rafts which can be slipped as the ship is foundering.
CHOKKA — Slang for fed-up.
CORTICENE — A type of heavy linoleum used to cover the steel deck.
CRACK — To open a valve quickly, and to shut it again immediately.
D.A. — Director Angle (torpedo firing angle).
D.R. — Dead Reckoning.
E-BOAT — The fast enemy motor torpedo boat.
E.T.A. — Expected Time of Arrival.
FIFTH COLUMNISTS — Traitors working inside one's own society.
FOCKE-WOLFE — German long-range reconnaissance aircraft.

FREE FLOOD — The open holes in the casing and tanks through which the water enters.

FRUIT MACHINE — A metal box into which all relevant attack data is fed, and from which the necessary information is extracted with which to carry out an attack.

GASH — Garbage.

GRATICULE — The fine centre-line and range calibrations which are marked on the lens of the periscope.

GROUP DOWN — Low speed on the main electric motors, thus using up little electric power.

GROUP UP — High speed on the main electric motors, thus using up the battery power quickly.

H.E. — High Explosive.

H.E. — Hydrophone Effect, i.e. propeller noise.

HEADS — Lavatory.

HEAT — Slang for a submarine at the receiving end of a severe depth-charge attack.

H.P. — High Pressure.

H.S.D. — Higher Submarine Detector; the rank of a skilled Asdic operator.

HYDROPHONE — Underwater listening device.

JIMMY-THE-ONE — Slang for First Lieutenant.

JOLLY ROGER — Skull-and-crossbones flag, upon which emblems of sinkings are sewn. Flown to denote successes.

LAYER — A difference of temperature gradients in the ocean.

LOOPS — A loop pf electrical cable lying on the seabed. The cable s connected to a galvanometer ashore, and if a submarine crosses the loop the galvanometer pointer swings.

MAIN BALLAST KINGSTON — Water into the internal tanks amidships is allowed to enter through the Kingston Valves.

MAIN BALLAST TANKS — The tanks which give a submarine its buoyancy. All are fitted with main vents, numbers 1 and 6 being external, the remainder internal.

MAIN VENTS — The large mushroom valves on top of the Main Ballast tanks. When the main vents are open, the water will rush into the tanks, but, if the main vents are shut, the air cannot escape when the Main Ballast tanks are blown, because the 'blow' is at the top of the tank and the free-flood holes at the bottom. Water is therefore forced out through the holes in the bottom of the tank, H.P. air taking its place.

MESSERSCHMITT — ME109; single-seater German fighter.

NAVIGATORI — Class of powerful Italian destroyers.

OLD MAN — Slang for Captain.

OUTSIDE E.R.A. — The Engine Room Artificer whose duty is at the panel in the Control Room, and who is therefore 'outside' the Engine Room.

PANEL — The conglomeration of valves, etc., all centralised at one position.

PERISHER — Slang for Commanding Officers' Qualifying Course.

PING-RUNNING — Acting as a 'clockwork mouse' to provide a target for training destroyers.

PRESSURE HULL — The cigar-shaped hull of a submarine which is tested to the safe diving depth. If any part of this structure is pierced, the submarine is unlikely to survive.

'Q' TANK — The emergency tank for quick diving. When flooded, the tank makes the submarine ten tons heavier than her normal dived trim. After diving, this extra water is blown out of 'Q' tank by high-pressure air. If this tank is required to be flooded when dived, its vent has merely to be opened, either into the submarine or outboard, and the sea will rush into 'Q' tank. In wartime, for obvious reasons, 'Q' tank is always kept flooded when the submarine is on the surface.

R-BOAT — The German equivalent of our motor launches, but with a slightly heavier armament. The Coastal Forces' 'maid-of-all-work'.

SQUAREHEAD — Slang for a German.

STICK — Slang for periscope.

THIRD HAND — The Third Officer in a submarine.

THROWERS — A type of mortar mounted on the quarter decks of destroyers. When fired they hurl depth charges well clear of each quarter.

U-BOAT — Enemy submarine.

URSULA SUIT — Waterproof overalls in general use, designed by the Commanding Officer of H.M. Submarine *Ursula*.

V-AND-W — A class of veteran destroyer built at the end of World War I but once more called into service, and whose names all began with the letters V and W.

VERNICHTUNGSWAFFE — War-winning weapon.

WIMPEY — Wellington medium bomber, British.

WOP — Slang for 'Italian'.

A NOTE TO THE READER

Dear Reader,

If you have enjoyed the novel enough to leave a review on **Amazon** and **Goodreads**, then we would be truly grateful.

Sapere Books is an exciting new publisher of brilliant fiction and popular history.

To find out more about our latest releases and our monthly bargain books visit our website:
saperebooks.com

Printed in Great Britain
by Amazon